UNDER LYING

ALSO BY JANELLE HARRIS

No Kiss Goodbye
See Me Not

UNDER LYING

JANELLE HARRIS

LAKE UNION
PUBLISHING

Text copyright © 2019 by Janelle Harris
All rights reserved.

No part of this book may be reproduced, or stored in a retrieval system, or transmitted in any form or by any means, electronic, mechanical, photocopying, recording, or otherwise, without express written permission of the publisher.

Published by Lake Union Publishing, Seattle

www.apub.com

Amazon, the Amazon logo, and Lake Union Publishing are trademarks of Amazon.com, Inc., or its affiliates.

ISBN-13: 9781542092630
ISBN-10: 1542092639

Cover design by Heike Schüssler

Printed in the United States of America

For Brian
x

*'There is nothing either good or bad,
but thinking makes it so.'*

– William Shakespeare

Prologue

Then

You died on a Saturday afternoon. The weather was filthy. The kind you loved and I hated. All wet, windy and angry. Sheets of lightning illuminated the whole sky followed almost instantly by the angry rumble of thunder. It was beautifully terrifying. But I wasn't scared. We were safe, together in our tiny student flat in Dublin. The weather forecast said the conditions were treacherous and people were urged to stay indoors. I suggested a movie marathon and a jammies day. You rolled your eyes, shook your head, and said the media were scaremongering. Scaremongering was your exact word. I remember because I had no idea what it meant, but I guessed it was something fancy you'd learned in your journalism class. You borrowed my umbrella and fetched your camera. You told me you were hoping to get some great shots of the lightning for your portfolio, but I knew you were after a story much darker and more sinister than the storm. You left our flat with a smile and wave. You promised you wouldn't be long. You never came back.

Chapter One

Now

The day everything changes doesn't begin especially differently to any other day. My alarm goes off at 8.30 a.m., like always. With my eyes still closed I stretch my right arm over the edge of the bed and pat my hand around my bedside table until I hit the right spot on my phone to shut the alarm off. I roll into the middle of the bed and flop on to my belly. I expect to find my husband's body heat clinging to the sheets on his side, but the white cotton under me is cool. I'm disappointed by Paul's absence, but I'm not surprised. I suspect he got up early to get a run in before Amelia, our soon to be three-year-old daughter, wakes. I sit up, drag my hands around my face and try to wake up fully.

There's a cup of coffee waiting for me beside my phone. The words *World's Best Mammy* wrap around the cream ceramic mug in swirly, purple font. It instantly became my favourite mug when Paul and Amelia gave it to me on my first ever Mother's Day. But before I dare to enjoy a sip, I tilt my ear towards the bedroom door. The house is blissfully silent. Amelia must still be asleep, I decide. Smiling, I take Paul's pillow and stuff it between my back and the headboard. I take my coffee in one hand and my phone in the other and slouch back against the mound of pillow to enjoy a lazy Saturday morning in bed.

I sip lukewarm coffee as I scroll through recent photos on my phone, choosing the best ones to share on Facebook. There's plenty of Amelia and me. At the park, out for a walk, in our garden. Our selfies are hilarious. Or at least I think so. We're always pulling faces or trying to make each other laugh. Amelia almost always wins, and I giggle first. Unfortunately, I don't have any shots of my husband. Paul always manages to duck out of shot just before the camera snaps. Which inevitably makes it impossible to get a family photo.

'Ah Susan, the state of me,' he says while running his hand through his floppy blond hair, which he's overly aware is thinning on top. 'Next time. Yeah? Get me next time. Let me get one of the two of you. My gorgeous girls.'

I've no doubt Paul's phone is awash with photos of Amelia and me, among screenshots of his Fitbit app. His perfect family and his perfect hobby. Everything about Paul is perfect. Or at least to the people who don't know him as well as I do it would seem to be.

Scrolling on, I find a shot of all of us in the park last week and I upload it as my new profile picture. My nagging wore Paul down and he actually stood for a photo. Unfortunately, my eyes are closed and Paul's face is obscured by a large tree branch and a cluster of leaves, but Amelia is smiling brightly and there's the unmistakable sparkle of childhood innocence in her eyes. I love it.

Gentle noise coming from downstairs hints that it's time to get up. Paul's voice like a gritty rainstorm and Amelia's giggles like the rainbow that follows make their way up the stairs to wrap around me like a warm hug.

I set my empty coffee cup and phone down on the bedside table, throw back the duvet and dangle my legs over the edge of the bed. I pause for a moment, trying to get the bubbles of nervous excitement popping in my tummy under control as I think of the day ahead.

I can tell it's a nice morning outside by the shapes and shadows the sun creates on my bedroom floor as it shines through the hideous floral curtains that came with our new home. I breathe a sigh of relief, confident in the knowledge that today is dry and warm; perfect barbecue weather.

'Today is so important,' I tell myself aloud as I slip my arms into the ivory silk dressing gown lying crinkled on the end of my bed. Standing up, I glance in the antique, full-length mirror that stands in the corner of my compact bedroom. My reflection stares back at me, smiling. My shoulder-length, mousy brown hair is messy and knotted but my eyes are sparkling and my skin is bright and fresh. *All this sea air has been good for me*, I think, my smile growing wider.

It was Paul's idea to sell our two-bedroomed apartment in Dublin and move to a quaint cottage in West Cork. I protested at first. Not just because I didn't want to leave the convenience of the capital city behind me. I mean, sure, that was part of it, but I also didn't want to move to the back arse of nowhere where I didn't know a single person and start my life all over again at thirty-five. But as soon as I saw our cottage with the little red gate that hangs slightly crooked, and the flower baskets dotted above every windowsill like pots of rainbow-coloured treasure, I fell in love.

Six months later, I've adjusted better than my husband to the move. Paul says he loves life in the country, and he swears the change of pace has been good for him, but I see nostalgia and regret in his eyes when we talk about our old lives. There is one thing we agree on, however – life on the Atlantic coast is good for Amelia. She loves the freedom of country lanes where she can run ahead without me shouting at her to get back and hold my hand, the way I did in Dublin. She loves the fresh air, and most of all she loves the ducks that swim in the stream behind our cottage. I'm quite fond of the ducks too. *Maybe we can feed the ducks later this morning*, I think, picking up the hairbrush from my dresser and dragging it through the stubborn knots on my head. My naturally ebony hair objects to being dyed several shades lighter and tangles like wire.

Today is the first Saturday in July. The weekend is defined clearly on the calendar hanging next to my dresser by messy red circles around all the dates that fall on a Saturday and Sunday this month. Paul took a red pen to my calendar a few weeks ago while we were mid-argument. I was on his case about how little time he spends at home since we moved. Between trying to get his accountancy business off the ground here in Cork and adhering to his strict running schedule, there are some evenings when he barely sees Amelia for ten minutes before she falls asleep. Other nights she just can't keep her little eyes open any longer and she asks me to give her daddy a goodnight kiss for her. In fairness, when I told Paul what Amelia said he looked broken-hearted and promised to make time for family. The days with red circles are Paul's attempt at an apology.

'The weekends are family time from now on,' he promised. 'You, me and Millie.'

So far, Paul has been as good as his word. Granted this is only the third weekend in his turned-over leaf but we've enjoyed walks in the countryside, picnics in the park and I've indulged in some much-needed lie-ins. This morning included.

I toss my hairbrush on to the bed I haven't bothered to tidy up and make my way to the landing. I curse when I bang my head, for the second time this week, against a solid timber beam holding up the low roof just outside my bedroom door. I rub my head and laugh at my silliness before carefully walking down the steep stairs. The cottage wasn't built with an upstairs in mind, but the previous owners have done a wonderful job opening up the attic and managing to create two small but comfortable bedrooms in the space. The original master bedroom was downstairs, but neither Paul nor I were comfortable sleeping on a different floor to Amelia, so we've made do with the much smaller upstairs space.

The smell of eggs and toast greets me from halfway up the stairs and my tummy rumbles excitedly in response. I pause on the bottom step and savour my view of domestic bliss. Paul is still in his running gear as he works hard in the kitchen. He doesn't notice me. I watch his slender arm stir eggs in a pan over the old-school stove and I smile at my idea to open up the entire ground floor. It had meant we lost two months in the building process because of complications with load-bearing walls and planning permission, but it was nothing that couldn't be fixed, much to Paul's disappointment. The idea of gutting an old cottage until it was unrecognisable didn't sit well with my conventional husband. But even Paul had to admit that the results of the renovation were spectacular. The stuff of magazines, he admitted recently.

Stepping off the bottom step and making my way across the highly glazed cream floor tiles leading into the kitchen area, I spot my daughter perched on a stool much too high for her, tucked against the kitchen island. Amelia sits with her back straight, her golden curls cascading over her shoulders as she watches her father cook.

'Good morning, little miss,' I say, waiting until I'm standing directly behind her before I speak.

'Mammy,' Amelia chirps, spinning round on the stool and almost falling off, just as I suspected she would.

I catch her.

'What are you doing up here?' I say sternly. 'You know these stools are way too high for you.' I'm speaking to my daughter but my eyes are on my husband.

Paul twists his head over his shoulder and looks at me while still stirring the eggs in the pan.

'You're a big girl now, aren't you, Millie?' he says.

Amelia looks at me, unsure, and I hate that Paul has confused her.

'You *are* getting so big, sweetheart,' I smile, clasping her waist as I swing her down. Her delicate, cheery lips turn downwards as the cold of the floor tiles hits her bare feet. 'But you're still not big enough for these high stools, okay? Soon though, I promise.'

'Okay, Mammy,' Amelia smiles and scurries over to sit at the table in front of the floor-to-ceiling window that overlooks our pretty little garden and the shallow stream running behind it.

'You can't keep her a baby forever,' Paul says, waiting until Amelia is sitting at the table and out of earshot.

'She *is* a baby, Paul. Still a baby. She won't be three for another couple of months.' I swallow hard, hoping to avoid another conversation about trying for a new baby. I shake my head and put the thought out of my mind. 'Breakfast smells good.'

'Millie is starving. Aren't you, honey?' Paul says, raising his voice enough to catch our daughter's attention.

'I like eggs.' Amelia smiles brightly, but her concentration is drawn to a colouring book and some crayons she's found on the table. 'I like blue. The sky is blue.'

'It sure is, sweetheart,' I say, making my way to stand beside her. 'And the sky is very blue today, isn't it?'

She twists on her chair and looks out the window. 'The duckies are sad, Mammy.'

I pull out the heavy oak chair next to Amelia from under the table, and no matter how much care I take not to scrape the tiles the legs squeak and protest against the floor.

'Why are the ducks sad?' I ask softly, sitting down and stroking my hand over Amelia's curls, but my attention is less on my daughter and more on the floor and the damage I've probably caused.

'Duckies like rain,' she explains, shaking her head to toss my hand away. She spins round and seeks out a green crayon. She swirls the bright colour around the entire page of her colouring book, ignoring all lines. 'Today is too sunny.'

'Ducks *do* like rain,' I smile. 'But they like sunny days too, you know.'

I pick up a pink crayon and begin to colour in the wings of a fairy on the page in front of Amelia, attempting to add some reasoning to the masterpiece.

She switches her green crayon for a yellow one and continues her haphazard style. 'Lellow is my favourite,' she explains.

'Ducks are yellow,' I say.

'Eggs are yellow too,' Paul adds, arriving next to us with a plate of scrambled egg and toast cut into triangles.

He places the yellow plastic plate with steam swirling from it in front of her.

'It's hot, Millie. You have to blow on it,' Paul says, walking back to the kitchen.

'Hot, hot, hot,' Amelia says, pressing her lips together as she attempts to blow away the steam.

I try not to laugh as I watch my daughter's technique for cooling her food, which involves spraying saliva all over her plate.

'Okay, sweetheart,' I say, taking the crayon from her hand. 'I think it's cool enough. You can eat up now.'

'We're fierce lucky with the weather today,' Paul says, placing a cup of coffee and a plate of eggs in front of me. 'It's going to be a scorcher. I was sweating to death on this morning's run.'

'Warmest day for five years, or something like that, according to the forecast,' I say, swapping the crayon in my hand for the cup of coffee. I turn towards the window and inhale the sight of the beautiful babbling stream, which looks as if it's jumped straight out of a Monet painting and positioned itself at the end of my back garden.

'It's global warming, that's what it is,' Paul says. 'We're not used to this heat.'

'Well, I'm delighted,' I say. 'I had visions of it lashing rain and the whole day being ruined. I couldn't sleep for ages last night worrying about it.'

'Ah Susan.' Paul bends in the middle to kiss the top of my head. 'You're working yourself into a tizzy over a silly barbecue.'

'It's not silly. Not to me. We're here six months now and I still don't really know anyone. Today is important,' I say, pushing some egg around my plate with the back of my fork. 'I want them to like me. To like us.'

'What time is everyone coming?' he asks, taking a seat opposite me with his eggs and a pint glass full of ice water. He gave up coffee six months ago when he began training for the Dublin marathon. He tried to encourage me to do the same. I wasn't having any of it.

'The invites said any time from three, with food around four. I hope no one arrives early,' I say.

Paul rolls his eyes. 'It wouldn't surprise me.'

'C'mon.' I shake my head. 'There's no point inviting all our neighbours around for a barbecue if you're going to be like that.'

'Be like what?' He shrugs. 'They're not my kind of people. That's all.'

'Paul, please,' I sigh, trying to ignore the fact that Amelia is spilling far more egg on the floor than she is getting in her mouth. 'You promised. You said you'd make an effort. If not for me, then do it for Amelia. I want her to have friends here. Please?'

He shoves a forkful of egg into his mouth. 'Fine.'

Chapter Two

Now

Paul's floppy hair dangles into his eyes and I grin when he tries to subtly blow it out of his way as he stands in our neat garden with his hands folded across his chest. I watch out of my kitchen window as my husband chats to a man and woman we don't know. I recognise the woman from my walks with Amelia but the man standing next to her is a complete stranger. He's her husband, obviously, and they're the couple who live a few houses and a couple of fields down from us, but I really don't know them. Of the fifteen to twenty people littered around my garden right now, I only know two of them. One is my husband and the other is our daughter. But I plan to get to know them today. All of them. I want them to like me. I need them to.

I hurry around my newly fitted kitchen with its bespoke ash cupboards, a carbon copy of the original layout. It wasn't easy to keep the feel of the old house once we opened up the ground floor, but I was determined to retain as much character as possible. The only stylistic change I made was swapping the rotten, warped timber worktop for highly polished black granite that sparkles when it catches the light. I take two glasses from the cupboard next to the sink and pour a glass of Chardonnay for Mrs Stranger and a gin and tonic for Mr Stranger. I reach for a third glass, fill it with tap water and fish around in my trouser pocket for a couple of paracetamol. I hope the medication kicks in soon and manages the migraine I've felt coming on all day. I was so enthusiastic when I started planning today but I had no idea that in practice it would be quite so stressful.

I glance out the window again. The sky is clear and blue but the leaves on the tall trees that separate our cottage from the farmland next to us rustle gently and I suspect a sudden wind has picked up. I grab Amelia's yellow cardigan from the shelf and tuck it under my arm. Taking the wine in one hand and the gin in the other, I make my way out of the open double doors into our garden.

'She's back with the good stuff,' Paul jokes breezily as he catches me out of the corner of his eye.

'Chardonnay, was it, Helen?' he asks, taking the glass of white wine from me and passing it to our neighbour.

'I hope it's cold enough,' I say, 'I forgot to put the wine in the fridge.'

'I'm sure it's lovely,' Helen smiles, pressing the glass to her lips.

'And a G&T, Larry, right?' Paul offers her husband the second glass.

'Won't you have one yourself?' Larry asks.

'Paul doesn't drink,' I say, and it comes out more snappy than I mean it to.

'Really?' Helen giggles, amused by the idea of a pioneer.

'Alcohol doesn't agree with me when I'm training,' Paul explains. 'It makes me sluggish.'

'Well, I must say, I admire your dedication, Paul,' Larry says. 'Wouldn't be for me, but to each their own, eh?'

'He doesn't drink coffee either,' I add, although I'm not sure why. I think I'm nervous.

'Wow,' Helen says, between sips of wine. 'My God, Paul. You're practically a saint. Susan, where did you get him, and are there any more like him?'

We all laugh. But I don't miss Paul's narrow eyes as he glares at Helen as if she is something unpleasant that he has scraped off the bottom of his shoe.

'I love what you've done with the place, Susan,' Larry says. 'This place was an absolute shambles before you got your hands on it. Helen nearly drove me round the bend, constantly bangin' on about how she'd love to give it a lick of paint. She loves a good fixer-upper.'

'Well, I married you, didn't I?' Helen laughs.

Paul and I glance at each other, equally uncomfortable by Larry and Helen's digs at one another. But we laugh too and brush it off as if our neighbours are hilarious.

'Yes. It was certainly in need of some TLC,' I say, running my eyes along the cream exterior of my cottage with its newly fitted windows. 'It was hard work, I can't lie, but I'm so pleased with the way it turned out.'

'I must admit, I had no idea the renovation was going to be quite so extensive,' Paul says, pressing the palm of his hand gently against the small of my back. 'Susan kept talking about light and space and opening the place up. We had workmen in the house for weeks on end.'

'But it was all worth it, wasn't it?' Helen asks, looking around, noticeably envious.

'It was expensive. That's what it was,' Paul says, and I know he's still pissed off that I went over budget. 'But anything for my Susan.' He dots a gentle kiss on the top of my head.

'I wish Larry would let me redecorate,' Helen says. 'I've been staring at the same bloody yellow kitchen for the past twenty-odd years.'

'What's wrong with yellow?' Larry says between large mouthfuls of gin. 'I like yellow.'

'I like lellow too,' Amelia says, appearing at my side.

'Well, hello there,' Helen says, bending down to Amelia's level.

Amelia takes a step back. I reach for her hand and she curls her small, sticky fingers around my palm.

'This must be your little girl,' Helen says, beaming.

'This is Amelia,' I smile proudly. 'Say hello, sweetheart.'

'Hello,' Amelia echoes, sidestepping so half her body is hidden behind my leg.

'She is just adorable, Susan,' Helen says. 'We have three boys. The youngest started college this year. It's just me and Larry at home on our own now.'

Helen doesn't look old enough to have grown-up children. I knew she was older than me, but I didn't think by much. But I've always been a terrible judge of age. I guess she must be closer to fifty than early forties as I'd thought.

'Amelia is almost three,' I say, crouching and wobbling on my unforgiving high heels as I attempt to guide her arms into her cardigan.

She wriggles and twists as I try to do up the delicate buttons. 'Can we feed the ducks now?' she asks.

'Not today.' I shake my head.

'But they're hungry.' Her blue eyes cloud over with disappointment.

'Amelia,' I say sternly. 'I said not today, okay?'

Her bottom lip drops and I know she's about to cry. 'We'll feed them tomorrow, I promise.'

Her frown turns into a bright smile once more and she nods her head enthusiastically.

'Okay, sweetheart,' I smile as my fingers fasten the last button on her cardigan. 'Do you want to play some more?'

Amelia looks up at me, her beautiful eyes sparkling as she nods and then runs off to join a group of slightly older neighbourhood children laughing and playing at the end of the garden.

'She's as pretty as a picture,' Helen smiles, sipping her wine casually. 'Enjoy every moment of her, before you know it she'll be old enough to answer back and will want to borrow the car.'

I exaggerate a frown. 'Something to look forward to,' I joke.

'Seriously though,' Helen says, 'how are you doing? I remember the early days at home alone with the boys when Larry was working. I thought I'd lose my mind with loneliness. Don't get me wrong, I love my kids. But sometimes we all need grown-up talk, don't we? It can't be easy moving into a new area with a toddler and not knowing a soul. I only live up the road, if you fancy popping in for a coffee anytime. I'd be glad of the company, really.'

'Amelia and I try to get out for a walk every day,' I say.

'Oh yes,' Helen smiles, 'I've seen you. Down by the lake, feeding ducks.'

I nod. 'Amelia is mad about the ducks. We feed them most days.'

'I had no idea we were neighbours,' Helen says. 'I should have introduced myself. You must think I'm awful.'

'Not at all,' I say, 'you weren't to know. And it's lovely getting to know each other now.'

'Well, you must let me make it up to you. And Amelia too, of course. You should call in after your walk. How does Monday sound? I'll bake some scones or something. We can get to know each other better.'

'Ah thank you, Helen,' I say. 'But Amelia usually goes for a nap after our walk. My only chance to get any work done is while she's sleeping. It's a long walk there and back, and it tires her out for a good couple of hours.'

'Oh, you work from home,' Helen says, thankfully unoffended by my decline of her kind offer. 'What do you do?'

'I'm a counsellor. Bereavement mostly.'

'Oh wow. How interesting,' Helen says. 'Like a doctor?'

'Not quite,' I blush. 'More like a good listener.'

'We'd make a good team, us two,' Helen says, pointing to me and then tapping her finger against her chest. 'Larry says I never know when to shut up. But it's only because I have to repeat myself no end. That man doesn't listen to a word I say.'

'Mmm,' I smile, wide-eyed, and shift my weight from one foot to the other. I try to catch Paul's eye, hoping he'll join our conversation.

Unsurprisingly, he and Larry are chatting like a pair of old friends. No doubt bonding over sport or cars, Paul's favourites. He's a dab hand at making people feel comfortable. Larry is so content he is blissfully unaware that his wife has just belittled him for a second time in as many minutes, in front of a complete stranger. I wonder how often Helen does that. They're such an odd couple, I decide, and I think it might be harder to make friends around here than I thought.

'Have you been in the counselling business long?' Helen asks.

'I worked full-time when we lived in Dublin.' I pause, relieved the conversation is moving in a more comfortable direction. 'It's been a big change moving here and giving up a permanent position. But I'm enjoying the freedom. I only have a couple of clients at the moment, but I've contacted local charities offering to volunteer an hour or two here and there, mostly at the weekends, when Paul can watch Amelia. It's slow progress getting word out about my services, but I'm embracing the challenge.'

'And do your clients come to the house?' Helen probes.

'Yes. For now,' I say, feeling somewhat unprofessional. 'But I'm hoping to take an office in the city when business picks up.'

'Larry, do you hear this?' Helen nudges her elbow into her husband's ribs. 'Susan is a counsellor.'

Larry turns his head towards me with an awkward smile.

'She talks to people who have lost someone,' Helen explains. 'It's her job. And you thought she was a photographer.'

'Really? A photographer.' I tilt my head to one side, intrigued. 'What gave you that impression, Larry?'

My eyes are on Larry's but it's Helen who answers, unsurprisingly. 'He noticed the lovely photographs hanging in the hall. The lightning strikes. He thought they didn't fit well with the rest of the house, so he assumed you'd snapped the shots yourself. I told him to mind his own business. What does a farmer know about interior design, right?'

Larry's puckered brow tells me Helen is making him uncomfortable. Him and me both, but most likely for very different reasons. Larry Mullin may look like a simple farmer, but I suspect there is nothing simple about this man.

'I'm not artistic at all, unfortunately,' I say, my eyes sweeping over Larry. 'I didn't take those photographs.'

'Well, they're nice pictures,' Helen says, 'wherever you got them.'

'Thank you. I like them,' I say.

'Ah c'mon, Susan. You more than like them. Be honest,' Paul says. 'She adores those bloody things. I don't see the appeal, personally, but she has better taste than me, so I take her word for it that they're fantastic.'

'I think the photographer was very talented to snap the lightning at the exact moment of the strike. It gives me chills,' I say.

'Yes,' Helen nods. 'Can you imagine how difficult it must be to click right at the exact moment? Sure, you only have a split second to get it right.'

'Exactly,' I smile. Helen has finally said something to help me like her.

'Women,' Larry snorts, trying to catch Paul's eye. 'Full of romantic notions, aren't they? Lightning is lethal. Anyone who sees anything other than Mother Nature's temper needs their head examined, that's what I say.'

'Jesus, Larry. You're a brave man,' Paul smirks. 'Susan will have your guts for garters talking like that. She loves those photos. Has for years. She found these old prints in a drawer in my apartment when we first started going out. I'd forgotten I had them, to be honest. She became obsessed with them. So I had them framed for her the following Christmas as a surprise. They've become her pride and joy over the years.'

'So, you don't see the photographer's talent, Larry?' I ask, trying hard to hide my offence, but my cheeks feel hot and I'm guessing my frustration is showing.

'Clickin' an aul button on a camera?' Larry rolls his eyes. 'Talent me arse.'

'We'll have to agree to disagree,' I grimace.

'Well, I agree with Susan.' Helen glares at her husband, warning him to keep his mouth shut. 'I think they're fantastic. They must be a great conversation starter when your clients come to visit the house.'

'Actually,' I say, pausing to envisage the photos, 'Larry is the first person to notice them in quite a while.'

'Do you hear that, Larry?' Helen asks. 'Maybe it's a sign. You should come for one of Susan's sessions. You could talk about your mother and all your issues.'

An unmissable redness creeps across Larry's face and I wonder if he's irritated or embarrassed. Probably both. I avert my eyes, finding myself agreeing with at least one thing Larry says . . . *Helen really doesn't know when to shut up.*

'Larry's mother passed away two years ago,' Helen continues. 'She was eighty-nine, but young at heart. It was sudden. Wasn't it, Larry?'

'I'm so sorry,' Paul says.

Larry shuffles on the spot and I wonder if I've been too quick to judge him. He's obviously dominated by his wife, and I can tell how much he misses his mother. The mere mention of her forces his eyes to the ground and his thumb is curled and stroking the tip of his little finger. It's a classic fidget. A distraction. Watching out for these traits is an occupational hazard. Larry is hiding something, I decide.

'Our house is the old family home,' Helen says. 'Larry grew up there. I'd love to do it up now that his mother has passed. You know, put our own stamp on it.' Helen's eyes sweep over our cottage longingly. 'I thought we could do something artistic, like you and Paul. But Larry won't hear of it. He says our house is just fine the way it is. But I think our boys are embarrassed to bring their friends around because of the state of the old place.'

'Jesus, Helen,' Larry grunts through gritted teeth.

'What?' Helen shrugs. 'Even *you* agree it's lonely in that big old house, just the two of us rattling around.'

Larry's square shoulders stiffen and he glares at me, as if it's my fault Helen is oversharing.

'That's the trouble with kids,' Helen sighs. 'They grow up. I miss the boys. We tried for another baby over the years, but it didn't happen. I always wished we'd had a girl, but I guess it just wasn't meant to be. *C'est la vie.*'

'We're hoping for another soon,' Paul smiles.

'Oh lovely,' Helen says, her enthusiasm punctuated by outstretching her arms. The remaining wine splashes over the rim of her glass and on to the grass. She doesn't seem to notice as she raises the empty glass to her lips, clearly disappointed when all she gets is the last dribble. 'It'll be wonderful for little Amelia to have a brother or sister soon.' Helen's eyes are on me, studying my reaction. I smile, but my eyes narrow as they shift to my husband.

'Will you excuse me, please?' I say. 'I really should put Amelia down for her nap.'

'But she's having such fun, Susan,' Paul says. 'Leave her to play for a while longer, yeah?'

My gaze shifts to the spot at the end of the garden where my daughter is playing contentedly with her new friends. Their giggles carry through the air like waves of childhood innocence. Their happiness is contagious, and I find myself grinning, absorbing their fun.

'Okay,' I nod.

'She probably wouldn't sleep with all this excitement and noise anyway,' Paul says. 'Let's throw routine out the window, just for today, eh?' He runs his hand up and down my upper arm encouragingly. 'It is a party after all.'

It's way past Amelia's naptime, but her bedroom is at the back of the cottage and the window overlooks the patio area where a group of elderly neighbours are sitting at our picnic table and chatting loudly.

'I wish I had half her energy,' Helen says. 'She's a little dote.'

'I'm going to pop inside and check on the appetisers,' I say, peeling my eyes reluctantly away from my little girl running around so much I know she must be exhausted, but she's determined to keep up with the bigger kids. 'I won't be long.'

'Okay. Cool,' Paul says. 'I'll keep an eye on Millie.'

'Make sure she keeps her cardigan on,' I insist. 'She keeps trying to take it off, and I don't want her catching cold.'

Paul looks at Amelia and shakes his head. 'She doesn't like that one.'

'It's her favourite,' I correct. 'It's yellow.'

'No.' Paul shakes his head again. 'She says it's scratchy.'

'Well, it will have to do,' I say. 'I don't know where her other yellow one is and she won't wear any other colour at the moment. Anyway, can you just make sure she keeps it on?'

'Ah Susan, do you really need to mollycoddle her so much?'

'There's a wind picking up and she's in the shade. She needs her cardigan. It's important.'

'You know best,' Paul sighs, defeated. 'If you need any help with the food just gimme a shout, okay?'

'Yeah. Okay.'

'I can help,' Helen suggests.

'Oh, not at all,' I say, waving my hand to politely dismiss her offer. 'You stay out here and enjoy chatting.'

'It's no trouble, honestly. I'd like to help,' she insists. 'And I'd love an excuse to inspect this new kitchen Paul has been telling us all about.'

'Great,' I lie, tucking a flyaway strand of hair behind my ear as I groan inwardly. 'Thank you.'

I really hope Helen isn't going to talk about babies and kids some more once we're inside. I already have to listen to Paul drone on about how lonely Amelia will be growing up as an only child. As if I don't understand better than anyone exactly what it feels like to be without a sibling.

'Paul,' I say, stroking my husband's arm. 'When you get a moment will you pop to the corner shop and pick up some cream for dessert? I wasn't expecting so many people and we don't have enough.'

'Sure,' he smiles, taking the empty wine glass from Helen. 'I'll just get Helen a top-up first.'

Helen touches her hands to her lips and blushes. 'Oh, I really shouldn't have another so early in the afternoon.'

'Ah go on, love,' Larry says. 'Let your hair down.'

'You'll have another too, Larry?' Paul says, looking at the nearly empty glass in Larry's hand.

'I will indeed,' Larry laughs, slugging back the last couple of mouthfuls of gin.

Chapter Three

Now

I'm busy in the kitchen, arranging steamed asparagus wrapped in Parma ham on a silver platter, when torrential rain erupts out of nowhere. Huge, heavy drops pound against the kitchen window and angry, dark clouds gather overhead, turning a summer's afternoon into a wintery evening. I forget the platter of fancy food and hurry outside, waving my arms as I encourage everyone to make a dash for the house. I quench the barbecue and turn round to find Helen behind me. She's skilfully covering salad bowls with plastic wrap and tosses raw meat into my best Tupperware, pressing the lids down firmly. I wince; the raw steak will stain the plastic and I'll never be able to wash the horrible brownish-red tinge off the lids. But I press on my best fake smile and thank her for her help.

'Keeps the air out,' Helen says, smiling, and despite the rain. 'You can stick these in the freezer. I do it all the time.'

I watch as the rain turns her pretty lemon sundress to a dreary mustard and I apologise, as if I'm somehow responsible for the weather.

'I thought Paul would be back ages ago,' I say awkwardly as I tuck a bowl under each arm and carry a tray of mixed breads towards the house.

'Ah, that's men for you,' Helen says, picking up the Tupperware. 'I sent Larry home to pick up my sunglasses. That was twenty minutes ago.' She rolls her eyes and I giggle. 'He's probably at home now, distracted by some game on the TV. He's useless at the weekends. Stick a bit of sport on the telly and I can't get him out of the house.'

'Does he play?' I ask.

Helen snorts. 'Larry? Jesus no. Running around is not his thing. He used to play football for the local team, but that was more than thirty years ago. He hasn't kicked a ball in years. And he gets annoyed when I give out to him about his lack of exercise. But I swear, Susan, that man's cholesterol is out of control.'

'Gosh,' I say, trying to sound sympathetic. 'Paul is the opposite. He's a fitness fanatic. He's obsessed with training for the Dublin marathon at the moment. He's run it a few times before, but this year he's determined to get his time under three hours. He gets pissed off any time I worry about how hard he's pushing it.'

'Men,' Helen tuts. 'I'm surrounded by them. You're so lucky to have little Amelia. She's gorgeous, Susan. A real treasure.'

'Thank you,' I smile.

'Our boys grew up so fast,' Helen sighs, her shoulders rounding. 'I miss when they were little.'

A dull silence hangs between us. I'm not sure what to say.

'You know . . . I'd be happy to babysit Amelia anytime you need, if you and Paul want to get out for dinner sometime. Or even just take a walk. I'd be happy to have her. I'd love to, actually.'

I take in Helen's genuine expression and the softness around her eyes that tells me she's spent years longing for a daughter.

'Sure,' I say, raising my eyebrows. 'Sounds good. Paul and I could use some grown-up time.'

'Great.' Helen rubs her hands together and I'm not sure if she's excited or just trying to warm herself up. 'Larry will be delighted too.

He'll never admit it, but I know he misses the kids around the house as much as I do.'

Her excitement makes me uncomfortable. I'm trying to like Helen. At least, as much as anyone can like a neighbour they're slowly becoming acquainted with. But I'm not about to leave my little girl with a stranger, no matter how kindly she offers. I concentrate hard to make sure my apprehension isn't written all over my face.

The house is now noisy and cramped. Our open-plan living space doesn't feel as spacious with so many neighbours dotted around. Some stand in corners chatting, some perch on the arms of the couch because there isn't any more room for them and some buzz like bees hovering from flower to flower as they work their way from person to person, gathering local gossip like nectar. Thankfully, conversation is flowing and there is a lot of laughter. Despite the sudden change in weather and Paul's prolonged absence, the party seems to be a success.

'You're saturated,' I say, pointing to Helen's dress. 'Can I get you something to change into?'

She looks me up and down, flashes a toothy grin and shakes her head. 'I don't think I could squeeze my thunder thighs into anything of yours, Susan. You're so slim, but thank you.'

Helen isn't overweight, but she's certainly bigger than me. Most people are, I suppose. I was born three months premature and I've always blamed being short and skinny on my early arrival.

'I'll dry off in a minute,' she smiles, trying to ease my concern. 'I'm used to a little rain, Susan, don't worry. You should see how wet I get some mornings tending to the cattle.'

'Okay.' I blush, suddenly feeling very much a city girl lost in the countryside.

'You run up and change,' Helen suggests. 'I'll chat to everyone down here.'

'I'm okay,' I lie, shivering from the cold seeping into my bones as my shirt and cropped jeans cling to my skin.

'Nonsense. You're soaked through to the bone. Don't worry about everyone down here. I'll top up their drinks and pass around the plates of finger food while you're gone.'

'Would you mind?' I ask, somewhat uncomfortable with Helen taking over as host.

'Course not. What are neighbours for? Now go on up and change before you catch a cold. Leave everything to me.'

'Thanks,' I say, suspecting that despite her pushy nature she means well.

I hope so.

I hurry to my bedroom, throw on my most respectable tracksuit and make a quick call to Paul's mobile. As I suspect, he doesn't answer but I leave a voice message, checking if he's okay and asking him to hurry.

Larry is back and chatting to Helen in the kitchen when I come downstairs. He's helped himself to another gin and tonic. His face is red and puffy and beads of perspiration dot around his receding hairline. He looks as if he's run a marathon instead of walking a couple of hundred metres up the road and back. I understand why Helen laughed earlier when I asked if Larry is sporty. The man is a walking heart attack, I think, and his fondness for gin isn't doing him any favours.

'Any sign of Paul?' I ask, glancing at my watch. 'He's been gone ages.'

Helen passes me a glass of white wine. 'Not yet,' she says, straining her eyes over my shoulder to glance at our oblivious neighbours, and I can tell she feels sorry for me being left to entertain them by myself.

'C'mon,' she says, linking my arm roughly and almost spilling the wine. 'Let's mingle. Bring that with you.' She nods at the glass in my hand. 'You'll be glad of that stuff once this lot start talking nonsense to you.'

'They can't be that bad,' I laugh. 'Everyone around here seems so nice.'

'Appearances can be deceiving.' Helen takes on a sudden seriousness that ages her. 'You've a lot to learn about this place, Susan. Ballyown has more skeletons than any graveyard in Dublin, you know.'

'Really?' I say, my eyes wide.

'She's taking the piss,' Larry says, slamming his empty gin glass on the countertop. I'm not sure if he's annoyed with Helen for talking nonsense or with me for being gullible enough to believe it.

Helen shakes her head as she reaches for the half-empty bottle of gin and splashes a generous helping into Larry's glass.

'Of course I'm joking,' she says, placing the bottle back down. 'Ballyown is lovely, Susan, and you're going to fit right in. Isn't she, Larry?'

Larry reaches for the glass and nods. 'Absolutely.' And I wonder if he loves Ballyown, or his wife, nearly as much as the clear liquid he's about to drink.

Untangling my arm from a tipsy Helen, I excuse myself and begin to work the room. I shake hands with almost everyone and express how excited I am to be the newest member of the community. The reaction is mixed. Some of the younger neighbours are excited too. Some of the older ones seem a little put out and the drunk ones don't seem to care about anything either way, as long as I'm topping up their glasses.

Minutes tick by slowly before Paul finally arrives back at the cottage. His clothes are soaked, and his mood is equally damp.

'It's raining cats and dogs out there,' he says, taking shelter in the porch as he kicks off his saturated shoes on the step. 'I got this wet just walking from the car to the door. I've been waiting in the car for twenty minutes for the rain to ease up enough to come inside, but I think it's down for the day. So much for our barbecue. I hope you're not too disappointed.'

I shake my head. 'It's been fine. Everyone has plenty to eat and drink. And now that you're back with the cream I can serve dessert.'

I look around at the picture of the entire community of Ballyown enjoying themselves in our home. 'They're all having a good time, Paul,'

I smile, 'and everyone thinks what we've done with the cottage is amazing. I wasn't expecting the rain but everything else has gone to plan. I'm really glad we did this.'

'That's great, Susan.' Paul kisses my cheek and rain trickles from his hair down my face.

'God, you're freezing,' I say. 'You need to change your clothes before you get sick.' I laugh inwardly as I hear Helen's motherly words echo in my own.

'Good idea.' Paul passes me the extra-large tub of cream. 'Here. I'll run upstairs and dry off. I won't be long. I could murder a glass of wine . . .' He pauses to glance at Helen. 'If there's any left, that is.'

'Really?' I say, surprised to hear my teetotal husband make the request.

He laughs. 'For the day that's in it, Susan. I'd like to raise a toast to my wife – interior designer extraordinaire, wonderful mother and the latest Ballyown socialite.'

'Stop teasing,' I giggle, enjoying his silliness.

I crane my neck, trying to see into the back of Paul's car, which is parked just before our little red gate. It's taken us a while to get used to roadside parking. Initially we thought about opening the front garden into a driveway, but it's such a tight space we'd only fit one car anyway and it would be a pity to lose the pretty trees and shrubs that have been growing here for years. Getting rained on the odd time seems a small sacrifice to keep such a pretty landscaped space. I shake my head. The tinted windows in the back of Paul's car don't allow me to see inside.

'Aren't you going to carry Amelia in before you change?' I call after Paul as he dashes past me to make his way up the stairs.

He stops midway and turns round.

'If she's still asleep we can put her into our bed,' I suggest. 'It's too noisy down here, all the laughing will wake her. I'll fetch the spare stair gate and put it across our bedroom door, that way she won't come flying down the stairs if she wakes, the way she nearly did last week.'

I don't like the look on Paul's face as he tilts his head to one side. 'Millie isn't in the car, Susan.'

'What?' I gasp. 'Where is she, then? You took her with you, didn't you?'

Paul's forehead wrinkles. 'You said you were putting her down for a nap.'

'You told me not to.' I set the carton of cream down on the hall table with more force than is needed. 'You said to leave her to play. Remember? You told me you'd watch her.'

'But then you asked me to go to the shop . . .' he mumbles sheepishly.

'I thought you had her,' I say, throwing my arms wide in frustration. 'What the hell, Paul? Where is she?'

'Here with you, isn't she?'

'Oh God. We all came inside when it started to rain. I thought you were watching her. Jesus Christ, Paul, why didn't you tell me?'

'Susan, calm down. Someone will hear you.' He winces as he glances around the open living space heaving with chatting neighbours.

'I don't care.' I shake my head. 'Amelia. Amelia . . .' I call, turning my back on my husband to hurry around the house. Sticky, clammy bodies are cumbersome and awkward as I squeeze past them, repeatedly calling my daughter's name. The house is buzzing with conversation and laughter. The neighbours' children whip past me as they chase each other; their voices and giggles are too loud for indoors. Amelia isn't among them.

'Have you seen Amelia?' I ask, catching the attention of one of the mothers sitting on the couch.

She looks at me blankly and I'm not sure she realises I'm the host, and she obviously has no idea who Amelia is.

'My little girl,' I say. 'She's about this high.' I hover my hand next to my mid-thigh. 'Cream dress, yellow cardigan. Have you seen her?'

The woman smiles. 'Oh, that's your daughter. She's a lovely little thing. She's been playing with my five-year-old all afternoon. They've had such fun.'

'Yes. Yes. Have you seen her recently? In the last hour or so?'

'I thought you put her down for a nap,' she says, her eyes softening, and I can tell she's picked up on my panic.

I exhale sharply, making myself light-headed.

'Sweetheart, have you seen Amelia?' she says, catching her daughter's arm as she whizzes by in the group of hyper children.

The girl shakes her head. 'She's not playing with us any more.'

'Well, where is she, then?' I snap.

The girl's eyes cloud over with tears as she shuffles closer to her mother. I've scared her.

'Where is she?' I repeat, finding myself shouting. 'Where is Amelia?'

'She doesn't know,' the mother answers, pulling her daughter close to her, clearly annoyed that I've raised my voice.

'Amelia?' I begin to shout. 'Amelia!'

'Millie!' Paul calls from the stairs.

I spin round and catch his eye. Suddenly he doesn't look worried about raised voices, but he does look worried. My panic is rubbing off on him.

'Millie, sweetheart.' His deep voice is so much louder than mine. 'I'll check upstairs,' he says. 'You check the garden.'

'Okay!' I shout back, startling some of our neighbours, who begin to look concerned.

'Susan.' Helen catches my arm as I rush towards the double doors at the back of the house. 'Is everything all right?'

'Have you seen Amelia?' I ask, my heart beating fast.

'No. Not for a while.' Helen's speech is slurred from several glasses of wine. 'Susan, are you okay? You look like you've seen a ghost.'

I shake my arm free and reach for the door handle. I jerk it open roughly and run into the garden. Heavy, cold rain pelts me all over and the wind blows strands of my hair across my face, blocking my vision. I rub my eyes and hurry towards the end of the garden.

'Amelia!' I shout, spinning round, trying to take in the whole space. 'Amelia, where are you?'

I feel the heat of Paul's body suddenly behind me as he presses his hands on my shoulders. 'She's not upstairs,' he says.

My chest tightens. 'The gate,' I say, pointing. 'It's open. Oh Jesus, the gate is open, Paul.'

'One of the older kids must have opened it,' he says, hurrying ahead of me.

'The ducks,' I cry. 'Amelia wanted to feed the ducks. I said no.'

Paul races through the gate. I'm right behind him, even though I can barely breathe.

The stream looks as innocent and unassuming as always. Raindrops dance across the surface, creating ripples between the large rocks protruding in haphazard places. The water is clear and I can see the pebbles at the bottom; it's not even knee-deep and only waist-high for Amelia. We paddled in it just a couple of days ago, but Amelia didn't like it when the water splashed her face. If she fell in she'd have been able to pull herself out, and she'd have come into the house crying with the cold and shock.

'There are no ducks here today.' I point towards a patch of green scum floating near the bank where the ducks usually feed.

'She loves those damn ducks,' Paul says and shakes his head.

Without another word he sprints down the narrow laneway that runs alongside the stream.

'Millie!' he calls. 'Millie!'

I kick off my heels and run after him. I don't feel the stony pathway beneath my feet. Normally I would struggle to keep up with Paul's speed and fitness but right now I'm just a couple of steps behind him.

We come to a fork. One path is narrow with tall trees blocking out the light. It scares me, so I know it would be terrifying to a two-year-old. The other path is wider and brighter and sweeps away from the water.

'This way,' Paul shouts, veering on to the dark path.

I shake my head. 'We've never been down this way. Amelia and I walk in the other direction.'

'I ran this way this morning,' Paul pants. 'This path leads to the lake.'

'I know. But it's dark and scary. Amelia wouldn't go down there. Not by herself.'

'She would if she was following the ducks,' Paul says.

'The fucking ducks,' I growl. 'Why didn't I just let her feed them? She only wanted to feed them. Oh Christ, Paul, where is she? Where is our baby?'

'C'mon,' he says and grabs my hand.

We run again. My hot breath dances across the air in front of my face like a cloud as I puff out, my lungs burning.

'Millie!' Paul roars, skidding on wet clay as he reaches the lake edge, almost dragging us both in. 'Millie, are you here?'

'Amelia! It's Mammy and Daddy.' I shake my hand free from Paul's and run along the water's edge, my breath shallow and laboured.

The water is angry. Twisting and turning as if the rain and wind have woken it from slumber.

'Do you think she's hiding?' Paul's voice breaks and his fear is palpable. 'Maybe she's playing. She loves hide and seek, doesn't she?'

I shake my head. 'The ducks.' I point to where several ducklings swim in a straight line behind their mother, not far from us.

'She can't swim.' Paul states what I already know. 'She wouldn't get in the water to play with them. She knows the water is dangerous. Haven't you told her it's dangerous?'

'Of course I have,' I shout. 'But what if she slipped? Oh Paul. I can't see her. I can't see our baby anywhere.'

Paul doesn't reply. He runs around, retracing his steps up the laneway and back. I don't move. I'm frozen to the spot, as if the chilly wind has turned me to ice.

'For fuck's sake, Susan,' Paul shouts. 'Don't just stand there. Look for her!'

I begin to cry. I wrap my arms around myself and sob loudly.

Some of our neighbours appear behind us. The looks on their faces tell me they've guessed what's going on.

'She can't have gone far,' Helen says, suddenly at my side.

'She's been gone for an hour at least,' I say. 'She's alone. She's all alone.'

I look up to the sound of splashing. Paul and some of the men have begun wading into the water. A succession of loud voices calling my daughter's name rings in my ears.

The mothers and children stand back. The hyper children are calm now – silent as their mothers hold their hands much too tightly, keeping them safely away from the water as everyone looks on in disbelief.

Helen passes me her phone. 'Has anyone called the Guards?'

'Oh God.' My eyes widen. 'The cops.'

'It's the shock, Susan,' Helen says, sober as she drapes her arm over my shoulder and holds me close. 'You didn't have time to think. Call them now.'

My hands shake as I try to dial. I hear Paul's voice above all the other men shouting. The sound of my husband screaming our daughter's name echoes around the trees and bounces back to punch me in the gut. I double over, almost dropping Helen's phone in some long grass.

'Here.' Helen takes her phone back from me. 'Let me help.'

I watch the activity in the lake as if it's some horrible film I wish I hadn't come to see. The water must be freezing, but no one acknowledges the cold as they wade deeper and deeper.

'Hello. Gardaí please?' I hear Helen say as a teenage boy emerges from under the water with a yellow, knitted cardigan in his hand.

Chapter Four

Then

My alarm goes off at 6.30 a.m., like always. Too sleepy to open my eyes, I pat my hand around my bedside table, searching for the button on the alarm clock to shut it up. Triumphant, I flop on to my belly and pray that my flatmate hasn't used all the hot water again. My flatmate is my twin brother, Adam. He's recently broken up with his girlfriend of two years, and he spends most mornings in the shower, wanking. I'm cool with him taking the hands-on approach against heartbreak, no pun intended, I'm just not okay with having to have a bloody cold shower every day because of his penis.

I love my brother, but the downside of being a twin is that every milestone you reach in your life your sibling reaches at almost the same time. Learning to walk, for example. Adam was marginally first, two days ahead of me, and he never lets me forget it. He proudly called me Snoozy Susie until last year. First tooth – according to our mother, I won this round by a whole month, but I also started losing my baby teeth before him, which meant Adam looked cute and loveable in our cousin's wedding photographs when we were seven while I looked gappy and goofy. Academically, our results are usually on a par. We're both high achievers, although the grades come easily to my brother while I work my arse off, but I'll never admit that.

Morning showers aren't technically a milestone. But since Adam and I have a lot of overlapping classes we tend to be heading for the shower at the same time as each other every morning. I'm most definitely not a morning person. Adam is. Which means that for four years of college he has beaten me to the bathroom every day. This morning I'm determined to win the battle.

I flop my legs over the edge of the bed and wince as fluff from the carpet – I badly need to hoover – sticks to my bare feet. I shake one leg at a time, shedding crumbs and bits of I-don't-even-know-what. I pull on my oversized green hoodie with the college logo printed across the front in giant navy letters and fish around on the end of my bed for the clean towel I know I left there last night. Unsurprisingly, I find it in a ball on the floor. I pick it up, shake it out and throw it over my shoulder. *A hot shower is mine.* I open my bedroom door and the smell of eggs and bacon distracts me.

'Why the hell are you up and cooking so early?' I ask, running a hand through my bed hair as I bypass the bathroom to investigate the delicious smell.

'We've a party to organise.' Adam flashes a goofy smile as he stands in his boxers in the tiny kitchenette just metres from my bedroom, stirring eggs in a pan. 'And I was awake anyway. Not all of us sleep all day, you know.'

I pull a face and point towards the poky living room window. The weather is filthy. Strong wind blows rain against the glass with temper. Thunder rumbles in the distance and I laugh inwardly because I'd heard the noise already in my sleep but I thought it was my tummy telling me that I'm hungry. It's the kind of day that makes you want to stay in bed bingeing on DVD box sets while eating too much chocolate and popcorn. It's not the kind of day you celebrate your twenty-first birthday.

'Do you think we should call off the party?' I say, more of a statement than a question. 'No one is going to want to come out in this crappy weather, are they?'

'What?' Adam scrunches his nose. 'No. Of course we're not cancelling. Are you mad? It's only a little rain, Sue. Anyway, Mam is already on her way.'

'She's driving in this weather?' I say.

Adam's eyes narrow and he looks at me seriously, seeming so much older than his twenty-one years. 'Sue, it's just rain, not bloody Armageddon. What's up with you? You're acting all stressed out or something. It's our birthday. You should be happy.'

I press my hands against my waist and stand nervously with a hip out. 'It's just this stupid thunder. It's giving me the creeps or something.'

'I think it's awesome,' Adam says. 'Look at that. How can you not love it?' He points towards the window as a sheet of lightning streaks across the horizon. It's followed almost instantly by a nerve-rackingly loud clap of thunder.

'I have a bad feeling.' I fold my arms across my chest.

'You're just nervous about the party,' Adam says. 'But you only turn twenty-one once, Sue. And tonight is going to be the best party ever. Just relax and enjoy it. No one is going to give a shit about a little drizzle when the DJ gets going. Trust me.'

I know my brother is right. Our friends won't care about bad weather, and they certainly won't miss out on a party because of it. Adam and I have been looking forward to this milestone for months. But I can't relax. The knot of anxiety in my stomach is not just pre-party nerves. It's silly, I know, and I can't quite put my finger on it, but something is making me edgy.

'Can't you put some clothes on while you cook?' I say, trying to distract myself from my concerns with something familiar and comfortable. Teasing my brother is about as comfortable as it gets.

'Eh? I did,' Adam laughs, dropping his eyes to his boxers.

'Ugh. Yuck.' I pull a face. 'I didn't need to know you sleep naked. What the hell, Adam? Overshare much? You're so gross, you know.'

He shrugs, ignores my disgust and continues cooking.

'Okay, next question,' I say as my nostrils widen, savouring the enticing aroma wafting from the kitchenette. 'Did you think it would be funny to set my alarm for stupid o'clock on a Saturday?'

Adam laughs. 'I didn't. You can't blame me if you were too lazy to reset it, Sue.'

I groan loudly, knowing my morning-person brother is right. I fell into bed last night sometime around 2 a.m., after a *Buffy the Vampire Slayer* marathon.

'But, it's sooooo early,' I protest, tossing my head back to stare vacantly at the ceiling. 'We don't even have class today.'

Adam sighs. 'It's 1.30 in the afternoon. And yes! If you're wondering if your alarm went off as usual this morning—' He stops stirring the eggs to turn and face me. 'It did. At 6.30. And want to know how I know that?'

I meet my brother's stare head-on. I know a lecture is coming no matter what I say.

'Because you weren't the one who turned it off, were you?' Adam says.

I grunt, knowing where this is going.

'I was,' Adam continues, turning his attention back to the eggs before they start to burn. 'It woke me, Sue. From the other bloody room. You were in a fucking coma and didn't hear it because you stayed up all night watching that vampire crap and drooling over the dude who needs to get a tan.'

'1.30?'

'Yup! I reset your alarm for lunchtime. I can't believe you didn't notice.'

'No wonder I'm starving,' I smile. 'Is there some for me?' I ask, yawning as I make my way into the kitchenette, which is barely big enough for two people.

'Yeah, s'pose,' Adam says. 'If I don't feed you, you won't feed yourself, will you?' Adam rolls his eyes, but he can't keep a straight face as he pulls the pan off the heat. He's laughing by the time he begins to plate up the eggs.

I'm older than my brother. Three minutes and eleven seconds older to be exact. Although, ironically, timekeeping hasn't been my strong suit since.

Adam and I were born twelve weeks early, twenty-one years ago today. And our mother loves to tell the story of how she nearly died in the process; how we all nearly died, and how we're lucky to be here at all.

'I was barely eighteen. Only a baby myself,' Mam says, as if Adam and I were very inconsiderate for gatecrashing her party lifestyle. 'It's not easy being a single parent. And you were such sickly little things,' she often reminds us. 'It's a miracle. You're miracles. I spent all my time worried about you.'

She always points to the fine lines around her eyes and tells us we're responsible. She's joking, of course. Mam is only thirty-nine, but she looks ten years younger. When she comes to visit Adam and me on campus, our friends often think she's our older sister, and she rarely tells them otherwise. Actually, people often think my mother and brother are related and I'm just a friend.

Mam and Adam are tall and broad. They both have brown eyes and fair hair. On the other hand, I'm short and too skinny for my own good. I have black hair and my eyes are a greeny-blue, like the Caribbean Sea. Adam sometimes teases me that there must have been a mix-up at the hospital and they brought me home by mistake. But while my brother looks like Mam on the outside, inside he's very different. He's quiet and placid – nothing like our mother. Or me. Mam and I are outspoken and opinionated. And not always easy to get along with. We don't always get along with each other. Thank God for Adam keeping the peace. Funny, that's probably one of the few things Mam and I have in common – our love of Adam.

Most people never believe we're twins. He's more than a head taller than me, ironic considering when we were born he was less than half my birth weight and the doctors warned my mother that he probably wouldn't make it. Mam hasn't stopped worrying about him since. While Adam spent the first three months of our lives in hospital on a ventilator, I was home after just five weeks. Those eight weeks are the longest we've ever spent apart. Adam is my twin but he's also my best friend, and I rely on him more than I'll ever admit out loud to anyone, especially him.

'Right, make yourself useful and make some toast,' he says, breaking into my thoughts as he throws a half loaf of bread at me.

'You're right beside the toaster,' I say.

'You are so lazy,' Adam says, knocking his shoulder against mine. 'Mam was right when she warned me if we shared a flat I'd end up taking care of your lazy arse.'

'I'm not lazy,' I groan, unfazed by my mother's dig. 'I'm just not good with cooking and shit.'

'Or cleaning,' Adam says, looking over his shoulder into the messy living area.

I follow his gaze. A bottle of my foundation is on top of the TV, missing its lid. There are several pairs of my shoes scattered around the floor and a small mountain of my clothes at one end of the couch.

'Whoops,' I say, spying my favourite black lacy top peeking out from the middle of my clothes monster. I hurry over to the couch to drag it out, knocking half the pile of clothes on to the floor in the process.

Adam groans, unimpressed.

'What?' I say, waving my top above my head like a flag. 'I've been looking for this.'

'Well, you need to clean this place up before tonight,' he grumbles, adding some delicious crispy bacon on top of the two plates of eggs.

'A few people will probably call round here for a drink before we head to the party.'

'Ah Adam,' I say, annoyed that my brother has obviously invited people to our flat without clearing it with me first.

'It's just a couple of the lads,' he smiles, knowing I'm on to him. 'I said it to your friends too, of course.'

'You what?'

'Well, I knew you wouldn't so—'

'Yeah, you're right, I wouldn't. We promised Mam we'd keep it simple. And you know if things get out of hand, I'll be the one she blames,' I say. Sulking, I tuck my top under my arm and walk back into the kitchenette to fetch my plate of food. 'I thought we could have a couple of glasses of champagne here, just you, me and Mam, and then head to the party together.'

Adam scrapes his fork against his plate and the shrill squeak hurts my brain. 'But that was before I was about to break the biggest, juiciest story ever,' he says.

I groan. Adam is always about to break the biggest, juiciest story – forever following a lead here and a hint there. I'm getting more and more frustrated that he can't give it a rest for one bloody night.

'I'm serious this time, Sue,' he says, reading me. 'All I need is a couple of incriminating photos and – boom! Exclusive has my name all over it. This story will be career changing. I want to par-TAY.'

'Career changing?' I snort. 'Adam, it's the college paper, not the national press. You're still a student, remember?'

'And Ms Mahon is still university president, but that doesn't stop her sleeping with students.'

'Fuck off,' I say, my hand covering my mouth.

'You should see your face,' he chuckles, polishing off his bacon. 'I told you this was a juicy story, didn't I?'

I can't form any words.

'Apparently she's been at it for years. The canteen. The library. Her office. She's a complete nympho. And, of course, her favourite students pass with flying colours.'

'That's so gross,' I say, gagging for dramatic effect. 'Isn't she like a hundred and ten or something?'

Adam rolls his eyes at my exaggeration. 'She's in her fifties, Sue. But that's still thirty whatever years older than the students she's banging. And she's married and has kids.'

'Wow. That is pretty fucked up.'

'I know, right? There's a couple of us on to her. But I'm determined to break the story first.'

I take a deep breath. 'Adam, are you sure about this?'

'Don't look so worried,' he grins. 'I've never been more certain of anything in my life. This story is mine.'

'Okay, okay,' I say. A sinking feeling in the pit of my stomach puts me off my eggs. 'But just be careful. She's the president of our university. If this goes wrong, it will go spectacularly wrong.'

'I know, but nothing is going to go wrong,' he says, shovelling a huge forkful of egg into his mouth and swallowing. 'Trust me.'

'Oh Adam.' I shake my head, unsure.

'Look, I'll tell everyone the pre-party is off. We'll meet them at the venue instead. Will that make you feel better?'

'Okay. Cool. Thanks,' I say, taken aback. I was certain he'd put up more of a fight.

'Don't be too smug about getting your own way, Sue. You can pay for the champagne. I'm broke. Stupid suit hire is costing me a fortune.'

'You're hiring a suit?' My eyes widen. 'Jesus, isn't that a bit fancy?'

'No. It's our twenty-first. Everyone will be dressed up.'

'Yeah. Our twenty-first, not our fiftieth. Suits are for old people.'

'Eh, listen to who's talking, Miss I want to drink posh champagne with my family instead of chilling with my mates,' Adam says in a terrible mimic of my voice.

'Right. Fine. Whatever.' I shrug, forcing the last of my eggs down. 'But I'm wearing jeans and this top I just found.' I pull my top out from under my arm and press the lacy fabric against my nose and sniff to make sure it's clean enough to wear later.

'You're disgusting,' he says, tossing his empty plate into the sink of soapy water. 'Right. I cooked, so you can clean. I'm going to pick up my suit now. If you give me some cash I'll get the champagne while I'm out.'

'What? Now?' I protest.

'Yup,' Adam nods. 'The suit hire place closes at four on Saturdays.'

'But the storm?' I grumble, pointing to the window.

'I'll bring an umbrella, okay?'

I don't bother to argue. Adam is becoming annoyed, I can tell, and I don't want to spoil the evening with a pointless argument over the weather.

I stuff a slice of bacon into my mouth to buy myself time while I try to think where I left my wallet.

'Do you just want one bottle of champagne?' Adam asks.

'Eh, yeah,' I say. 'That stuff's expensive. Actually, maybe Prosecco.'

'Okay. One bottle. Of cheap Prosecco,' he says, holding in a laugh. 'I can tell by your face that you've no idea where your wallet is, so you can just pay me back when I get home. And clean up, yeah? This place is disgusting.'

'Hey,' I moan, tossing my empty plate into the sink where it clinks against Adam's. 'Who made you the boss?'

He shrugs cockily. 'So don't clean. I won't be the one who has to listen to Mam's moaning about the state of the place when she gets here.'

'Ugh.' I wrinkle my nose. 'I hate it when you're right.'

'I'm always right,' Adam laughs, snapping the towel from my shoulder before racing towards the bathroom. 'And I'm always first in the shower.'

'Arsehole,' I shout after him as he locks the door.

Several minutes later Adam is by the front door, wearing the same hoodie as me, except his fits him. He has the strap of his fancy and expensive camera slung over one shoulder and my hot-pink umbrella is tucked under his arm.

'Before you say anything . . . I left you hot water,' he smiles.

Lightning flashes and engulfs our entire living area in a purple-blue hue for a split second, followed almost instantly by a loud clap of thunder.

'Don't look so worried, Sue,' Adam says as he opens the door. 'I won't be long. This is going to be the best birthday ever. I promise. See you soon.'

The wind slams the door shut behind him with an aggressive thud and I shake my head, wondering how my twin brother and I have grown up to be such different people.

Three hours later I'm hot and clammy from cleaning. My fingers feel flaky and grubby where the inside of the cheap rubber gloves has started to crumble against my skin because I've been scrubbing so hard. My efforts have paid off; the kitchenette is spotless. The countertops actually sparkle. I sorted and put away all my clothes. In the process, I found a black cocktail dress I'd forgotten about and decided to wear it tonight. *Adam won't be showing me up in his suit after all*, I think. My bedroom is clean and tidy and I even changed the sheets on my bed, realising it's pretty disgusting that I can't remember the last time I did that.

Exhausted, I peel off my gloves and throw them in the bin. I thought Adam would be back ages ago. I wonder if he's lost track of time taking photos of the storm. I hope he got some good shots. I decide I'll try to get my hands on his camera when he's not looking and have the best ones printed off and framed. I haven't had a chance to get him a birthday present yet, so this would be perfect.

I make the most of having the flat to myself. I spend ages in the shower, and when I get out I put *Buffy the Vampire Slayer* on the telly and plug in my hair straightener in the living room. Adam would go crazy if he caught me. I've already burned several holes in the carpet in my room, and he says the landlord will freak and we'll lose our deposit when we move out. Adam worries about all the wrong things, I think, staring out the window at a tree blowing furiously in the storm. I try to take my mind off my overzealous brother hunting for a great shot. I pull on my little black dress over greyish-blue underwear that used to be white, and flop on to the couch to make a start on my make-up.

I must have fallen asleep, because when I open my eyes again the thunder and lightning have stopped and the rain has reduced to a depressing drizzle. Adam was right not to cancel the party. I was worrying over nothing. The storm has blown over in time. Bubbles of excitement pop in my tummy as I look forward to the night ahead.

When my phone rings I expect to find my brother's name onscreen, but I'm not surprised to see my mother's instead – I was expecting her to be here at least an hour ago. The weather must be playing havoc with the traffic, I think. I try to hit answer but I'm sleepy and uncoordinated. The ringing stops and seconds later my phone beeps, informing me that I have a voice message. I listen.

'Sue, it's Mam. Please, please call me as soon as you get this. There's been an accident. A terrible accident.'

Chapter Five

Now

TEN DAYS LATER

The news comes on the telly and I close my eyes and cover my ears with my hands. 'Blasted thing,' Helen says. 'I'll turn it off.'

I wait a couple of seconds before I lower my hands and open my eyes. 'Thank you,' I say, choking back tears. 'I just can't listen to them talk about Amelia any more. It's too hard.'

'I know. I know,' Helen says, placing the remote control on the coffee table next to a freshly made sandwich.

'Are there reporters still outside?' I ask.

She walks over to the window and parts the drawn curtain just enough to peek through. 'Nope. No one. Oh wait, hang on . . . a girl with a fancy camera. I think she's taking pictures of the house.'

I shake my head.

'Will I tell her to go away?' Helen asks.

'No point,' I shrug. 'She'll just come back later. Or tomorrow. They always do. There's always someone here, isn't there? If it's not the cops, it's the press, or a curious neighbour. I wasn't prepared for this. I didn't know there would be so many people. So many questions. I can't breathe.' I tug at the collar of my blouse, loosening it, but it doesn't help and I still feel choked.

'Ah Susan,' Helen says as she lowers herself on to the sitting room couch next to me. 'How could anyone prepare for this? You're doing great. And you don't have to answer anyone's questions. Not if you're not up to it.'

I can see her thigh brush against mine and she places her hand on my knee, but I don't feel her touch. My whole body is numb, everywhere is stiff and without feeling – except for my head. My head hurts. It pulses like it might explode as I replay in my mind the image of my teenage neighbour pulling Amelia's cardigan out of the water.

'Susan, won't you eat something?' Helen asks, her voice slicing into my thoughts.

I shake my head. Food is the last thing on my mind as I stare at the blank television screen where an image of Amelia shone back at me moments ago. I don't remember Paul giving a photo of Amelia to the police or the reporters. Did he give them a photo of me too? I know he'd never provide one of himself. Paul can't abide having his photo taken.

'Susan.' Helen says my name in a sing-song voice. 'You haven't eaten in days.'

'What day is it?' I ask.

'Tuesday,' Helen says. 'It's Tuesday, today. Can you remember the last time you ate? You must be hungry. Please just try a little bite. I'm worried about you.'

I shake my head as I glance at the ham sandwich and glass of ice water in front of me on the coffee table. The food turns my stomach as if it has sat there for days. I guess Helen must have brought it from her house. I don't have any fresh bread. Or ham. But my fridge *is* full of food. Mostly lasagne and quiches.

'Anything that will hold for a couple of days and keep you going,' my well-meaning but nosy neighbours say when they arrive at my front door carrying a tray of home-made offerings.

I always accept the food that I know I'll never eat, and I manage the words 'thank you' before I close the door without inviting them in.

The only people who have been inside my house since Amelia disappeared are the team of police and Helen.

Helen is here almost all the time. She arrives early in the morning and leaves late at night, when Larry finally finishes work on the farm and comes to walk her home in the dark. He usually stinks of gin and can barely stand up straight. And I can hear him shouting profanities at her before they reach the gate.

Helen has taken on the role of a mother figure in my house. I'm not sure if she's trying to help me or herself, and I'm too exhausted to try to figure it out. I have no idea how Paul feels about her constant presence. Paul and I haven't properly spoken in a while. He's rarely at home. And when he is here, I barely recognise him and the way he's acting.

He took down all Amelia's paintings from the fridge without asking me. I'm not sure exactly when I noticed they were gone. It may have taken me a couple of days. I was furious at first. And hurt. Then I found them under his pillow. But I don't know why he keeps them there. He doesn't sleep in our bed any more. He falls asleep on the couch or at the kitchen table, usually in the early morning, after pacing the floor for hours. As soon as he wakes, he pulls on running gear and leaves the house. He never says goodbye. The slam of the front door behind him is the only clue that he's gone.

Paul can't seem to be here. And I can't be anywhere else. It's as if every piece of furniture reminds us of her. As if the walls whisper her name and torment us. Our little cottage that we've grown to love is lonely and enormous without the sound of childhood laughter filling it every day. Last night I watched my husband rock back and forth on a kitchen chair all evening. His hands covered his ears as he said our daughter's name over and over while tears streamed down his flushed cheeks. I didn't go to him. I didn't try to touch him, or hold him or kiss him. I can't bear to be near him. Paul, with his eyes of glacier blue and hair the colour of desert sand – just like Amelia.

I jump as I feel Helen's hand press firmly on my shoulder.

'Jesus, Susan. I'm sorry. I didn't mean to startle you.'

'It's fine,' I say, shaking a little.

My heart is beating furiously, and I'm aware of the sound of my blood coursing in my veins as it swishes inside my aching head.

'Where's Paul today?' Helen asks quietly, looking at her watch.

'Running,' I reply, hating how defensive I sound. 'Paul likes to run.'

'I know. But he's been gone a long time, even longer than yesterday. Do you want me to send Larry to go look for him?'

I shake my head. I don't need Larry to look for Paul. I know where my husband is. It's the same place he's been every day for the past ten days. He's down at the lake. And I know what he does there; he stands at the water's edge and waits for Amelia, as if she'll float up to him, take his hand and come home.

'You shouldn't be alone, Susan,' Helen says. 'Paul should be here with you. I know he needs the fresh air and time to clear his head, but I haven't seen him much since . . . since . . . well—' She clears her throat. 'I just think you need each other at a time like this.'

I pull my shoulder away from under Helen's hand and turn so I can look her in the eye.

'He thinks she's dead, you know,' I say. 'Paul thinks Amelia drowned. He thinks she fell in looking for those damn ducks.'

Tears prick the corner of Helen's eyes. She hasn't cried in front of me. Not once. She's probably the only person in the whole village who hasn't broken down and offered me their condolences, as if they're so damn sure my baby is dead. But I can tell she wants to. I can tell Helen wants to cry her eyes out, because it's just so bloody wrong that a beautiful little girl was running around the garden on a sunny afternoon and suddenly she's not here any more.

'You can say it, you know,' I sigh. 'Everyone else has. I've heard the rumours. People saying I'm a bad mother. I blow into the village, more concerned with making friends and keeping up appearances than watching my own daughter.'

Helen shakes her head and the tears she's battled to hold back begin to fall. 'Listen here to me, Susan Warner. You are not a bad mother. You loved that little girl. It was an accident. A tragic accident. No one is to blame. No one.'

'You think she's dead too, don't you?' I swallow. 'You think she drowned, just like everyone else in this miserable village.'

'Susan, it's been ten days,' she whispers, reaching for my hand. 'I can understand you clinging to hope. Lord knows, I'd do the same myself. But . . .'

'Someone took her, Helen,' I snap, pulling my hand away before she touches me. 'Someone stole my baby.'

'Who, Susan? Who would take a little girl from her own garden with the whole neighbourhood watching?'

'A monster.' I drag my hand through my hair, my fingers catching in the knots. 'Someone has my daughter, Helen. I'm going to bring my baby home. And I'm going to make the bastard who took her pay. I'm going to make him pay for everything he's done. He deserves to pay, doesn't he?'

She nods and tries to smile as she reaches for my hands and lowers them slowly. Her fingers curl around my palm, attempting to be positive, but her wrinkled brow and cloudy eyes tell me how fearful she really is.

A couple of firm knocks sound on the front door. Helen lets go of me, and it's only then I realise I've been holding my breath.

'I'll get it, if you like?' she says as she runs the tips of her fingers under her eyes to catch some tears.

I nod.

'Hello,' she says, opening the door of the cottage to a man and woman.

I stand up as soon as the man speaks. I recognise his voice and I make my way to the door.

'Oh God,' I say. 'Have you news? Have the divers found something?'

'May we come in, Susan?' Detective Connelly asks, his voice steady as always, offering no clues about what he's thinking.

I nod and walk back to the couch, pleading with myself to remain calm.

'Can I get anyone tea or coffee?' Helen asks, and I guess she's realised the strangers are the Gardaí assigned to Amelia's case.

'No, thank you,' the young female detective says.

'Speak for yourself, Langton,' the older man cuts in. 'I'd appreciate a coffee, thank you.' I watch his eyes sweep over the sandwich and water I haven't touched. 'Susan, you'll have a coffee too, won't you?' he asks.

There's a distinctly father-like quality about him, and sometimes I feel as if he wants to wrap his arms around me and tell me everything will be okay. And I think I'd like it if he did. I presume he has children my age. Maybe he has grandchildren too. Grandchildren like Amelia.

'Yeah, coffee,' I nod, sitting down. 'Coffee would be good, Helen – thanks.'

'Ah good,' Helen says. 'And I'll make some tea for myself. If you change your mind, Miss . . . Miss . . .'

'Fiona,' the female Garda says. 'And, thank you, but I really am okay.'

'Fiona,' I repeat silently in my head, thinking how the name suits her. Fiona Langton.

I'm sure the pair of Gardaí standing uncomfortably in my home have told me their first names before. Maybe many times. But I don't remember. Detective Langton and Detective Connelly refer to each other by their surnames. It's obviously an occupational habit. I wonder if they do the same outside of work. If they bump into each in the supermarket aisle, do they still assume the same formalities?

Fancy seeing you here, Langton.

Oh, I just popped in for some frozen peas, Connelly.

I like Connelly. He's considerably older than Langton. Old enough to be her father. He's overweight, but his suit tells me he wasn't always that way. It's a tight fit and his jacket struggles to button up over his a-few-doughnuts-too-many belly. The tailoring is dated, and the pin-stripe is wide and out of fashion. I suspect his suits are serving Connelly as long as he's been serving the force. He wears black. Always. The only splash of colour is his fat tie that looks like it's escaped from an 80s romantic comedy. But he smiles at me often and his eyes tell me how much his heart breaks every time he's assigned to the case of a missing child. He squeezes my hand sometimes, and it feels as if he's promising he'll find my little girl.

Langton is entirely different. She looks at me with unsure eyes and I wonder if she has children of her own. She's about my age. At most she's a year or two older. I think that might be unusually young to be a detective but I'm not well up on that sort of thing. She has a neat, strawberry-blonde bob and fair skin, the kind that burns after just a couple of minutes outdoors in the summer. Freckles sprinkle across her nose like cinnamon on an apple tart and her lips are narrow and dark red – serious, always, like a stern headmistress. Her pencil skirts sit respectably below her knee and her jacket plunges tastefully, reveal-ing a crisp pastel blouse. She oozes perfection. She looks like someone who has never had a bad hair day in her life. A woman who doesn't make mistakes, and certainly not the type of mother who would ever lose a child. Her clear eyes sweep over my dishevelled appearance, which is a stark contrast against my perfect home. She tries, and fails, to hide her disapproval with professional composure, but I can feel her judging me, wondering how I could possibly be so negligent. Wondering how any mother could be so caught up by sudden bad weather that she neglected her own child. Wondering if this is all my fault. But, mostly, I see her wondering if I'm broken. And the answer is written all over my face.

'Is Paul here?' Connelly asks, lowering himself to sit next to me, and the cushion behind him puffs out in protest under his weight.

I shake my head.

'Okay.' Connelly sighs. 'Will he be home soon?'

I shrug. I can feel Langton's eyes burn into me and I should be embarrassed that my husband appears to have abandoned me when we need each other most, but I don't have the energy.

'We were hoping to speak to both of you,' Langton explains, folding her arms.

'Paul is out running,' Helen says, appearing from the kitchen area.

She carries my cherished, hand-painted china tray in her hands and matching cups with steam swirling out the top rattle and clink with each unsure step she takes towards us. There's a plate of chocolate biscuits too. I don't know where Helen found them. Maybe one of the neighbours dropped them in.

'This is beautiful.' Langton points to the tray that seems to fit effortlessly in my home.

'Thank you,' I say, glancing at the blue swallows painted above bright green foliage that work their way across the china set. 'It was a gift from my mother. A few years ago.'

I neglect to mention that at the time my mother gave it to me I stuffed it under my bed for months on end, horrified by the sight of the kitsch thing.

'Ah, lovely. Thank you,' Connelly says as Helen leans over the coffee table, lifts the biscuits and hot cups off the tray and places them on the table.

Helen clears away the untouched sandwich and glass of now lukewarm water and sighs as she looks at me. 'I made your coffee extra strong, Susan. You need it.'

'Thank you,' I say, relieved as she walks back towards the kitchen.

'Paul goes out running a lot,' Langton says as soon as Helen is out of earshot.

'Yes,' I agree, reaching for the cup of coffee nearest to me. It's much too hot to drink.

'Has he always been a keen runner?' Connelly asks.

I smile. Connelly's approach is much softer. More likeable. He manages to ask the same questions as Langton but in a more human way.

'As long as I've known him. Yes,' I say.

'And how long is that?' Langton asks.

What a strange question, I think as I stare her down with bloodshot eyes and I'm sure my expression tells her as much.

She elaborates awkwardly. 'Are you married long?'

'Four years,' I say. 'Five this summer.'

'And how did you meet?'

'We bumped into each other in a coffee shop, but it took him a long time to finally work up the courage to ask me out.'

'A true romance.' Connelly smiles. 'Ah, young love. You can't beat it, can you?'

'Did you know Paul before that?' Langton asks.

I shake my head, distressed. 'I'm sorry, these questions . . .'

Connelly shoots Langton a look that warns her to back off. I'd put money on her next question being about Paul's past. And I'm certainly not about to discuss that. Not now. Not ever.

'Are you a runner too?' Connelly asks, impressively deflecting, and I let on as if I don't notice him pulling rank.

'No. Just Paul.' I answer his question but I keep my eyes on Langton.

I don't like her and I definitely don't trust her.

'Paul is training for the Dublin marathon,' I explain. 'He's run it every year since we've been married, and every year he tries to beat his previous time. He's fast. Top two per cent, or something like that.'

'And is he going to run it this year?' Langton says.

It's not what she says but the way she says it that makes the hairs on the back of my neck stand on end. She doesn't only think I'm a bad mother. She thinks Paul is a lousy father too. As if we're self-absorbed parents who deserve to lose a child. *Paul busy running. Me busy trying to fit in. Amelia didn't stand a chance.*

'I don't know.' I shrug. 'Maybe. We haven't discussed it. Paul was training hard before . . .' I cough and take a mouthful of coffee. It's scalding and it stings as it makes its way down my throat like liquid fire.

'Do you know where he runs? The route?' Langton says.

'Not really. Down by the lake sometimes. The road into town isn't safe. There's lots of bends and blind spots. I don't like him running there. I've asked him not to.'

'How far does he run?' Langton continues. 'Four, maybe five kilometres?'

'God no.' I shake my head. 'Ten most days. Fifteen sometimes.'

'But it's only a couple of kilometres to the lake and back,' Langton says.

'Yeah . . . and . . .' I twitch.

'And where does he pick up the remaining thirteen kilometres?'

'I don't know,' I say, my eyes seeking out Helen in the kitchen.

She has her back to me as she leans over the sink, washing dishes that have been there for days.

I want to believe Langton is trying to make conversation until Paul comes home. I want to believe she's simply taking an interest in my husband's hobby, but there's something about the determined glint in her eyes that tells me this is more than just an awkward chat. She makes me uneasy and maybe I'm too tired to hide it.

'Are you married?' I ask, a single eyebrow raised accusingly.

I glance at her wedding finger and I don't see a ring. But that doesn't answer my question. Maybe she doesn't wear her ring at work.

Her eyes meet mine and she shakes her head. 'No.'

'Kids?' I mumble, the word passing my lips before I have time to think.

Langton remains silent but I don't miss the twitch of her lips. *She's a mother all right.*

'Susan, I know this isn't easy for you,' Connelly interjects. 'We're just trying to gather as much information as we can, to paint a picture for ourselves. It helps sometimes.'

'Does Paul ever go running in the woods?' Langton asks.

I shift uncomfortably on the couch and turn towards Detective Connelly. He's helped himself to a cup of coffee and half the plate of biscuits is gone. Telltale crumbs sprinkle his tie.

'What woods?' I ask.

'It's not really a wood,' Connelly explains, using the back of his hand to brush the crumbs off his tie and on to my plush cream rug. 'It's really just overgrown agricultural land.'

I squint, trying to visualise the area he's talking about.

'There are some tall trees on the far side of the lake, they stretch for a couple of miles before they reach the nearest farm,' he continues.

'It's no place for a runner, up there,' Helen says, once again returning from the kitchen area, this time wearing my rubber gloves, which are much too small for her. 'It's mucky and hilly up there. Paul's hardly going to risk a broken ankle when he's training for the bloody marathon.

Susan, don't worry, Paul hasn't run off into the woods. Jesus.' Helen squeezes my shoulder gently with a soapy, gloved hand before she walks back towards the kitchen sink, shaking her head and muttering under her breath.

'Why are you asking these questions?' I say, setting my coffee cup down before my shaking hand spills some.

'There's no body, Susan,' Langton says. 'Our divers have been over every inch of the water and there's nothing.'

'So . . . What are you saying? Have you come here to tell me you're giving up? You're just going to stop looking? Is that it?'

'No. Absolutely not,' Connelly cuts in, his eyes burning into Langton's like hot coals. 'We'd never give up looking for a missing person. Least of all a child.'

'Susan, we want to find Amelia,' Langton says, following Connelly's lead, and I think I can hear her voice breaking. 'But we do have to tell you that the divers are pulling back. I'm sorry. It will probably be on the news later, when the reporters notice, and we wanted you *and Paul* to hear it from us first.'

'Amelia is two.' I begin to cry. 'She's two years old and you're sitting on my couch eating biscuits and telling me that you're not going to look for her any more?'

Langton's face is laced with emotion.

Angry, tearless sobs burst out of me. 'She's a baby. Just a baby.'

Helen hurries back. She looks like she might cry too.

'Susan hasn't been watching the news,' she explains, making it obvious she's been listening to our conversation all along despite busying herself with the washing up.

'I can understand,' Connelly says, tilting his head to one side and looking at me with knowing, sad eyes. 'Reporters can be unintentionally insensitive.'

'Unintentionally my arse,' Helen snorts.

Connelly shifts slightly as he switches his attention to Helen. The leather couch squeaks under him and the noise hangs in the air for a moment.

'They took photos of Amelia from Susan's Facebook page,' she says, audibly disgusted. 'The cheeky bastards. They splashed them in all the papers. How is that unintentional, huh?'

Connelly's forehead wrinkles and he shakes his head.

'Some of the locals even gave interviews to the papers about this poor family.' Helen points a single finger in my direction. 'People around here barely know Susan and Paul, but that didn't stop them talking. The papers don't care. They just want a headline. They'll print any old nonsense.'

'Susan, I can assure you everyone wants Amelia found,' Connelly says. 'The Gardaí, the press, your neighbours . . .'

He's speaking to me but looking at Helen. I can see him losing patience as he tries to quench her fire with calm words and a firm tone. But Helen is on a roll.

'And is any of this going to help find Amelia?' Helen goes on. 'No. Of course it's not. Reporters just want a story. They're using a missing child to sell bloody papers. It's disgusting.'

'I can understand how upsetting that must be, Susan,' Connelly says. 'As you know, we issued a statement when the case first broke, asking the media to show discretion and respect your privacy.'

'Well, the media ignored you,' Helen grumbles.

'The press will always print the strongest story,' Langton says, keeping to the facts and keeping emotion out of her tone. 'It's their job at the end of the day. It can be very distressing, for any family. It's certainly not ideal, but it is all very normal under the circumstances, I'm afraid.'

Helen nods. She opens her mouth ready to speak but the two Gardaí stare her down and she closes it again, obviously thinking better of it.

'We will of course issue another statement this afternoon, after the divers pull back,' Langton says. 'It will most likely dominate the news channels and papers tomorrow. It will be online too, of course. You and Paul need to be prepared for that, Susan.'

'It said on the news that she drowned,' I say. 'One reporter stood on the verge of the lake and pointed into the water as he said, "She went to her watery grave." Watery grave,' I snort with disbelief. 'Those were his exact words.'

'I'm sorry,' Connelly sighs, reaching for the last biscuit. 'The media can be damn right cruel sometimes.'

'And in the absence of facts they often run with their own, do they?' Helen says, unable to help herself butting in again.

'What do you think, detective?' I tilt my head to one side, watching him eat, my own stomach churning. 'Do you think my baby drowned?'

Connelly doesn't answer me. Instead he takes my hand and gives it a gentle squeeze, as if he's offering me his condolences. I wonder if that's his answer.

'When will Paul be home?' Langton asks suddenly, her eyes small and curious.

'I don't know.' I drag my hand away from Connelly and wrap my arms around myself. 'I honestly have no idea.'

'It really would be good if we could speak to you *and* Paul,' Connelly says.

'I know. I know,' I say.

'Susan, this is our third visit to the house,' Langton says. 'Last time we stayed for almost two hours. Where does Paul go in all that time? Where is he right now?' Langton folds her arms and shakes her head.

'Running,' I say. I let my head fall forward and I barely have the energy to keep my eyes open. 'I told you, he goes running.'

'For two hours?' Langton asks.

'For however long he wants,' I say, lifting my head to meet Langton's gaze. 'For however long it takes to outrun the pain.'

'Okay, Susan,' Connelly says, 'take a moment. Catch your breath.'

He reaches for my cup of cooled coffee and passes it to me without a word. I take it, but I don't want coffee. The china is tepid and more comfortable to hold now. I stare at the black liquid as my whole body shakes.

Every part of me knows Langton and Connelly are playing me. Their good cop, bad cop routine is faultless. I want to slap Langton across the face and I want to bear hug Connelly, as if he can make everything all better. It's textbook stuff and they pull it off brilliantly. I understand the technique. I just don't understand why they're using it now. On me. My child is missing. *Surely, they know I have nothing to hide.*

The front door creaks open and Paul appears. He's wet from head to toe. His running pants and vest cling to him like a wetsuit. His face is gaunt and stubborn dark circles sit under his eyes.

'Langton. Connelly,' Paul nods, clearly more familiar with their names than their faces. I doubt he knows who is who. I doubt he cares. He kicks off his mucky runners on the porch before stepping inside.

'Coffee, Paul?' Helen asks.

'Water. Water would be good. Thanks,' Paul says. His face is flushed and strands of his wet hair are sticking to his forehead.

'Paul,' Langton says. 'We have some questions.'

'More questions? But still no answers, eh?'

'Paul, please,' I say, standing up.

I'm about to walk over to him, but he raises his hand and I know he doesn't want me to come any closer. He never wants me to get close now.

'Perhaps you'd like to sit down?' Connelly asks.

'In a minute,' Paul says. 'I just ran fifteen kilometres, I need a shower, a change of clothes and a glass of water.'

'This won't take long,' Langton says.

'Neither will this,' Paul replies, taking the stairs two at a time.

'Paul, they only need a few minutes,' I call after him.

Paul pauses mid-flight and turns around. 'A few minutes is a long time, Susan,' he says, his eyes vacant, as if his body is present but his mind is somewhere else entirely. 'A lot can happen in a few minutes. For example, a child could drown.'

I stare at my husband. He stares back, and neither of us bother to hide our growing resentment of each other in front of the detectives.

'Grab a shower, Paul,' Connelly says. 'We'll wait.'

Chapter Six

Now

Paul makes his way downstairs more than thirty minutes later. He's changed into jeans and a T-shirt that's lost its shape from too many washes. He doesn't sit. Instead he stands, facing Connelly, Langton and me with his arms folded across his chest. His eyes are red and puffy and I wonder if he's been crying in the shower again.

'So, to what do we owe the pleasure of today's visit?' He glares at the Gardaí sitting in front of him as if they're responsible for our daughter's absence.

'Paul, we understand your frustration,' Langton begins.

He cuts her off before she has a chance to say another stupid word. 'Really?' He tilts his head to one side. 'You understand what it's like to hold your newborn daughter in your arms and whisper into her tiny ear that you will always protect her and keep her safe?'

'I have kids,' Langton confesses.

'So you do . . . you do understand.' Paul sways on the spot. 'You know what it feels like to love someone – this little child who burst into your life – more than you ever thought it was possible to love someone.'

'Yes.' Langton swallows, and at least she has the good grace to blush. 'I love my children. Yes, I do.'

'Good,' Paul nods. 'We're all supposed to love our kids until the day we die. We're not supposed to lose them. We're not. But it happens. It does happen. And then what? What the hell are you supposed to do then?'

'I don't know,' Langton says. 'I honestly don't know.'

Her sincerity jolts me. I don't quite know why.

'Paul, where did you go running today?' Connelly asks.

'I ran into town.' He glares at me, defiant. Amelia sometimes looks at me with the same expression. I pull my eyes away from him and drop my gaze.

'Did you talk to anyone?' Connelly asks. 'Did anyone see you?'

'I was running, detective. I wasn't out for a chat.'

'Okay,' Connelly nods.

'But you'd know that, wouldn't you?' Paul says. 'Because you passed me on the way here. Langton, you had the courtesy to wave, at least.'

'I don't recall,' Connelly says sharply.

Connelly clasps his hands and drops them into his lap. His eyes narrow as he glares pointedly at my husband. The squidgy around the edges, father-like man is so different around Paul than he is around me. He's stern and authoritarian.

I don't like the version of Connelly that Paul seems to bring out. And I can't help but wonder what he knows about Paul that makes him dislike him so much.

'Well, I recall just fine,' Paul says, his face redder than when he came back from his run. 'You nearly ran me off the road. Now, what the hell is going on here? You're asking me questions about where I've been when you damn well saw me out running. You're calling around to my house every second day and distressing my wife.'

He takes a deep breath as if he's run out of oxygen. Neither Connelly nor Langton speak. Hostility hangs in the air like a dark rain cloud ready to burst.

'Paul, please,' I say, my voice cracking like static on the radio. 'This isn't helping anyone.'

He doesn't even look at me.

'Will I tell you what's really going on here?' he continues. 'You two can't do your fucking job. Where is my daughter? Where is she? You know as well as I do she's in that bloody lake, why has no one found her yet? Why can't you bring her home? Please, just bring her home.'

'Paul, sit down,' Langton says.

Connelly shifts to the armchair next to us and makes room for Paul to sit beside me. I feel the heat of my husband's body radiate against me. And I want to move away. I'm already sweating.

'They've tried to find her, Paul,' I say. 'The divers. The police. The volunteers. You know they have. But they can't.' I turn towards Connelly. 'You can't, can you? That's what you're going to tell us, isn't it? You're not here to tell us that the divers can't find Amelia. You're here to tell us that *you* can't find her either. You really have no idea where our daughter is, do you?'

Paul begins to cry. I watch his slender body curl and shrink.

'I can't stop thinking about how scared she must have been,' Paul sniffles, dragging his arm under his nose. 'When she fell into that fucking lake. The water is freezing. She can't swim. We were going to start her in lessons soon. Weren't we, Susan? We talked about it.'

I nod.

'But with the move and everything, we didn't get a chance. We were trying so hard to settle in . . .' Paul trails off and a silence falls over us all. 'We never should have moved here, Susan. I'm sorry. I'm so sorry. We shouldn't have come here.'

Langton's expression softens. 'The lake leads out to sea, as you know,' she says.

'And what the hell does that mean?' Paul says.

'Bodies float, Paul,' Connelly says, in a voice deeper and more serious than I'm used to hearing from him. 'Given enough time, they do.

And little Amelia, well . . .' Connelly coughs. 'Well, we thought we'd have seen her by now.'

'We've spoken to everyone who was here that day,' Langton says, and I can see heartbreak written in her eyes. But she's not upset for me. Or for Paul. Her heart is breaking for Amelia. A little girl, lost and alone. 'Everyone seems to agree that the last place they saw her was playing in the garden, and—'

'Not everyone,' Paul says, cutting across Langton. 'You haven't spoken to everyone.' I swallow roughly. 'You haven't spoken to Deacon.'

'Deacon?' Langton echoes.

Connelly pulls a pen and notepad from his inside jacket pocket. He uses his teeth to pull the lid off the pen and spits it into his hand. He rests the paper on his knee, ready to take notes.

'Deacon O'Reilly,' I offer, before Paul has a chance to say another word. 'He's a client of mine.'

'A client?' Connelly's eyes narrow, and for the first time I see something in him that unsettles me: judgement. He must be wondering why I haven't mentioned Deacon sooner.

'He wasn't at the barbecue,' I explain. 'He's not from Ballyown. The barbecue was just a neighbourhood thing. We wanted to get to know people around here. Make friends, really.'

'But Deacon *was* here,' Paul says, standing up. 'I saw him. I spoke to him.' He paces in front of the unlit open fire. 'Not for long, just a couple of minutes at the start. I wondered what the hell he was doing here.' Paul comes to a standstill and turns to face me. 'I just assumed you'd invited him, Susan.'

'I didn't see him. I didn't know he was here,' I say.

'Oh c'mon,' Paul snorts. 'You must have known he'd come.'

I shake my head. 'I didn't invite him.'

'Why was he here, then? Why was that man in my fucking house?'

'You don't like this man?' Langton asks.

'I don't know him,' Paul admits. 'But he certainly spends a lot of time with my wife. Sometimes I think Susan spends more time with Deacon than she does with me.'

I shift on the couch. I want to get up and pace too, feeling as if I'm being interrogated. Langton, Connelly and Paul's eyes are all on me.

'I told Deacon about the barbecue,' I say. 'I mentioned it at one of our sessions. I told him we were trying to settle in. We are, aren't we, Paul?'

'So Mr O'Reilly has become a friend?' Langton asks.

'Deacon is a client. Just a client,' I say. 'I keep it professional. Always.'

'A client who followed you from Dublin,' Paul says.

'Mr O'Reilly travels from Dublin to Ballyown for your sessions?' Connelly asks. 'How often do you see him? Weekly? That's a lot of travelling.'

'Deacon lives in Cork now,' I explain. 'He has for a few months.'

'He moved here,' Paul says through gritted teeth. 'Not long after us. Susan was his counsellor when we lived in Dublin. She'd see him three times a week. Far more than she saw most of her clients. Then we moved. And suddenly Deacon has moved here too. And he's seeing Susan again. Three times a week. Like always.'

'Do you have an address for Mr O'Reilly?' Connelly asks.

I shake my head.

'But he is living locally,' Langton adds.

'He's from Cork. Originally,' I say, staring my husband down. *What is he trying to suggest?* 'It's just coincidence. We moved. And a few weeks later Deacon decided to go home.'

'Did he talk to you about this potential move?' Langton asks. 'Previously, at your sessions. Did he express his desire to move home at any time?'

'I'm sorry.' I sit straight. 'I can't discuss what my clients talk about. I could lose my licence to practise. And I think you know that.'

'Sure,' Langton says, staring at me as if she's desperate to know what I'm thinking.

'Deacon has nothing to do with any of this,' I say. 'He's never even met Amelia. She's always napping when he comes to the house for his sessions. And he's gone before she wakes up.'

'Oh Susan, stop. Just stop. Your obsession with this guy is driving me crazy,' Paul snaps, clasping his hands and pressing them down hard on the top of his head. 'I told him to leave the barbecue. He had no business being there. He wanted to talk to you. He said it was *soooo* urgent,' he mimics, 'but you were busy with the food. I didn't see him pass through the house. He must have gone out the back gate. Deacon was the one who left the gate open. It was him, I'm sure it was. Deacon O'Reilly is the reason Amelia drowned.'

I glare at my husband. Langton and Connelly are watching me. I'm not looking at them, but I can feel their eyes studying me. Searching for something in the lines of my face, the tears in my eyes, the crack in my voice. But all they must see is my frustration and desperation as my fiery stare burns into the man I married and the father of my child. 'Why don't you say what you really mean, Paul?'

He tilts his head to one side. And equal distaste smoulders in his eyes.

'Deacon was here because of me,' I gasp. '*Me!*' I tap my index finger against my chest. 'You're blaming me. You think this is all my fault. You think our baby is dead and you think I'm responsible.'

'Yes,' Paul barks, stomping his foot as saliva sprays past his lips. 'It's all your fault, Susan. This is all your fucking fault.'

Chapter Seven

Then

I stand outside the gates of my old primary school and take a deep breath. I haven't been back here since I was twelve and my senior class made the transition to secondary school. My last memory of this place is laughing as a couple of the more boisterous kids from my year spray-painted *Mrs Smyth smells* across the back of the principal's car. They got in terrible trouble, but I smile, thinking of those days when Adam and I were inseparable.

The slap of tarmac under my runners is painfully familiar as I cross the schoolyard. So familiar I almost feel my brother walking beside me the way we did every day for eight years when we were pupils here. It hurts to feel him so close and at the same time know that his presence is nothing more than a figment of my imagination now.

Tears prick my eyes as I read the sheet of A4 paper stuck to the main doors. Someone has written *Bereavement Group* in large black letters across the paper and stuck it against the glass with a blob of Blu-Tack. I know tomorrow there will be another equally haphazard sign in the same place. It'll spell out something different. Pilates, maybe. Or Aerobics. The school has hired out the hall for evening classes for as long as I can remember. Adam and I used to joke about the sad, lonely people with no lives who spent their evenings here. Oh how the irony stings as I take a deep breath and pull the doors open. *No turning back now.*

My shoes squeak as I cross the shiny, rubbery floor in the hall, but heads don't turn, not like how you see in films. In real life everyone is too preoccupied with their own loss and emotion to care about some newbie wearing all white runners with overly shiny soles. I make my way towards the circle of ten or so plastic chairs in the centre of the floor. My arms dangle by my sides as if they're not part of my body. I'm not entirely sure what to do with them. Fold them, clasp my hands, leave them by my side.

In an effort to create a near perfect circle, the plastic chairs that they've borrowed from a nearby classroom are slotted painfully close together. I shuffle between the two seats with the biggest gap between them. Heads finally lift and suddenly there are a lot of eyes on me. I really wish my brother was here with me.

There's only one vacant seat, between a dapper, elderly man and a girl my age – a girl too young to be here. A girl just like me. It feels as if they've been waiting for me. And for a moment a numbing sense of relief washes over the hall when I sit down, completing the circle of miserable people with long faces and heavy hearts.

The regimental plastic chair attacks my spine just as I remember from school and forces me to sit unnaturally straight. I cross my legs, trying to appear relaxed, but my eyes are on the exit. It's hard to believe I ever spent any time in this hall before. It's hard to believe I ever belonged here. And that Adam did too.

'Hey,' the girl beside me says, 'you're new. Welcome. It's been ages since we had anyone new join us.'

I acknowledge her with a nod but I don't reply. I don't know what to say. I don't even know why I'm here. Why I chose today to come.

'I'm Jenny,' she says, smiling brightly. Her bubbly personality surprises me and I wonder why she's so happy – considering the group we're all attending.

'Well, Jennifer, actually,' she continues. 'But I don't like that name, so everyone just calls me Jenny. Jen sometimes, I suppose. What's your name?'

'I'm . . .' I swallow and pause for a moment, as if I've forgotten my own name. 'I'm Susan.'

'Good to meet you, Sue.'

'No, erm, just Susan. Really.'

'Okay, Susan. Not one for abbreviations. That's cool. This is Wayne.' Jenny points to the man next to me. 'His wife died from cancer two years ago. They had three kids. Two boys and a girl. His kids are grown up and they all live abroad now. I think they have kids of their own. But I'm not sure. Do you have any grandchildren, Wayne?' Jenny leans across me and raises her voice as if Wayne isn't sitting right next to me.

He shakes his head.

'No. He doesn't have any grandchildren,' Jenny says.

'Okay,' I say, wishing the empty chair had been situated beside someone else, any of the other silent people here.

'I'm sorry to hear about your wife, Wayne,' I say, catching his eye.

He doesn't reply. I don't say anything more. I just smile, unsure.

'What brings you here?' Jenny asks.

It takes me longer than it should to realise Jenny means *who*. *Who brings me here?* Who has died and left me as washed out and heartbroken as the rest of the people in this circle?

'My brother,' I say, holding back his name defensively.

I can feel Jenny's eyes on me, but mine stare straight ahead. I don't want to see her feel sorry for me. That's the only way people look at me now. They don't see their friend, their classmate, their student. They only see what I've become. A shell.

I stare ahead and focus on the stage at the top of the hall. Children's artwork hangs across the white wall behind the stage. There are small handprints in various colours splattered on to one large sheet of stiff card and some near-illegible writing says something about *growing up*.

The side wall is covered in more artwork. Definitely by older children. I can easily make out that the cotton wool stuck on crepe paper creates a delightful bunch of sheep. The sheep are complete with googly eyes, and painted-on legs. They're really rather impressive. Except for the one-eyed sheep whose other googly eye has fallen on to the floor. That sheep is creepy, and reminds me of similar artwork Adam and I brought home when we were little. For years my mother proudly displayed our art on the fridge, only taking one down when there was another, even more colourful offering brought home from school to replace it. Neither of us was the next Rembrandt but at least our mother could guess what Adam had created. My masterpieces were little more than glitter splashes on paper. I was often jealous of my brother's art and every now and then I would accidentally on purpose spill black paint on his work or get too enthusiastic with the scissors. Adam would cry, of course, but I won his forgiveness with Jelly Tots and He-Man stickers.

'You're not a talker,' Jenny says, bright faced and giddy once again. I shake my head.

'That's okay,' she smiles. 'I talk enough for everyone.'

Jenny seems hyperactive and I wonder if she has some sort of condition that makes it difficult for her to sit still. My eyes fall to her knees bouncing up and down like a jackhammer. Maybe it's a coping mechanism, I think. Maybe she twitches and bounces to shake off her grief. I hope for her sake it works.

I wish I could find something that worked for me. I spoke with the college counsellor last week. He said that everyone grieves in different ways, as if that wasn't obvious. He said my mother's sudden decision to move to the South of France was her way of coping. I think it's running away, personally. And it's definitely abandoning me. The counsellor said it's okay to be angry and it's okay to direct my anger at my mother. He also said that when I find my own outlet I'd feel much better. I left after that bullshit advice, but nonetheless I find myself slap bang in the middle of a bereavement group. And while I don't believe that it will make me feel any better, I really want it to.

'Sometimes I wish I could shut up but it's a nervous habit, I guess,' Jenny rambles on, and I realise she's been talking all the time, oblivious that I'd zoned out. 'This group always brings out the chatterbox in me. I don't usually talk this much. Well, actually, I do, but I'm not usually this annoying—'

'Have you been coming here long?' I cut her off.

'Five years next month. I lost my mother when I was seventeen.'

'I'm sorry,' I say genuinely.

I do the maths in my head and work out that I guessed correctly – Jenny and I are the same age.

'It must be hard to have lost your mother when you were so young,' I say. 'I'm twenty-one and I still struggle to cope without mine.'

'I'm so sorry to hear about your mam's passing.' Jenny's knees stop bouncing and she suddenly seems very serious. 'Was it at the same time you lost your brother?'

'It's complicated,' I say.

I don't want to talk about my mother, but Jenny's eyes are burning into me and she's waiting for me to say more.

'You only get one mother in this life, and it feels so unfair when she's not around you any more,' I sigh.

And for the first time since I sat down Jenny is calm. She nods and drags the sleeve of her coat over her hand. I know that move: I create makeshift handkerchiefs with the edges of my clothing all the time lately. I look away. I'm sure Jenny would like to dab her teary eyes without an audience.

I curse myself for upsetting her. And I almost wish she'd go back to being loud and chatty. I don't really know why I came out with something so profound about mothers. It's not me at all. Adam was the one who was good with words, not me. But there's something about the atmosphere in this group. It makes me want to talk. Certainly not as much as Jenny. But for the first time since Adam died I want to be around other people.

I decide I like Jenny after all, but I don't tell her that my mother is still very much alive – it's our relationship that's dead. Mam can't bear to look at me since Adam died. My brother and I were nothing alike in appearance or personality, but we were two halves of a whole. Like sugar and spice, sweet and sour. My mother can't be around me; she can't talk to me or hold me. She can't cope with having one twin without the other. Everything about me is a constant reminder that one half – her favourite half – is gone. My mother didn't die in a freak accident along with my brother, but she might as well have, because I lost her the day I lost Adam.

'Time helps,' Wayne says, finally lifting his head. 'I know you've probably heard it from a bunch of people who don't know what they're talking about. But take it from someone who knows – it doesn't get easier. I won't lie and rattle off that kind of nonsense, but it does get bearable. You never stop missing them, you just learn to live with that feeling every day.'

'But I don't want to live with this feeling,' I say.

'Tough,' someone says. 'Tough shit.'

'Excuse me?' I say, whipping my head round, trying to find the owner of the voice.

'That's Deacon.' Jenny offers an introduction as she points to a guy three seats down from me. 'Deacon O'Reilly.'

Deacon glares at me with an anger I don't deserve. Instinctively, I look away. Other heads have turned my way.

I seek out the exit behind Deacon's shoulder. But my eyes are drawn back to his face. He's still watching me. *What the hell is this guy's problem?* Something about his clenched jaw tells me he's not happy about my presence in *his* group. My heart is beating furiously but I glare back and silently argue with him to back down. I win and Deacon's eyes find their way to the floor.

'Deacon's not a talker either,' Wayne explains, loud enough for Deacon to overhear.

'We don't even know why he comes,' Jenny whispers. 'He must have lost someone. But he's never said who. He never even told us his name.'

'How do you know who he is, then?' I ask, wishing I could pull my eyes away from Deacon, but I just can't. He's so sombre. Everyone here is gloomy, of course, but Deacon is a whole other level. He looks tortured.

'We used to wear name tags,' Wayne says. 'Back a couple of years ago. But it made people uncomfortable, so we voted to stop. Now we let people introduce themselves in their own time. Well, most of us do. Jenny likes to drag their names out of them before they've even sat down. Don't you, Jenny?' Wayne smiles affectionately, and I can tell he has a soft spot for her.

She shrugs. 'It's true. I do. I'm a people person. I can't help it.'

I guess there's a lot of things Jenny can't help. Her nervous twitch, her noisy nature and her eyes that seem to see me better than I want them to.

The hour-long session ticks by surprisingly quickly. Members of the circle take it in turns to stand up and speak. They talk about profound loss in one breath and in the next sentence they're waffling about running out of teabags the last time a neighbour called around for a cuppa. It's strange. I find myself close to tears one moment and holding my sides from belly laughing the next. I'm not sure how the session makes me feel, and when Jenny asks me if I'll be back next week I hesitate before I answer.

'Ah, please say you'll come again. Everyone else is as old as the hills – no offence, Wayne.'

Wayne smiles and shakes his head, clearly used to Jenny's unintentional insults.

'It would be good to finally have a friend my own age,' she adds, 'and you look like you could use a friend too.'

She keeps talking, no doubt rattling off an annoying list of reasons why I should come back, but I've stopped listening.

It's Deacon who helps me decide. I wonder how long he's been coming. How many sessions have gone by without him saying a word, and most of all I wonder who he lost that their absence has stripped his heart from this world.

'Yeah,' I say, watching him stand up to leave. 'I'll be back next week.'

Chapter Eight

Now

I sit cross-legged on the floor in Amelia's bedroom. My eyes are closed and if I concentrate I can feel her chubby arms around my neck. I can hear her laughter. I can smell the shampoo in her hair. She picked it out herself the last time we were in Tesco. She likes it because it comes in a pink bottle with a yellow cartoon fairy printed on the label. I like it because it smells like raspberries and reminds me of summer picnics.

'Hey, there you are,' Helen says, popping her head around the door. 'I've been looking all over the house for you.'

I open my eyes and uncross my legs. I try to stand up but pins and needles dart from my knees and my feet are numb. I didn't notice Helen arrive. I wonder if she's been here long. Paul must have left the front door unlocked again when he went out running. It's becoming a bad habit. I've tried talking to him about it, but he just rolls his eyes and walks away whenever I bring it up.

'Your mother is on the phone,' Helen says, holding her thumb against her ear and her baby finger against her mouth.

I'm dazed. I stood up too suddenly on an empty stomach and circles of white light spin in front of my eyes. Feeling is starting to return to my feet and it stings. I really wish Helen would just go away.

'I don't want to talk right now. Can you tell my mam I'll call her back later?'

'That's what I told her yesterday, Susan. And the day before.'

'I don't want to talk, Helen,' I repeat firmly.

I should probably be irritated that Helen has answered the phone in my house without me even hearing it ring, but I don't have the energy to care about that right now.

'Okay. I'll tell her you're not up to it.'

'What does she want anyway?' I sigh.

'She's worried, Susan. She says the news stations in France aren't carrying any coverage of Amelia's drowning. And you haven't replied to her texts. She just wants to know what's going on.'

'Disappearance,' I snap. 'Amelia disappeared. There's nothing to confirm anything about a drowning. Jesus Christ, why does everyone insist on saying she drowned? She didn't. I know she didn't.'

'Of course, I'm sorry. I've been listening to the news too much.'

'My mother hasn't seen Amelia in eight months,' I say. 'And it was six months the time before that. If she was so worried about her only grandchild I think she could make an effort to visit more often, don't you?'

Helen shakes her head. I can't tell if her disappointment is with my aggression towards my absent mother or my mam's failings as a grandmother.

'I'll ask her to call again tomorrow, okay?' Helen suggests as she walks out of the room.

'Fine. Whatever.'

I turn back and take one of Amelia's T-shirts out of the top drawer of the tall, freestanding dresser. The dresser is an antique I painstakingly refurbished shortly after we moved in. I spent hours stripping back the varnished oak and painting it white. Amelia helped, of course. The yellow handles were her choice. I've become quite artistic over the years and the dresser turned out better than I could have imagined.

It's beautiful, but I always worry about its size. It's three times as tall as Amelia. I've asked Paul several times to secure it to the wall in case she tries to climb it or, worse, knocks it down. 'You can never be too careful with a toddler,' I say so often I even irritate myself.

Still staring at the dresser, I place the baby-pink cotton T-shirt under my nose and take a deep breath. It doesn't smell like my daughter. It smells like the new fabric softener I bought on special offer a couple of weeks ago. I ball the T-shirt up and shove it back in the drawer and slam the drawer shut with an aggressive bang. The dresser wobbles and I know Paul never got around to securing it to the wall. I exhale sharply. I'm frustrated, but I'm not surprised.

Paul says that I'm a worrier and I see danger in everything. I don't argue about that, there's no point. When Amelia first started to walk, I spent most of my time walking backwards a couple of steps ahead of her with my arms outstretched, ready to catch her if she tumbled. And when she started feeding herself I'd spend so long cutting her food into tiny pieces that it was always cold before she could eat it, simply because I feared that her milk teeth couldn't master chewing properly. Paul said I was overprotective. I said he was too relaxed. We often have arguments over our different parenting techniques. *But don't all couples?*

We had a whopper just recently. I came home from grocery shopping to discover Amelia in the garden on her tricycle without her helmet on. I was furious and gave Paul a piece of my mind. He freaked out and said I was insinuating that he was a bad father. I don't think that. I think he's a fantastic dad. Amelia is a lucky little girl. But Paul wouldn't let it go. He said I was stifling her and that she would grow up afraid to make mistakes or take risks. I said he was careless and complacent. And that if Amelia followed his example she would grow up reckless and selfish. It escalated from there. I bitched at him about all the time he spends working or running. He let rip about the money I've spent on the house. He added something obnoxious about at least one of us earning a real living. I lost it a little after that and it got messy. Amelia overheard us shouting. We scared her. I felt terrible, and Paul did too. We put our harsh words aside to reassure our little girl that everything was okay.

It was. Paul skipped his evening run that night. I cooked his favourite dinner and we all ate together. We read a story together. All three of us squashed into Amelia's bed and cuddled, enjoying family time.

Later, when Paul went back downstairs and Amelia and I were alone, snuggling, she asked me, 'Mammy, do you love Daddy?'

I nodded involuntarily, her grown-up question catching me by surprise.

'Do you love Daddy the same much as you love me?' she added.

I didn't answer that question. I simply kissed my little girl on the forehead and said, 'Sweet dreams, darling.'

That night Paul and I made love in the sitting room for hours after Amelia fell asleep. I watched my husband as he lay next to me on the soft cream rug. His naked, clammy body pressed against mine as he fixed a stray strand of my hair behind my ear.

'You're a great mother,' he said, kissing me. 'I mean it, Susan. I can't wait to watch our little girl grow up. I hope she grows up to be just like you.'

Paul's words play over in my mind now, as they do often. He couldn't possibly have imagined that less than two weeks later we'd be robbed of the chance to watch our little girl grow up at all.

I shake my head as if I can toss the memories from my mind, and I'm about to follow Helen downstairs when I notice some photographs scattered on the floor at my feet. They must have fallen out of the drawer when I took out Amelia's T-shirt. I bend down and gather them up, taking care not to dog-ear the corners.

'They're fantastic,' Helen says, picking one up.

'Don't touch it,' I growl, grabbing the photo out of her hand.

Helen jumps back, narrowly missing spilling the cup of coffee in her hand all over her blouse.

'Sorry.' I quickly lower my voice.

She looks at me as if I'm a stray dog she's not sure she can trust.

'I'm sorry,' I repeat, whispering now. 'I'm just a little emotional. I didn't mean to bite your head off. I know you're only trying to help.'

Helen smiles, unsure, but she takes a step forward.

I instinctively clutch the photos against my chest. 'I thought you'd gone back downstairs,' I say, trying to justify my skittish outburst.

'I had, but I thought you could use a coffee. Your mam says she'll call you again tomorrow.'

'Okay. Is Paul back yet?'

'Not yet,' she says as she sets the cup of coffee down on Amelia's bookshelf and turns to walk out of the room.

'Helen,' I say.

She turns back to face me.

'Where do you think Paul goes?'

She shakes her head. 'He's running, isn't he? Training for that big race in Dublin.'

'No one can spend all day every day running,' I say. 'He goes somewhere. Not to work, he's taken leave, obviously.'

'Maybe he goes to the pub?' Helen says. 'Larry likes a drink most days. You'd find half the men in Ballyown in the pub on a Saturday afternoon.'

'No,' I sigh. 'Paul rarely drinks. Alcohol isn't good when he's training.'

'Ah yes, I remember you said that previously.' Helen smiles sympathetically, and I wonder if she thinks I'm deluded assuming my husband doesn't drink like most of the other men around here.

'The Guards asked me where I think Paul goes,' I say, dragging my finger over the top of the photographs I hold against my chest. 'They asked me what I think he does during all those hours he's away from the house every day.'

Helen looks at me blankly. Her eyes are glassy and bloodshot and I think she might be hung-over.

'It wasn't what they said, it was the way they said it, you know?' I continue, staring at her, wondering if she's hearing me. 'As if they thought there was something suspicious about Paul spending so much time away from our home.'

'I won't lie,' Helen says, suddenly astute, 'I think Paul's place is here with you at a time like this. The police are barking up the wrong tree, Susan. The completely wrong tree, if they think Paul has anything to do with Amelia falling into that lake.'

'No. No,' I say sternly. 'They didn't say that. That's not what they were implying.' I shake my head. 'Never mind. I shouldn't have mentioned it.'

'The police have nothing to go on, that's their problem,' Helen says. 'Don't let them drive a wedge between you and Paul with silly questions that won't help anyone. Sit down tonight and talk with Paul. Tell him how much you need him near you.'

I press the photos tighter against me, close my eyes and breathe slowly. A tight knot sits in my chest.

'Paul should be here for you, Susan. That's all there is to it. I'll have a word with him, if you like?'

I open my eyes and watch her with trepidation. 'Where's Larry?' I ask. 'Doesn't he mind you spending every day here?'

Helen clears her throat with a dry cough. 'No. He doesn't.'

'But what does he do all evening in that big old house? It was nearly eleven o'clock when he came looking for you last night.'

'He does his thing, I do mine,' she says.

'And what's your thing?'

'I like taking care of people. I like making sure they're okay. I like making sure you're okay.'

'Helen, maybe you should go home,' I say. 'You've been very kind, but . . .'

She shakes her head and I can see tears in her eyes. 'Larry and I aren't the picture-perfect couple we pretend to be, you know.'

I didn't think for one moment that Larry and Helen were perfect. I think they torment each other with snide comments and backhanded insults. I wonder if that's why Helen is so pushy and interfering. She has little control in her own home so she's looking for it in mine. I smile, realising that I spend most of my time trying to read people instead of actually getting to know them. Occupational hazard, I think. I need to work on that.

'I don't think any marriage is perfect, Helen,' I say.

'I'm sorry, I've upset you now, haven't I?' Helen says. 'I should learn when to shut up. Larry says my mouth is the biggest part of me. And he's right. I doubt you want to hear about my marriage troubles when your own worries are so great. Gosh, Susan, I'm sorry. Look at me, a silly woman. You're right, I should go home.'

I take a deep breath and set the photographs face down on the dresser. I'm desperate to kiss the back of the top photograph, the way I do every time I let Adam's work out of my hands, but I restrain myself in front of Helen. I walk over to the bookshelf and pick up the cup she left for me. I take a mouthful and pull a face.

'Let's go downstairs,' I say. 'I'll make some fresh coffee. No offence, Helen, but this stuff is terrible.'

Chapter Nine

Now

I sit at the kitchen table with my back to the window. Initially, I was sitting at the opposite side of the table, but I couldn't bring myself to look out the window at the view of my pretty, well-kept garden and the stream running behind it. I asked Helen to switch places with me. She knew why.

'I've lived in Ballyown for twenty-five years,' she says. 'And I think you're the first *real* friend I've made.'

'Twenty-five years is a long time to go without any friends,' I say.

'Yes. Yes, it is,' Helen admits. 'But I had my sons. And three boys will keep you busy with all the mischief they get up to. And then there was the farm. Farms are hard work, you know. There's always something to be done. I never had a free minute over the years.'

'And now you do?' I say.

Helen throws her head back and cackles. 'Are you going to charge me for this session, counsellor?'

'You said we were friends.' I keep my voice level, wondering why she's suddenly so jumpy since we came downstairs. She's almost spilled her coffee twice. 'Don't friends talk about their problems?'

'They do.' Helen brings her head back. 'But I don't feel right talking about my troubles . . . when, well, you know . . . when . . .'

'Helen,' I interrupt her. 'I really can't talk about myself any more. It would do me good to hear something about someone else. Please. Just talk to me. Let me listen. I need the distraction.'

'Okay.' Helen smiles. 'I could use a chance to talk, if I'm honest.'

'In your own time.' I wince and almost bite my tongue, hearing the cliché I use in my sessions. I hope Helen doesn't pick up on it.

'First of all, I should explain that I like where I live.' Her eyes meet mine. 'I just don't love it.'

I tilt my head to one side.

'I don't fit in,' she rushes to clarify.

'You haven't settled in Ballyown in twenty-five years?' I ask, worrying that I may be in Helen's shoes some day.

She looks embarrassed.

'I have,' she back-pedals. 'Of course, I have. But it's not me, Susan. Not the real me. This place, Ballyown, it changes you.'

'We all change, don't we? Over time?' I suggest, picking up my coffee and walking towards the sitting room.

'Yeah, sure,' Helen says, following me. 'But do we really want to? *Or*, do we feel we should?'

I hide an uneasy gulp as we sit down.

'I mean, I love my husband,' she continues, oblivious to my crisis of conscience. 'I'm just not in love with him. Not any more.'

'Has Larry done something to hurt you?' I ask.

Helen laughs again. This time it's less sarcastic and more a nervous giggle. 'He doesn't mean to. He's just selfish. His mother had him spoiled, you see.' She pauses and takes a deep breath and I can tell the confession is painful for her. 'She always treated him like a little boy, even when he was in his thirties.'

'It's not as uncommon as you'd think,' I say. 'Lots of grown men live at home, especially if they're single. They just need to meet the right woman.'

'But that was the problem,' Helen says, her eyes glassing over. 'Her interfering didn't stop when he met me. If anything, it got worse. She did his laundry, cooked huge meals for him, even when she knew we were going out to dinner. She'd even choose his clothes. It was crazy.'

'Wow,' I sigh. 'She sounds intense.'

'She was. She really was,' Helen says. 'She did everything in her power to break us up, and when it didn't work and we got married, the old bitch was furious and made my life hell. I hated her. And Larry knew it, but we still had to live with the cranky old battleaxe until she died.'

'God, Helen, I had no idea. I've heard in-laws can be a nightmare, but both of Paul's parents were dead before we got engaged. I never had his family to deal with.'

'Count yourself lucky,' Helen snorts. 'I spent years dealing with that woman. Nothing I ever did was good enough. I wasn't a good enough cook. I didn't muck out the pigsty right. I mean, how can you possibly criticise someone for the way they shovel shit?'

I giggle sheepishly.

'It's funny looking back on it,' she says as she rolls her shoulders and straightens her back, 'but at the time I wanted to belt her in the back of the head with that goddam shovel.'

'It sounds like even after you were married she still tried to drive a wedge between you and Larry,' I say.

'She did. Every bloody chance she got. And that's why I spent twenty years daydreaming about topping off the aul bitch. A little weed killer in her tea, or fertiliser in her biscuits,' she says with a sadistic grin.

'Oh Helen,' I sigh. 'I hope your daydreams helped.'

'They did. For a while. Until she found my weakness. I couldn't give her a granddaughter. She told me often enough she had a son of her own, what did she want three grandsons for.'

'That's a terrible thing to say,' I whisper, taking a large mouthful of coffee, grateful for its warmth as I hear my mother's voice in my head telling me how lucky she was to have a boy and a girl. *One of each*, she'd say, hugging us. Her perfect family. 'I hope your boys never heard her.'

'No, of course not,' she says. 'She was as sweet as pie around them. She had them all fooled. Worst of all, she had Larry brainwashed. He spent years craving a daughter. Not for himself. Or even for me. For his bloody mother. Can you believe that? If the bitch wasn't dead now I think he'd still be pestering me to try for a girl. Imagine.' Helen taps her chest with her fingertips. 'Could you imagine me pregnant at forty-six? No bloody thank you. Last thing I need is a child in my life now.'

I sip my coffee, but my eyes peer over the top of my cup, watching her.

When I first met Helen I honestly thought she was a bored housewife content to spend her days gossiping with the locals and her evenings drinking Chardonnay that she hadn't bothered to chill. But I'm slowly realising that Helen is like an onion: you have to peel her back one layer at a time and what you find brings tears to your eyes. But I'm not sure if that's a good or bad thing just yet.

'Oh Susan, I'm sorry. Jesus, that was very insensitive of me, mentioning a child like that. I'll shut up. I'll shut up now.'

'No. Don't.' I put my cup down. 'I asked you to talk. So don't feel you need to censor what you say. Please?'

Helen's eyes widen and I can tell I confuse her.

'It's just, it's good to hear someone not holding back what they say,' I explain. 'Everyone else in the village is tiptoeing around me, afraid to open their mouths in case they say something that upsets me. I actually think the neighbours are secretly glad when I don't answer the front door. They only knock because they feel obliged. As if that's what good neighbours should do. But I barely know them. They don't want to talk to me as much as I don't want to talk to them.'

'S'pose people just don't know what to say,' Helen says. 'But they mean well, Susan. They really do. People around here are nice. Nosy. Very nosy. But nice.'

'I get that. I *do* understand. But don't become one of those people. Please, Helen? I need someone to talk to or I'll crack up.'

'Okay,' she smiles, staring into her coffee. 'Would you mind if I made another cup? I was so busy nattering, I've let this one get cold.'

'Sure,' I nod.

'Will you have another?' Helen asks, standing up.

I shake my head, distracted by the sound of the handle on the front door turning.

Helen makes her way towards the kitchen area just before the door swings open. Paul stands in the doorway. He's saturated again. His usually floppy hair is flat against his head and strands stick to his face. His lips are slightly blue around the edges; it's noticeable even from a distance.

'Hi,' I say as he closes the door behind him with unnecessary force.

I know he heard me but he doesn't reply as he slips off his wet runners. He's gone through three pairs this week. The last two are still drying out on the kitchen windowsill.

He doesn't bother to look up at me. He leans one hip against the door as he pulls his sock off the opposite foot.

I turn my head, forcing myself to look outside for the first time today. The sun is shining brightly and there's nothing more than a couple of white clouds as thin as candyfloss dotted sporadically overhead.

'Was it raining?' I ask, knowing it wasn't.

He pulls off his other sock and stuffs them into his runners. 'I'm going upstairs to change,' he grunts.

'How did you get wet?' I say, the legs of my chair scratching against the floor tiles as I push it back abruptly to march towards him.

Paul ignores me. The bottom step of the stairs creaks as he steps on it. He grabs the banister and I gasp as I notice the dried blood smeared across his knuckles.

'What happened?' I ask, racing towards him. 'Did you fall?'

'Susan, I'm going upstairs to change my clothes,' he says with his back to me. 'Give me some fucking space, will you?'

'I give you nothing but space, Paul,' I say softly. 'You're never here.'

'You're right.' Paul turns. 'But Amelia isn't here either, is she?'

'Please, talk to me,' I beg. 'Where do you go?'

'Well, right now I'm going for a shower. Is that allowed?' His eyes narrow and sparkle like glazed almonds. 'Do you want to call the cops and tell them *that*, since they're so interested in my every move?'

'Paul, I didn't know they were going to ask those questions yesterday,' I say. 'They caught me as much by surprise as you.'

He rolls his eyes. 'Susan, I'm wet and cold. I'm going for a shower. Please just leave me alone.'

I watch him climb the stairs two steps at a time. He doesn't look back at me. I press my lips firmly together and count backwards from five in my head, blushing when I turn round and see Helen making her way to the table.

'I'm sorry you had to hear that,' I say, dragging my hands around my face, mortified.

'Hear what?' Helen shrugs. 'I was boiling the kettle. I didn't hear a thing. Is everything okay, Susan? You look very pale all of a sudden.'

'I'm fine,' I lie, brushing off her concern. 'I see you're really getting to know your way around my kitchen.'

Her reply comes in the shape of a smirk and wide eyes. It's really rather irritating and unhelpful right now. Helen also didn't make coffee, which is equally annoying. Instead, a couple of wine glasses dangle upside down between her fingers and she's holding a bottle of Chardonnay by the neck in her other hand. I have no idea where the wine has suddenly come from. Helen plonks the bottle and the glasses on the table. I want to get coasters before the glass scratches the table, but I shove my hands into my pockets and try to keep under control. I wonder if Helen hurried back to her house for the wine. Maybe she really didn't hear Paul and me talking.

'You're shaking,' Helen says, pouring the first glass and offering it to me.

I take it and slug a huge mouthful. It's chilled and tastes crisp but not too sharp; it definitely hasn't come from my fridge.

'Thirsty,' Helen says, pouring a second glass for herself. 'Was that Paul's voice I heard?'

'I thought you didn't hear anything?' I lower my glass.

'Well, I mean, I didn't hear what you were saying, Susan.' Helen smiles and I know she's lying. 'I don't like to eavesdrop, but I did hear voices. Is Paul home?'

I swirl the wine around my glass and look at her. Helen can't be in two places at once. If she noticed Paul was home, she didn't have time to pop out to grab a bottle of wine. She confuses me. All my training and I can't read her. Ironically, the more she tells me about herself, the less I feel I know her. It's weird. I sip the wine and try to appear relaxed. I was going to tell Helen about Paul's scratched knuckles. I was going to confide in her that I found a broken tile in the shower and I think Paul punched it after Langton and Connelly asked too many questions. I was going to confide that I'm worried about his frustration and temper. But I've trusted the wrong people in the past. I hold my tongue.

'This is nice,' I say, pulling my eyes away from Helen to look at the yellowy-green liquid in my glass.

'Glad you like it,' she says. 'Larry dropped it in a few moments ago, and I thought, to hell with the coffee, Susan needs booze.'

'Larry was here?' I ask.

'Yeah,' Helen nods. 'About ten minutes ago.'

'I didn't see him.' I cough and clear my throat.

'Ah, he was in his wellies, he didn't want to come in and drag muck all over your beautiful house.'

'Still, he could have come in. I haven't seen him . . . since that day. I suppose he doesn't know what to say.' I exhale, frustrated. 'He probably thinks I'm a bad mother. Everyone around here does.'

Helen sits down. 'Larry doesn't think that, Susan. No one does. You're just punishing yourself with those kinds of thoughts.'

'He's been avoiding me since the barbecue.'

'He's just socially awkward, that's all,' Helen explains. 'He doesn't mean anything by it.'

'He seemed fine at the barbecue.'

'Ah, that's because he was talking to Paul.' Helen smiles, but there's an uneasy twitch at the corners of her lips that I can't miss. 'Men! Yapping about sport and training and all that kind of thing. Larry is a man's man. He's not great around women. Ironic, since he's been pining for the daughter he never had.' Helen makes a face. 'Like I said, we can blame his mother for that. He was afraid to open his mouth for years, she had him so under her thumb. The only females Larry is comfortable talking to these days are the heifers on the farm. I swear, he's better with those bloody cows when they're calving than he was with me when I was in labour with his sons.'

I laugh for the first time in days. I stop as soon as I catch myself, but it was glorious for the split second it lasted. In that second, I was free. In that moment, I wasn't the mother of a missing child. Reality hits hard.

'It was nice of Larry to bring the wine over. Tell him I said thank you, won't you?' I say.

'Yes, it was nice of him, wasn't it?' Helen smiles. 'But to be honest, I think he's just trying to get rid of me for the rest of the evening. There's a match on the telly tonight, you know. Galway are playing Kerry. Whoever wins takes *us* on in the final. Everyone is talking about it. The whole of Cork will be watching the game tonight. The village will be buzzing with excitement. I've no doubt Larry will end up in the pub. They have a big screen there. Will Paul go down for a pint?'

'Erm,' I wince, realising that Helen isn't planning to go home any time soon. I really need to talk to Paul. I need to ask him what happened to his hand. And most of all, I just need some time alone with my husband. 'Paul's not really into Gaelic sport,' I say eventually.

'Oh Jesus.' Helen's eyes widen. 'Don't let people around these parts hear you say that.'

'Really?'

'God yeah,' Helen sniggers. 'Folks are hurling mad round these parts.'

'Right.' I smack my lips together and pull them apart again, making a popping sound; it's louder than I mean it to be. 'Well, you're welcome to stay, unless you want to catch the game too . . .' I haven't finished my insincere sentence before Helen is filling a second glass of wine.

'There's another bottle in the kitchen, Susan, don't look so worried.' Helen scrunches her nose. 'I'm not going to drink it all. After all, I think you need this more than I do.'

I'm not so sure I do.

'You know, I lost a baby too,' Helen blurts, slugging on her second glass. 'It was a while ago now. But it still hurts.'

My jaw gapes. 'I had no idea. I'm so sorry. I don't know what to say.'

'It's not the same as you losing Amelia, I know.' Helen drains her glass, but I snatch the bottle before she pours another.

I top up my glass and set the bottle down on the table. My hand has barely let go when Helen reaches for it and pours the remainder into her glass.

'It was a late miscarriage,' Helen continues. 'Eighteen weeks. Larry was out on the farm, like always, and I was in the house with the boys. His mother was there but I would have preferred to be alone. It started as light bleeding, really. But by the time we fetched Larry and got to the hospital there was no heartbeat.'

'I'm sorry,' I say.

'We'd had the scan just a few weeks earlier,' Helen says, tears pricking the corners of her eyes. 'They didn't say if it was a boy or a girl. But I had my fingers crossed. Larry took the news harder than I did. He hit the drink.'

I eye the empty bottle of wine and the near empty glass in Helen's hand.

'And you didn't drink back then?' I say.

'No. Not then,' Helen snorts, and I wonder if she's admitting she drinks too much now. 'Larry pestered me for a long time to try again, but my heart wasn't in it.'

'Was this recently?' I ask.

'Seven, almost eight years ago. But Larry can't seem to get past it. It killed our marriage, if I'm honest. We stopped being intimate when he kept making it about trying for a baby.'

I guzzle a large mouthful of wine. Helen could be talking about Paul and me. Paul is constantly nagging me to try for another baby. He doesn't want Amelia to be an only child.

'I'm sorry, Helen, that sounds hard,' I say.

'It is,' she says, standing up and walking away without excusing herself, and I know she's going to fetch the other bottle of wine.

The floorboards overhead creak and I realise Paul is out of the shower. Considering the mood he was in when he came home, I'd rather he didn't find our noisy neighbour drunk in our house when he comes downstairs.

'I never wanted kids,' I say, as Helen wobbles back towards me with a second bottle cradled in the crook of her arm like a newborn baby.

'Really?' she says, unscrewing the cap.

'Nope, never.' I tilt my head, turning my ear to the ceiling as I listen to Paul walk around our bedroom. 'It was Paul who really wanted to start a family. I don't have a good relationship with my mother. She lives in the South of France and only comes home once in a blue moon.' I surprise myself at how easily the truth slips off my tongue. 'I didn't want history to repeat itself.'

'I understand,' Helen says. 'I worried our kids would get Larry's mother's genes and turn out to be little arseholes. Thankfully they didn't. They don't look like the old witch either,' she laughs.

I laugh too. Grateful that Amelia is nothing like my mother . . . or me.

'It is a pity you and your mother don't get along,' Helen sighs.

'It's complicated,' I say.

'Isn't life always?'

'Yeah,' I nod. 'It is.'

'Did she take those photographs? The pretty ones you have hanging in your hall?' Helen asks, pointing behind her in the wrong direction, but I know what she means. 'Is your mother a photographer? Or was she, before she retired to France?'

'Hmm?' I say, only giving her half my attention. I'm busy concentrating on the noise of the creaky wood that maps out my husband's every move above me.

'Your mother, Susan. Is she a photographer? I don't mean to be nosy, but I noticed the photographs in Amelia's room earlier and they're a similar style to the ones hanging in the hall. They're all really very good.'

I don't mean to be nosy, I think. Christ, I should get Helen a T-shirt with that printed across the front. It's her catchphrase.

'No. My mother's not a photographer,' I say.

The floorboards overhead stop creaking. Paul has stopped moving. I wonder if he's listening to me, just as I'm listening to him. The walls and floorboards of this old cottage are paper-thin. Sound travels like grains of sand through a sieve.

'Do you want to go for a walk?' I ask suddenly.

'But the wine.' Helen's eyes widen. 'I've only just opened this bottle.'

'Let's bring it with us.' I scoop the wine bottle off the table and screw the lid back on. I don't bother to pick up the glasses. 'I could use some fresh air and a chance to stretch my legs.'

'What will Paul say?' Helen asks, unsure. 'He only just got home.'

'Who cares?' I shrug. 'He's never home when I want to talk. Let's see how he likes a taste of his own medicine.'

Chapter Ten

Then

I'd been staring out my bedroom window for over an hour when I notice Jenny arrive outside my flat unexpectedly. She's dressed head to toe in black and looks even thinner and tinier than usual. She doesn't know I'm watching her when she checks her reflection in the side mirror of a parked car and tucks some stray hair behind her ear. She spins round on to the footpath and rings my doorbell. She presses it incessantly until I reluctantly make my way from my bedroom to answer.

'Jesus, you have no patience,' I say, rolling my eyes dramatically as I open the door. 'Good thing I live in the bottom flat. What would you do if you had to wait for me to make my way down from the top floor?'

'Ta-da!' Jenny throws her arms out and twirls slowly around. 'What do you think?'

'Well, hello to you too,' I say.

'Yeah. Yeah. Hello.' Jenny spins, completing a full circle to face me again. 'Now tell me, what do you think? Do you like it?'

'What do I think of what?' I step back to take in a better view of the black cloak covering my best friend from head to toe.

'My costume, silly.' She reaches behind her head and pulls up an oversized hood.

'Oh Christ, you're not dressing up, are you?' I shake my head.

'Hell yes! It's Halloween.' Jenny bounces. 'I'm the Grim Reaper. Fitting, eh?'

I pull a face. 'You're seriously going to dress as the Grim Reaper for the bereavement group's Halloween meeting?' I ask.

'Yup. Fuck it. You have to laugh, Susan, don't you?' Jenny says.

I shake my head again. 'No. No you don't.'

I've spent a lot of time getting to know Jenny over the past year. I would say I know her well. Her tongue-in-cheek sense of humour and no bullshit approach takes some warming to, but I'm used to her quirky ways now. She still scares the crap out of newbies at their first meeting, but her oddball personality is about the only thing saving the group from becoming a snore fest. Jenny would probably say she knows me well too, and she does, in so much as I allow anyone to *really* know me.

'I haven't forgotten it's your birthday too,' she says, reaching behind her cape to produce a sparkling, pink gift bag.

'Wow,' I say, caught off guard as she passes it to me. 'I didn't think anyone would remember my birthday.'

'What?' Jenny squeaks, throwing her hands in the air. 'Of course I remembered. Open it. Open it. Open it.'

I reach inside and pull out a rectangular grey box. Flabbergasted, I lift the lid. Inside, I find a silver locket and chain neatly presented against cream velvet.

'The locket's empty,' Jenny says, 'but I thought maybe you could put one of Adam's photographs inside or maybe a photo of you both together. I dunno, just an idea . . .' She trails off, adopting her default fidget. 'I just thought you'd like it.'

'I do. I really do,' I say, barely able to form words. 'It's . . . it's . . . unexpected.'

I lift the chain out of the box with trembling fingers. The shiny silver heart tumbles and swirls, coming to a sudden stop at the end of the chain. It swings back and forth for a few seconds, like the arm on a metronome, before it comes to a standstill.

'There's something written on the back,' I say excitedly.

I read the inscription aloud.

Twenty-one years together
Never really apart.

Never really apart? The phrase scratches across my mind as if it's being engraved into my brain just as it is on the locket. I feel heat in my cheeks and my chest tightens as a familiar wave of anger washes over me. *Never really apart?* Except that we are apart. Adam is dead and I'm here; that's about as apart as it gets. I curl my fingers tightly around the locket until I feel the trinket dig into the fleshy part of my palm. I close my eyes for a moment and take a deep breath. Counting backwards from five, the urge to toss the locket across the road passes.

'Susan?' Jenny calls, and I open my eyes. 'You okay? I didn't mean to upset you. I know this is hard.'

'It's a very thoughtful gift,' I say, calmer and more in control. 'It's beautiful. Thank you.'

She shrugs. 'It's nothing, really.'

'It's something special. It must have been very expensive, you didn't need to . . .'

Jenny blushes and drags the front of her hood over her eyes, hiding. My rhapsodising is making her uncomfortable. But that's what people do when they receive an unexpected gift, isn't it? They gush. Even if that gift feels as if someone has pulled your heart clean out of your chest and stomped it into the floor. I stop talking, fold my arms and wait for Jenny to pull her hood back.

A sudden gust of October wind finds its way past us and into my flat. I shiver.

'C'mon in,' I say, turning to walk inside where it's warm.

I smile when I hear the door close, followed by Jenny's footsteps behind me. We're sitting face-to-face on the couch before she finally takes the hood off her head. She crosses her legs and bobs her top foot at the ankle. The whole couch bounces as a result. Jenny can never sit still; it's as if her body just won't allow her any downtime.

'How are you doing?' she asks.

'I'm okay,' I lie.

'Really?' She tilts her head. 'Because I wasn't okay on my mam's first anniversary. I don't believe for one second that you're okay on your brother's. If you don't want to talk about it, that's cool. Tell me to piss off, shut up, whatever. But please don't lie to me.'

'Okay.' I shake my head. 'I'm not okay. Maybe I'll never be okay again. But I still don't want to talk about it. Now, will you help me fasten this chain, please?' I open my hand and stare at the pretty locket again.

'You don't have to wear it,' Jenny says. 'If . . . if it's too soon.'

I want to ask her why she bought it if she thought it was too soon, but I don't bother. She'll just fidget or mumble or bounce around the room talking shite for twenty minutes, and I won't get a comprehensive answer anyway. Besides, I know she didn't mean to upset me and I should appreciate the gift. Jenny is kind.

'Just put it on for me, Jenny, yeah?' I try hard to smile and keep the emotional quiver out of my voice.

'Sure,' she says, twisting on the couch.

I turn my back to her and slowly guide the silver chain around my neck.

I can feel her hands shaking against my neck as she fiddles with the clasp. I forgot how difficult a task like this is for her. Her dexterity isn't good, especially not with intricate things like fastening a delicate necklace. I once watched her struggle to get the battery back into her phone for half an hour before she finally let me do it for her. I wonder how long this is going to take.

My neck begins to ache.

'This is a tricky feckin' thing,' Jenny says. 'Just there . . . almost . . .'

'It's okay,' I say, reaching up to place my hands over hers. 'I can try it on another time.'

'Just give me . . . two . . . more . . . seconds . . .'

'Jenny, just leave it,' I say, my neck actually hurting now.

'Hang on, I nearly have it.' She's fooling herself but not me. 'Anyway, I might as well keep trying while I tell you my news.'

'Oh?' I say, intrigued. 'News? What news?'

'Sit still,' Jenny scolds. 'I nearly had it and then you moved.'

I didn't budge. And Jenny didn't nearly have it, but I play along. I want to know her news.

'Sorry,' I say. 'I'll keep still.'

She tuts and tries again.

'So, this news, then?' I continue. 'Sounds exciting, eh?'

Jenny and I share news all the time. World news. Like what's happening on CNN and what Sky is reporting. We chat about the latest TV shows and rant when our favourite characters get killed off unexpectedly. We have an insane number of text messages dedicated to our obsession with *Desperate Housewives*. But we never have any real news. Nothing personal or current. Because there's never anything to tell.

'I, erm.' Jenny pauses, and I think I can hear her chewing on her lip as she concentrates on the clasp. 'Got it,' she announces, triumphant. 'I got the little bugger.'

I feel the weight of the locket dangle around my neck as Jenny lets go on her end, and my hands automatically reach for the silver heart to settle it between my collarbones.

'Thank you,' I say, spinning back around to face her. 'How does it look?'

'Fabulous,' she grins. 'I knew it would suit you.'

'I really do love it, Jenny,' I lie. 'Thank you. Thank you.' I take her twitching hands in mine and, as always, physical touch has a calming effect on her jitters.

'So are you going to tell me your news, or keep me in suspense all night?' I finally say.

She pulls one of her hands free to scratch her ear. The effort is so vigorous she makes the skin on the tip of her ear turn red. I'm so used to Jenny's oddities it takes me longer than it should to realise her agitation now is different. Something is really affecting her. She's nervous. Whatever she's about to tell me is huge. I swallow hard and prepare myself for bad news.

'Jenny,' I say cautiously, 'is everything okay?'

She clasps her hands together as if she's rubbing invisible moisturiser into her skin. 'I've started seeing someone,' she mumbles.

'No way,' I squeak. 'Who is he? Do I know him?'

'Wow, Susan,' she says, blushing. 'Calm down. It's nothing to get excited about. It's early days.'

'Oh c'mon.' I pull up my legs and tuck them against my chest, infused with giddiness. 'Don't pull that "it's early days" nonsense, this is the best news I've had in ages. Who is he? What's his name? Do I know him? Oh my God . . . tell me everything. Everything.'

'You *do* know him.' Jenny lifts her shoulders to her ears and locks them there, embarrassed.

'No way? Who, oh my God, who is it?'

Jenny and I don't have any mutual friends. And when we go out I rarely see her talking to anyone. I can't think who it could possibly be. I immediately wonder if he's imaginary.

'Deacon,' Jenny says, flashing her tobacco-stained teeth.

'O'Reilly?' I jerk my head back. 'Deacon O'Reilly. You can't be serious?'

'I know you don't like him,' Jenny says, lowering her shoulders. 'But he's a great guy. Honestly. He's been through some tough shit. We connect.'

'I never said I don't like him. I just don't know him, Jenny,' I say. 'A year of group sessions and he hasn't said a word. No one knows him. It's odd. He's odd.'

'We've talked,' she says, the apples of her cheeks rounding with satisfaction. 'I like him, I like him a lot. I think this might be the real deal.'

I chew on a fingernail, a habit I've picked up in the last twelve months. 'Okay.'

'Really?' Jenny smiles. 'You're okay with this?'

'Sure.' I shrug. 'It's not up to me who you go out with, is it? I just want you to be happy. Isn't that what being friends is all about? Wanting each other to be happy.'

'You're really okay with this?' she says, obviously suspecting I'm lying.

'I said I am, didn't I? Just be careful, okay,' I say, tilting my head to one side. 'I don't trust him.'

'You don't trust anyone,' Jenny laughs.

I don't reply. She's joking but her jab saddens me because she's right.

'So you just want me to be happy?' she says, thankfully sidestepping how quiet I've suddenly become.

'Oh God.' I press my hands against my face. 'What have I walked myself into?'

'Try fancy dress?' Jenny claps, way too excited. 'Please? Dress up with me. Just because we're a bunch of people who love dead people doesn't mean we can't have fun at our meetings. Halloween is all about the dead, after all. It's like our national holiday.'

'Your logic is so messed up,' I say. 'You do know that, right?'

'You think?' She gives me a guileless smile. 'So, you'll do it then? You'll wear a costume?'

'Fuck no,' I snort. 'But nice try.'

'Please?' she says, dragging out the e-sound as if she's a humming bird stuck on a single note.

'No, seriously, Jenny. I'm not in the mood,' I say, losing patience. 'Thank you for the lovely gift, but I really just want to forget it's my birthday and forget it's nearly Halloween.'

'Why?' She takes on a seriousness that isn't like her. 'Because you won't let yourself ever have fun because of Adam? Because your brother died and you're terrified to go on living?'

'Jenny,' I snap. 'I don't want to talk about this.'

'Susan, I'm your best friend and all I know about Adam is his name, that you were twins and that he died on his twenty-first birthday. Why don't you ever want to talk about him?'

I look at Jenny with a mix of anger and sadness. Her desperation to feel needed is written all over her face. 'Fine,' I hiss. 'What do you want to know about Adam? Ask. I won't hold back.'

'Everything, I want to know everything.'

'Okay. I'll tell you Adam's story. I'll tell you everything. And when I'm finished I have one question for you.'

'But you know everything about me.' Jenny shuffles on the couch. Her cape jars under her bum and pulls the neck so tight she baulks and has to stand up, adjust it and sit back down.

'I didn't say it was about you.'

'Oooohhhh,' she says with curious excitement. 'Intriguing. Okay, Susan Arnold.' She stretches her open hand towards me and it takes me a moment to realise that she wants to shake. I press my clammy palm against hers and we strike a deal. 'You tell me what you've been bottling up for a year and I'll answer any damn question you want,' Jenny smiles.

I let go of her hand and clasp my palm around my new silver locket. I take a deep breath, close my eyes and begin.

Chapter Eleven

Then

'I was napping on the couch when the call came in. *Buffy the Vampire Slayer* was playing in the background, and—'

'Vampires?' Jenny cuts in. 'Really? You watched that crap?'

'Jenny!' I shake my head. 'You asked me to open up about my dead brother, and vampires . . . vampires are what you want to talk about? Seriously?'

'You're right. Sorry, go on,' Jenny says, twirling the string of her cape around her finger melodramatically. 'I'm listening.'

I close my eyes and smile, inwardly accepting that if I'm finally going to open up I'm glad it's with Jenny.

'It was our birthday,' I begin. 'The big Two-One. We'd been planning the party for ages. But when the big day finally rolled around the weather was shit. I mean a full-on storm. Trees blowing all over the place. Power lines down. Rivers bursting their banks. I thought about cancelling the party. But Adam was so cool about it. He was all like "It's just a bit of rain, Sue . . . blah, blah, blah." That was Adam all over. He was never afraid of anything.'

'He sounds amazing,' Jenny says, pulling her feet on to the couch to sit cross-legged. She slouches a little, places her elbows on her knees and lowers her head until it rests on top of her clasped hands. Her back arches like a comma and she looks uncomfortable, but she's smiling and willing me on with her contagious enthusiasm.

'He was,' I sigh, remembering.

'Tell me more,' Jenny says. 'Tell me it all.'

'It was still raining when the call came,' I continue. 'But the thunder stopped as I put the receiver to my ear, as if the bloody weather was waiting with bated breath for the words my mother would whisper – the words that would change me profoundly.'

'It was your mother who broke the news to you?'

'Yeah.' I shudder, hearing my mother's sobbing as clear in my head now as I did that day.

'Is that why you're not close to her?' Jenny asks. 'Because you blame her for breaking the news to you?'

What kind of a fucking question is that? I think, tempted to reach across the couch and slap some sense into Jenny.

'No. God, no,' I say, calm instead. 'That's not it at all. I guess we just both miss him and we don't know how to deal with it. It was always the three of us. The three amigos. And without Adam,' I exhale roughly, 'without Adam it's different. It's broken.'

'Right, fuck this,' Jenny says, hopping up off the couch as if the cushion under her has suddenly caught fire. 'I need a drink. Do you have anything to drink in this place? You need one too, don't you?'

'There's some beer in the fridge,' I say. 'It's been open for a couple of days though. It probably tastes awful.'

'It'll do.' She hurries away.

I should have known not to talk about my mother in front of Jenny. I know how much she misses her own mother. She says that after being tossed out of foster care after just a year, my hot–cold relationship with my mother is a walk in the park compared to the crap she went through. Of course that pisses me off, but I let it slide because our mothers are not something either of us want to talk about. Jenny didn't take it well when I admitted that my mother was, in fact, alive, just dead inside, and I haven't mentioned Mam again since. Not until now.

I can hear Jenny pottering about in the kitchenette and if I look up from staring at the carpet I'll catch her movements out of the corner of my eye. But I don't want to look up. I'm staring at a cigarette burn I made in the carpet less than a week after we moved in. Adam lectured me for another week about my reckless, teenage behaviour. We were eighteen. We were kids, really, but Adam had such a sensible head on his shoulders. Always. It makes me wonder what the future would have held for him. I bet it would have been amazing. But it wasn't to be. Twenty-one years to the day was all the time Adam Arnold was granted in this life. But the bastard who ran him over is still out there, living his life. It's so unfair.

I close my eyes and listen to the noise Jenny is creating in the kitchenette. It's nice to have background noise, for a change, as my mind wanders towards thoughts of the day I lost my brother. Was it ironic that the rain pelted against the windows of our flat like teardrops as I listened to my mother cry over the phone?

'There's been an accident. A terrible accident,' she'd said. 'It's Adam.'

The days that followed are still a blur. Even now when I close my eyes and concentrate I only have snippets of memories from Adam's funeral. I remember the black dress I wore. The same one I'd chosen to wear to our birthday party. It was the perfect little black dress and I'd been excited to show him. I never should have had to wear it to his funeral instead. I remember the violin solo that my cousin played as they lowered Adam's coffin into the hole in the chalky, brown earth. Her hands shook so badly I thought she would drop her violin into the open grave after Adam. I remember countless people shaking my hand and telling me they were sorry for my loss, as if my brother was my favourite teacup that I'd dropped and shattered, or a treasured hat that had blown off my head on a windy day. But Adam wasn't lost. He was stolen. A drunk driver snatched my brother from this world with his selfishness and irresponsibility.

Jenny comes back from the kitchen with a bottle of beer in her hand.

'Does the Grim Reaper drink?' I joke, choking back tears as I look up at my best friend's ridiculously distasteful costume.

'If you had his job, wouldn't you?' Jenny presses the bottle to her lips and gulps down the last couple of mouthfuls.

'Yeah. S'pose,' I say. 'Wonder if it pays well.'

She laughs. 'I'd say he's been *dying* for a promotion for years.'

I shake my head and grin. 'That was a terrible joke.'

'I tried,' she says with a shrug. 'Right.' She drops the bottle into the bin next to the coffee table. 'You've no more booze. And I need a drink before tonight's meeting. If we go now we'll make it to the pub for a quick pint before the meeting starts.'

'I think I'll give tonight's meeting a miss, Jenny. I'm really not feeling it. I'm sorry.'

'I knew you'd say that,' Jenny says. 'Anniversaries and birthdays are the hardest. And you've the two combined. Jesus, that's tough. But it's also the very reason you need to go tonight. You don't want to stay cooped up in this tiny flat all alone. All those thoughts floating around your head. It's not good for you.'

'Actually, that's exactly what I want. I just want to be alone. I need time to think about stuff.'

'Well, I don't want to be alone. Please come with me. Please?' Jenny makes puppy dog eyes at me and she's trying very hard to come over as adorable, but one of her eyes is twitching. I'm not sure she notices. 'Besides, I've told everyone it's your birthday,' she adds. 'They'll be disappointed if you're not there.'

'Jesus, Jenny,' I say. 'I didn't want any fuss.'

'It's not fuss, Susan. Just a few cards and some gifts. It'll be nice, I promise.' She's bouncing on the spot, delighted with herself. 'And I thought maybe you could finish telling me about Adam.'

'At the meeting?' My cheeks flush.

'Well, yeah, that's kind of the point of bereavement counselling. You know, to talk about your bereavement.'

'Okay.' I fold my arms, defiant. 'I'll talk about Adam, but only if Deacon agrees to talk about whoever he lost.'

'Susan, c'mon,' Jenny pleads. 'You can't force someone to talk if they don't want to.'

'Oh, like you're forcing me, you mean.'

Jenny blushes. 'Ha! Yeah. I guess you're right. Well, I'll tell you what, if you can get Deacon to open up tonight I'll clean your whole flat from top to bottom. This place is absolutely filthy.'

I glance around at my messy flat. I've always been untidy, but without Adam here to keep my grubby habits in check the place really is bordering on disgusting.

'Okay, deal,' I nod.

'Before we go,' Jenny says, still looking around at the mess of the place, 'what was the question you wanted to ask me?'

'I've changed my mind,' I say. 'I'm going to ask Deacon instead.'

Chapter Twelve

THEN

Criminally Negligent Manslaughter. The words weigh heavy in my mouth as I repeat them aloud on the steps of the courthouse eleven days before Christmas. Jenny places her arms around me and I cry. The judge used complicated language that hurt my brain to try to understand. But I understood when he said Adam's death was a terrible tragedy, one that had impacted his family profoundly. Fourteen months after my brother's death, someone had finally said the words out loud that have plagued my conscious and subconscious every day. *Adam shouldn't be dead.* The judge said he was simply a young man in the wrong place at the wrong time. He said Adam was on the cusp of adulthood, doing what young people do – buying alcohol. He said Adam's only mistake was assuming that the driver would stop at the pedestrian crossing. Driving conditions were horrendous because of the storm, and the driver didn't see him in time to brake. Apparently, he had pulled over immediately and assisted Adam, flagging down passers-by to call for help. The driver hadn't been that much over the legal limit, his barrister tried to argue. The stiff-upper-lipped barrister tried to imply that the crash was Adam's fault for going out walking in such bad weather.

'The conditions were treacherous,' he said, 'braking distance was almost non-existent.' He shook his head, as if drink-driving during a storm somehow made more sense than walking sober. As if the weather somehow made the driver's actions justifiable and forgivable.

Outside the courthouse, reporters line the steps like vultures waiting for the convicted drunk driver to be brought out. They will snap his picture and print it all over the papers tomorrow, as if he's a celebrity who's earned his notoriety.

'Four years,' I say, leaning against the low wall at the side of the courthouse as I struggle to breathe. My mouth is open and my chest is heaving but I can't seem to get enough air into my lungs. 'That's all he got. Four bloody years. And God only knows how early he will be out with good behaviour. He could be a free man in just a few months.'

'It's shocking,' Jenny says. 'In four years that bastard will be out living his life again. But Adam got a life sentence. He's never coming back. I'm so sorry, Susan. Christ, what kind of justice system do we have in this country? It's a joke. A bloody joke, that's what it is.'

'It's so unfair.' I'm shaking all over.

A young journalist notices us huddled in the corner. I recognise her as she breaks away from the other reporters and photographers and crosses the steps to approach us. She's a girl from Adam's journalism class. I can't remember her name right now, but I definitely know her. She's been to parties in my flat. She was Adam's friend.

Jenny steps in front of me like a protective mamma bear as the girl gets close. Jenny isn't much taller or broader than me. I can't hide in her shadow, even though I want to. Nonetheless, I step to the side valiantly and lock eyes with the girl, whose name is on the tip of my tongue.

'Susan. Susan Arnold,' she says, shoving a small silver voice recorder towards me. 'Do you have any comment for us? How are you feeling? You must be disappointed by the lenient sentencing?'

I shake my head. I thought she was going to say something kind. Something about Adam, about what a good friend he was, or how he was a much-loved classmate. I wasn't expecting a barrage of cold, professional questions.

'Are *you* disappointed?' I ask, straight-faced. 'Adam was your friend, wasn't he?'

Her eyes glass over and there is a fleeting moment when I think her professional façade will crack and she'll wrap her arms around me, tell me how much she misses Adam and suggest we grab a coffee soon or something. But she turns her head towards the group of huddled reporters. None of them even glance our way. They don't know I'm Adam's sister. That advantage is reserved solely for . . . Rebecca, yes, that's her name. I remember now. Becky Clarke. What a huge advantage it must be over her senior colleagues to personally know the sister of the victim. She must be so confident she'll scoop the story. She'll stop at nothing for an exclusive. I know; Adam was the same.

Becky turns her head back. Her eyes meet mine and she half smiles. 'Surely you must have some comment, Susan? Take this chance to have your say. Tell the world how you're feeling.'

Becky's professionalism is impressive. She certainly looks the part of a well-groomed reporter, complete with tailored outfit and designer glasses. She works hard on her image, no doubt. This is a very different Becky to the girl throwing up tequila shots in my bathroom last year. She did well to land a job straight out of college. I have no doubt that story she wrote exposing the university president's sordid affairs with senior students earned her a cushy internship with a national paper. But Adam's name should have been on that story. He'd been rambling on about our president's inappropriate behaviour – piecing together clues, seeking out sources and snapping candid photos. I've no doubt Adam was the one who tipped Becky off about the story, and after he died she ran with it, doing the whole sordid affair spectacular justice. But she never gave Adam any credit. She doesn't give a shit about Adam, she's just after another great story. *Well, her greed stops here.*

I *was* going to comment. I was going to tell Becky how much I miss Adam and how miserable I am without him. But if a so-called friend cares more about a juicy story than about missing Adam, I quickly realise that the world doesn't care either. Sure, my words might make the front page. The story might pull at the heartstrings of some empathetic strangers over their morning coffee. People will devour his story on their commute to work and then toss the paper in a bin or leave it behind on the train. For the general public, Adam's name is synonymous with tragedy. They will forget my brother's name almost as soon as they've read it. But for me, and my mother, Adam's name is all we have left.

'Have you anything you want to say to the man who took Adam's life?' Becky asks, placing her hand on my shoulder. 'Surely there must be something you want to say to him. For Adam, Susan. Say the words now that Adam can't.'

I want him dead. I want to wrap my hands around his throat and squeeze every last breath out of him. I want to watch him kick and buck and struggle for air that I won't allow him. I want to watch him die. And most of all, I want him to go to hell for what he's done. I shake my head as salty tears trickle down my cheeks. 'Words won't bring my brother back,' I say.

'You heard her. She said she has no comment, okay?' Jenny growls. 'Jesus. Let it go. Have you no heart? Can't you see how upset she is? C'mon, Susan. Let's go.' Jenny drapes her arm around my shoulder. 'Let's get you home.'

'Okay,' Becky nods, slipping her hand into her trouser pocket to pull out a business card, 'but if you change your mind and you'd like to talk, my email and mobile number are on this. Please do get in touch anytime.'

Becky forces the crisp card into my hand.

'I really hope you'll be okay, Susan,' she says. 'Adam was a great guy. And a good friend. He is missed very much.'

I watch as she walks away and rejoins her colleagues. I crumple the card in my hand and my eyes search for a bin. But I'm distracted by an angry mob gathering at the foot of the steps. There aren't more than twenty people but they chant so loudly it seems like there are hundreds of voices.

'Murderer. Scumbag. Bastard,' they shout.

Some of them are waving their hands in the air and others are stomping their feet. They've attracted the attention of the camera crew among the newspaper reporters. The mob's voices grow even louder and their faces seem angrier once the camera is on them.

'What are they doing?' I ask, moving to the side to make sure I'm out of camera shot.

'Showing their support,' Jenny says, stepping the other way to make sure she *is* in camera shot. 'Look.' She points to one particularly boisterous shouter. 'Someone has made a *Down With Drink Driving* poster. That's awesome.'

My heart aches.

The camera pulls away from the crowd as quickly as it appeared, much to their disappointment. There's a sudden silence before boos and roars resume, even louder than before.

'What's happening?' I say, overwhelmed.

'They must be bringing him out now,' Jenny says, reaching for my hand to squeeze it gently.

My tummy somersaults.

The journalists race around the corner with their microphones poised and ready. Their enthusiasm makes me sick.

'Do you want to watch them take him away?' Jenny asks. 'It might help to see him go. To finally see him get what he deserves.'

This isn't what he deserves. 'It won't help.' I press my hands against my ears, trying to block out the shouting from the protesters.

'I don't want him to see me,' I say. 'I don't want to look into his eyes. I can't.' I begin to cry.

I sat at the back of the courtroom today. My mother was up front, with her legal team. Every so often she would glance over her shoulder and check I was still there. I would nod and smile, but I couldn't bring myself to get any closer. Not when I noticed her shoulders shake and I knew she was crying. Not when the judge read out the sentence and I watched her break down completely. And especially not when she let the man who took Adam away from us see her heartbroken and weak. She let that monster see how devastated she is; she let him have that power over her. I can't do that – not ever. I can't let him look into my eyes and try to offer me an apology that I don't want to hear. I can't give him anything more than he has already taken from me.

More commotion ensues on the steps. I spin round and see my mother has appeared at the main doors. Her legal team surrounds her like the Knights of the Round Table. Their expensive suits are modern-day armour. They are valiant and brave, or cocky and arrogant, depending on which side of their argument you stand on.

The reporters who held their ground on the steps are rewarded as my mother speaks at length about what a wonderful person Adam was. I find myself nodding as I listen. Her eyes are on a piece of paper she's holding, but her hands are trembling badly. She can't possibly be reading from such an unsteady page, and I wonder how often she has mulled over these words, certainly often enough to know them by heart. She speaks for about three minutes, faltering only to choke back tears. I wish she'd spoken longer, said more wonderful things about Adam, but it's long enough to give the tabloids plenty to print tomorrow. Finally, as my mother wipes her eyes and looks up, she notices me and we share a smile. I know she'll probably be flying back to Provence tomorrow, but I hope she comes by the flat later for a chat. I miss my mother as much as I miss Adam.

When that drunk bastard smashed his car into my brother he didn't just steal Adam, he stole my mother too. He took my entire family away from me in one foul blow. I wish he was dead.

Chapter Thirteen

Now

Helen and I sit at the edge of the lake, our toes daringly close to the water lapping the shore. It's getting dark. The sun has disappeared behind thick clouds, which is a pity as I long to watch it set over the horizon. I pull myself to my feet and take a couple of steps backwards. The sway of the water is making me dizzy and I realise I've forgotten to eat again today.

'We should get back,' I say.

'What? Why?' Helen says. 'We only just got here.'

'It's getting dark.'

'So?' Helen dismisses. 'I love the dark.'

'I don't,' I say.

Helen unscrews the cap on the wine bottle tucked between her legs. She takes a swig. Then another. And another. She finally drags the bottle away from her lips and reaches her arm out towards me. 'Want some?'

'No.'

Helen shrugs, unfazed. 'More for me, so.'

I watch her guzzle like a rebellious teenager, except she's my forty-something neighbour with a smart blonde bob, sensible walking shoes and a figure you can tell was once enviable but that she's noticeably let go over the years. Despite all my time attending a bereavement group,

Helen is the saddest person I've ever met. I'm wondering if I should give her a hug, when I'm distracted by something rustling in the trees behind us.

'What's that?' I jump.

Helen shakes her head. 'Oh Susan,' she sniggers, 'it's just a bird. Or a mouse maybe. Don't worry.'

'Yeah, you're right.' I twitch, unnerved. 'I'm still not used to the sounds of the countryside. Especially when it's getting dark.'

I walk back to the water's edge, distancing myself from the disturbing rustling behind me. I crouch on my hunkers and dip my fingers into the water. The icy bite against my skin startles me and I want to pull my hand out instantly, but for some reason I don't.

'It's cold,' Helen says, as if I can't feel for myself.

'I thought it would be warmer,' I say, feeling stupid. 'It's summer.'

'It leads out to the Atlantic, Susan,' Helen says. 'No amount of miserable Irish sunshine can heat it up.'

I stare at the water in front of me. It's blue-grey close to the shore but it darkens into a depressing navy-black as you cast your eyes further out, and I can tell it gets deep quickly. Locals call this spot the beach. But that's ridiculously optimistic and totally overselling it. It's nothing more than a picturesque horseshoe where the sea has eaten away at the rocks over the years to form tiny pebbles that long to be sand but fail miserably.

'You know they say once you get to a certain point of cold your muscles just seize up and you can't feel anything. You just go numb, so it doesn't hurt,' Helen says.

'What doesn't hurt?' I turn my head to glare into her glassy eyes. I doubt she notices my frustration.

'They say it's just like falling asleep,' Helen continues. 'Amelia wouldn't have felt any pain, Susan. It would have been just like going for a nap. I can see the way you look into the water and I can understand that your heart is breaking, but take some comfort in knowing that she would have slipped away peacefully at the end.'

My anger bubbles to spilling point and I'm about to scream in Helen's stupid face when the rustling behind the tree grows louder and more unwavering. I snatch the wine bottle from her hand. I turn it upside down and spill the remaining wine all over the ground.

'Where are you doing?' she says, swaying on her drunken feet.

'I need this.' I raise the bottle above my head. 'Someone's hiding behind that tree. They're watching us.'

A sudden snap hangs in the air from a stick breaking underfoot and I hear a deep, low voice like a hum. A male voice.

'Be careful,' Helen says. 'Be careful.'

I edge towards the tree slowly. My grip on the bottle tightens.

'Who's there?' Helen shouts from behind me. 'We're not afraid of you.' The tremor in her voice says otherwise.

There's more rustling and a high-pitched squeal that lasts less than a second.

'Jesus, Susan. Who is it?' Helen says, grabbing on to me and making it hard to move. 'I'm scared.'

I shake her off.

Something black moves behind the tree. I'm ready to bring the bottle down. Helen grabs me once more and I can feel her hot, drunken breath on the back of my neck. She's not as easy to wriggle free from this time.

Dusk is falling quickly and it's hard to make out the exact shape behind the tree. The large black figure bends forward, scoops something small and wriggling into its arms and runs away. The crunch of stones and leaves underfoot is unmistakable. It's definitely something on two feet, a person and not an animal.

'Oh my God,' Helen says, finally letting go of me to flap her arms about unhelpfully. 'Oh my God. I can't believe it. I just can't. Did you see that?'

'Yeah.' I shake my head, unsure of what the hell just happened. 'I can't believe it either.'

'It was Amelia,' Helen says, 'wasn't it? That man had Amelia in his arms, didn't he?'

'Helen, you're drunk,' I say.

'Come back,' she shouts, holding a pointed finger in the air. 'Come back here!' She begins to run after the shadow. 'We saw you. We know you have the little girl.'

She stumbles on the uneven ground and falls. Her knees land on some jagged stones. It must hurt but she's on her feet again in an instant, ready to keep running. I grab her hand and pull her back roughly. She trips again and I let go. This time she comes down on her back and hits her head. She doesn't get up. She lies still with her mouth gaping and she's making a rattling noise when she breathes. Her eyes are wide with shock and glassy from wine, but there's a sparkle of excitement dancing in them too.

'Helen. Take some slow, even breaths,' I say. 'You're winded.'

'Susan, I saw . . .'

'Stop it,' I growl. 'You're drunk. Look at you. You can't even stand up, for God's sake. And you're talking gibberish.'

'No, no, Susan.' Helen's arm shoots up and she grabs my hand so tightly it pinches. She tugs on my arm, dragging me forward until I have to bend in the middle and the fog of her wine breath hits me in the face.

'I know what I saw. Trust me,' she says, looking up at me. 'You were right, Susan. Amelia *is* still alive. We have to go to the police. We have to tell them. This is such good news. Oh Susan, I wish you'd seen her too.'

'Oh Helen.' I shake my head. 'I wish you hadn't.'

Chapter Fourteen

Now

I wake up on the couch with a splitting headache. Light is glaring in through the window. I had to take down the ugly polka dot curtains that came with the cottage when we moved in because there was mould growing around the stitching and I was worried it would make Amelia sick. I replaced them with cheap, flimsy ones when the renovation budget ran over. I'm regretting that decision now as my eyes sting.

Clattering cups and banging plates let me know Paul is preparing breakfast. I wonder if he's getting ready to go running or if he's just back. I sit upright and a wave of dizziness washes over me. I grab the edge of the couch and steady myself. Memories of last night play over in my mind. Helen drinking too much. The navy-black water in the deepest part of the lake. The sinister sense of someone watching us. And, of course, Amelia. Helen thinking she saw my little girl has rattled me. And now I can't get out of my head the look on Helen's face as I walked away.

'You're awake,' Paul says, walking towards me with a glass of water in his hand.

'No thanks,' I say as he stretches his arm out to me. 'I'll make some coffee in a minute.'

He sighs and places the glass of water on the coffee table in front of me. He puts two paracetamol tablets on the table next to the glass.

'Here, you should take these,' he says. 'They'll help your hangover.'

I'm not hung-over. Helen guzzled the lion's share of the wine last night while I barely managed a glass, but I don't bother to explain as my husband stares at me, exaggerating his disapproval as he shakes his head. I wait for him to blame Helen's bad influence. He doesn't.

It takes me a moment to realise Paul is in regular clothes instead of his running gear, which I've come to think of as his second skin. Low-cut jeans hang off his hips in a way they used not to. He's lost weight that he really didn't have to spare. An old grey T-shirt with a Ribena stain on the side, from the time Amelia spilled her juice on him just after we moved in, makes him look sloppy and careless. My usually dapper husband is slowly falling apart.

'Are you not going running this morning?' I ask.

Paul looks at me as if I'm making him as sick as the smell of eggs wafting around is making me.

'How could I leave you here on your own?' he says. 'The state you were in. I thought you'd throw up and choke on your own vomit or something.'

'Excuse me?' I gasp.

'You were hammered last night, Susan,' Paul says. 'Or should I say this morning, when you fell through the door.'

'I was not,' I say, swiping my hand through the air to dismiss Paul's irritating assumption.

'Really?' he blinks. 'You were shaking all over and you couldn't string a sentence together, for God's sake. And you were paranoid as hell, shouting at me to close the door in case someone saw you come home. To be honest, I'm surprised you even remembered where you live, you were that out of it.'

I try to think of an explanation for my behaviour, but I stop myself: I know whatever I say Paul doesn't want to hear it.

It wouldn't be unreasonable for any woman in my shoes to hit the bottle. In fact, it probably seems weird that I haven't before now. When Adam died, days blurred into nights and weeks into months because I was drinking so heavily. I thought alcohol would take the pain away, but it only made it worse.

'This is that Helen woman's influence,' Paul says.

And there it is, my husband's answer to everything – *blame someone else*. I resist the urge to start an argument. I feel a headache coming on and I squeeze the bridge of my nose, trying to relieve some of the sinus pressure. The smell coming from the stove is overpowering. *Paul and his goddam eggs every bloody morning.*

'She's bad news,' he continues. 'Always hanging around here. Why? She barely knows us. She's just a nosy busybody. I don't want her here any more, Susan. Certainly not all the time.'

'I . . . I . . . she's my friend,' I say, exhausted.

Helen has inserted herself into our lives so intrusively and so suddenly that Paul has every right to be frustrated about it. I can't argue with that.

'For fuck's sake, Susan,' he grunts. 'I can't do this.'

He picks up the paracetamol and tosses them into his mouth, washing them down with a large gulp of the water. He slams the empty glass back on the table with unnecessary force.

'Helen is my friend,' I repeat, staring at the glass.

'A friend like Deacon?' Paul says.

'Oh Paul, don't start this again,' I groan, the pressure in my sinuses becoming worse.

'Don't you think it's weird that you haven't heard from him since the barbecue? Not once. And the cops said he's not at his flat. But hey, he's your friend so he's a good guy, right?' Paul hisses.

'He *is* a good guy,' I snap. 'And I never said he was my friend. I expressly told you he's a client. And he's not obliged to *check in* on me,' I mimic, raising my hands to add air quotes. 'I haven't had calls or texts from any of my other clients either, Paul, but you don't seem to have any problem with that?'

'Whatever,' he shrugs. 'I don't trust him.'

'You don't trust anyone,' I say. 'Deacon. Helen. The cops, for Christ's sake.' I pause, unsure whether to say the next words. 'Do you even trust me, Paul?'

'We can't get rid of Helen most of the time,' Paul says, pulling a face and sidestepping my question. 'And then when you're drunk out of your head, she finally pisses off and leaves you on your own. Bloody hell! What kind of friend abandons someone like that? Especially when you're grieving. You really do have the best of friends,' he adds sarcastically, before rushing back to the stove and the sudden smell of burning eggs.

'I'm not grieving,' I mumble, before he's out of earshot.

I glance over my shoulder as Paul paces in the kitchen. He throws the eggs into the bin, tosses the burned pan into the dishwasher and uses his heel to slam the door shut, taking out his frustration on the appliance. His lack of respect for my pristine kitchen is infuriating, but I don't say anything. My coming home so late last night must really have pissed him off. Maybe now he understands how it feels when he disappears for hours on end. The less attention I pay, the more frustrated Paul seems to become as he cracks fresh eggs into a mixing bowl, takes a fork out of the drawer and whisks like crazy.

Finally, I pull myself to my feet and run my hands over my clothes, as if I can straighten out my emotions as I straighten out my blouse. My neck is on fire on my left side every time I turn my head. The last time I slept on a couch all night I was in college. I smile, despite the pain, realising I haven't thought about my college days in a while. I rub the back of my neck, easing some of the tension, and run my hand through my hair. I wince as my fingers catch in the stubborn knots at the back. I remember I had an appointment to get my hair done a few days ago, which I forgot to cancel. The hairdresser never called me. But the whole village is talking about me, so I've no doubt they know why I missed the appointment. Bad hair is the last thing on my mind right now.

'Today,' Paul says, coming towards me with the spatula in his hand. 'You need to talk to Helen today. I can't cope with her any more . . .' He pauses and his breath seems to get stuck in his throat as he edges closer to me. 'What's that on your hand?'

He drops the spatula on the coffee table. Runny uncooked egg trickles off the top and on to the polished mahogany. I groan inwardly and hide my disgust.

'What?' I turn my hand over to examine my palm.

Dried blood is trapped in the lines and creases on my fingers. I see more blood around my nails and across my knuckles. It's flaking and brown and revolting.

'Oh Jesus, Susan, what's happened to your head too?' Paul points.

His eyes are wide with concern and I notice how bloodshot they are. His cheeks are puffy and red. He must have been crying in the kitchen before I woke up.

'Nothing, it's nothing,' I say dismissively, curling my fingers into my palms before I shove my fists into my pockets.

'It's in your hair.' He reaches for the back of my head and I feel him pull on the same knots that were bothering me moments ago. 'Oh Christ, you're bleeding.'

Paul takes his hand back and examines small flecks of blood that have come loose from my scalp and stuck to his fingers.

'If it's bad you might need stitches,' Paul says, placing his hands on my shoulders as he tries to turn me around to investigate the back of my head. 'What happened? Where did you fall?'

'I didn't fall,' I say, holding my ground and shrugging his hands off me.

'You really expect me to believe that?'

'Yes. Yes, I do. I expect you to listen to me, Paul. But, to be honest, I don't care any more if you do or you don't. I'm tired. So tired. I'm going for a shower and maybe a lie-down.'

'Susan, you disappeared for half the night, and you've come home with blood in your hair and on your clothes.' Paul points at my cream blouse. 'Don't you think I deserve some sort of explanation?'

I take a step back and my teeth grind. I really thought I'd cleaned myself up when I got home last night. But I was tired and I guess I missed a bit. I glance at the tiny patch of blood on my blouse.

'Oh for God's sake, Paul. It's two drops,' I groan.

'Susan . . .' He says my name in a sing-song voice. I really hate it when he does that. Mostly because he uses the same melodic approach to call Amelia's attention to something dangerous or to correct her behaviour, and I'm not his child to scold. But also because it makes him sound like a smug prick and it's super irritating.

'Fine,' I say, throwing my hands in the air in mock surrender, knowing he won't let this go, and I really need a shower. 'As I said, I didn't fall. Helen did. Last night, down by the lake.'

'You went to the lake?'

'Yes, Paul.' I exhale. 'You're not the only who thinks about Amelia all the time. Yes, I went to the lake. Is that bloody okay with you?'

'Of course, Susan.' His stiff shoulders relax. 'I didn't mean . . . it's just . . . I didn't know.'

'Well, you wouldn't know,' I sigh. 'You're never here.'

I can't resist the dig, and I'm somewhat satisfied when I see it get to him. I flop back on to the couch and think about Amelia. I can tell Paul is thinking about her too. His breathing is laboured. His eyes are closed as he shakes his head. Our house is such a different place without the sweet voice of a little girl lighting up every room.

'What happened?' Paul finally asks, sitting next to me. 'How did Helen fall?'

'Isn't it obvious?'

'She was drunk,' he says.

'Yeah. She was drunk,' I nod. 'She'd had a full bottle of wine at our house earlier and she was guzzling her way through the second down by the lake when she stumbled on some rocks and banged her head.'

'Oh God,' Paul says, covering his mouth with his hand.

'I must have got some of her blood on me when I helped her up, but I wasn't paying attention, to be honest. I just wanted to make sure she was okay.'

'So this is Helen's blood?' Paul looks disgusted as he points at the crimson stain on my blouse.

'Yes.'

'And you're not hurt?'

'No. I'm not.'

'Well, that's good, then,' Paul sighs. 'And is Helen okay? I mean, it must have been a nasty bang if she got blood on you as well as herself.'

'Paul, I'm tired and stressed out. I really just want to get in the shower.'

'Sure.' He nods, but there's a look in his eyes that unsettles me. 'We can talk more about this later.'

Chapter Fifteen

Now

I'm making my way up the stairs when incessant pounding on the front door threatens to knock it off its hinges. There's no way Paul can't hear it, but he doesn't come from the kitchen to answer it. I know he thinks it's Helen.

'Fuck's sake,' I mumble under my breath and make my way back down the stairs, expecting to find someone from the police team at the door. 'Just a minute. I'm coming,' I shout as I quickly tuck the blood-stained part of my blouse into my jeans.

I swing the door open and flinch when I find Larry standing there.

'Where's Helen?' he puffs, and a cloud of his tobacco breath hangs heavy between us.

I don't know what to say. He takes a step forward and I move back instinctively but I keep my fingers curled around the doorknob. His broad shoulders occupy most of the doorway. He's wearing his farm coat and wellies, but they're pulled on over checked pyjamas. His face is blisteringly red. I turn to seek out Paul in the kitchen. He's busy washing up and doesn't look my way.

Larry's hand smacks against the door and I lose my grip on the knob.

'Is Helen not at home?' I say, turning my head back so my eyes can settle on Larry's shovel-like hand. His fingers are sprawled wide against the door and his arm is straight and rigid at the elbow.

'Would I be here if she was at home?' Larry wheezes, his laboured breathing demanding a better answer.

Paul appears behind me and places his hand protectively on my shoulder. 'Everything okay, Susan?' he asks.

'I thought Helen would be here,' Larry says, letting his hand slip off the door. 'She didn't come home last night. Never, not in twenty-five years, has she not come home.'

'I'm sure—' Paul begins.

'You.' Larry cuts across him, pointing his finger in my face. 'This is all you. She's changed since she's been around you. She's saying and doing things she never would have before. Picking holes in our marriage. Talking bullshit about painting the kitchen, and about the daughter she never had. That's all your counselling talk.'

'Helen isn't my client,' I say, standing straighter and folding my arms. 'I don't counsel her.'

'You talk to her.' Larry stomps his foot and his face grows even redder. 'That's enough. You've messed with her head.'

'Larry, that's very unfair.' Paul takes a step forward, placing himself between Larry and me.

'Look,' Larry says, 'I'm sorry for your troubles. No couple should ever lose a child. But I don't want Helen coming round here. Not any more. It's not good for her head. I'm putting my foot down.'

'Well, I'm sure you can tell her that . . .' I say, 'when you find her.'

Larry turns his back sharply on Paul and me and storms down the path without another word. He flings open our crooked little red gate, almost knocking it off its hinges.

'Susan. Where *is* Helen?' Paul asks.

'Okay, hang on,' I say, tilting my head to one side. 'A minute ago you were telling me to stay away from Helen, and now you want me to be her keeper?'

'Her blood is on your blouse.' Paul points to where my blouse is tucked inside my jeans. 'And her husband has no idea where she is – for the first time in almost thirty years. It's a bit weird, that's all I'm saying.'

'She's an alcoholic,' I snap. 'They're always acting weird. It's actually very sad.'

'Well, there's that,' Paul says. 'I knew from day one she was a hopeless case. I don't know how he stays married to her.'

'Jesus, Paul,' I say. 'Can you please keep your voice down or her dickhead husband will hear you.'

'Fuck 'em,' he snorts. 'He's just as bad. Our daughter is missing, for God's sake, and he's storming round here like he owns the place. Who the hell does he think he is? And at this hour of the morning.' Paul checks his watch. 'It's not even nine o'clock.'

I don't reply. My eyes are on Larry's back as the last few days play over in my mind like a tsunami, dragging my emotions on the crest of the wave. I keep watch until he turns a corner. Paul must have been watching too because he slams the door as soon as Larry is out of view.

'Arsehole,' Paul says, sliding his arm around my waist. 'Oh Susan. You're shaking like a leaf.'

'I'm fine,' I lie.

'I really wish you'd tell me what happened last night. Susan, I'm not stupid. I know you and you weren't yourself when you came home. What did Helen do? Did she upset you? Did she really fall, or did you push her? Did she say something about Amelia? Is that what happened? God knows I'd have pushed her under a bus long ago. Nosy bitch. I'm guessing the silly cow has run off somewhere to lick her wounds. Serves her right. She needs to learn to back off. Maybe now she'll leave us alone.'

'Oh, she'll definitely leave us alone,' I say.

Paul smiles, unsure.

'Do you think Larry will go to the police?' I ask.

'The police?' Paul says. 'C'mon, you're working yourself into a state. Helen will come home when she's good and ready. I wouldn't worry about her. Anyway, like you said, she's an alcoholic, nobody will believe a word out of her mouth.'

'But do you think Larry will report her missing?' I ask. 'He seemed worried, and that's only going to get worse the longer she's gone.'

'The only person missing is our little girl.' Paul's voice cracks. 'Larry is out of line. Way out. He had no right to upset you. Aren't we dealing with enough without our neighbours dragging us into their marriage problems? Larry and Helen are bad news, Susan. Do you believe me now? This is what I've been saying all along.'

'Yeah,' I nod. 'Yes. You're right. Bad news.'

'So we're agreed?' Paul asks. 'You won't see Helen any more?'

'I definitely won't,' I say.

'Good.' Paul kisses my forehead. 'That's good.'

He stuffs his hands in his pockets and shuffles slowly towards the kitchen with his head low. I make my way up the stairs.

'Susan?' he calls when I'm halfway up. 'You don't think . . . nah, never mind.'

'What?' I turn round.

Paul is standing at the bottom step drawing invisible circles on the tiles with his foot. His eyes are round and glassy and I know he's think-ing about Amelia. He's always thinking about Amelia.

'Nothing. It's crazy. Never mind,' he says. 'Grab your shower.'

'Doesn't sound like nothing.' I walk back down the stairs, and as I reach the bottom step Paul gathers me in his arms and holds me tight.

We haven't been this close in days. Not since Amelia went missing. We sway back and forth for a while, and every now and then I feel a shudder in his chest and I know he's silently crying.

'You don't think Larry and Helen had anything to do with Amelia going missing, do you?' he finally says, rushing the words out with a single exhale.

What happened to blaming Deacon? Paul is grasping at straws, I realise. He has no idea who took our daughter, or if anyone took her at all. I pull my broken husband a little closer to me and sigh.

He lets go of me and takes a step back so he can study me, as if he didn't have faith in his own theory until I didn't disagree. 'You don't, do you?'

I shrug.

'Christ, listen to me.' Paul shoves his hands into his hair and tugs. 'This is insane. I'm accusing our neighbours of kidnapping, for God's sake.'

'Oh Paul,' I whisper.

Paul shakes his head. 'Sorry. I'm sorry. It's crazy, I know. I'm crazy. I mean it, Susan. I think I'm actually losing my mind. I just miss her so much and it's killing me not knowing where she is. Not knowing if she's even alive or . . . or . . .'

It's easy to become swept up in Paul's hysteria. He's so fragile right now, as though if I hug him too tightly he might snap like a twig underfoot.

'Maybe it's not so crazy,' I say. 'Helen was saying all this stuff about how she and Larry always wanted a girl, and she kept telling me how cute Amelia was.'

'Amelia *is* adorable.' Paul smiles and a sparkle dances in his eyes and I wonder what lovely memory of our daughter he's thinking of.

'Helen said I was so lucky to have a daughter,' I add.

'Okay,' he says, raising an eyebrow, and I can tell he thinks that was an odd turn of phrase.

'She kept going on and on about it,' I say. 'As if she was obsessed or something. I thought it was just because she was drunk.'

Paul clears his throat and I know he wants to reiterate that Helen is trouble, but he doesn't say a word. I'm on a roll and I have his full attention.

'You said it yourself – Helen and Larry barely know us. And we invited them into our home. We invited everyone. It was my idea. I just wanted to fit in around here. I'm sorry, Paul. I'm so sorry.'

He doesn't reply. His eyes are focused on the floor but he's listening. He's processing. I know because the vein in his neck that pulsates whenever he gets upset or stressed out is going crazy.

'It does sound mad. You're right about that,' I say, 'but maybe it only *sounds* mad.'

Paul's eyes shoot up to meet mine.

'Just look at them,' I say. 'Helen is a miserable alcoholic pining after her grown-up children who clearly want nothing to do with her, and Larry is a stereotypical, detached farmer. It's a bloody film script. Could easily all be an act, couldn't it?'

Paul takes a deep breath, holds it for a while and then puffs it back out while shaking his head sadly. 'Blaming them is too easy, Susan. C'mon. We're better than that. I don't think our neighbours are the answer.'

A laugh rattles in the back of my throat. 'You're right. It's mad to even think about it.'

'We just need answers, Susan,' Paul says. 'We need to know where Amelia is. Before we both lose our minds.'

'But Helen is missing. And Amelia is still missing . . .'

I stop and let Paul figure out where I'm going with the equation.

He cups my elbow with his hand. 'C'mon, let's get you a coffee, and then you need a shower. You'll feel better after a shower and a lie-down.'

Chapter Sixteen

Now

I thought Paul would never leave the house. He was fussing over me all day like a mother hen. He kept wanting to make me coffee or rub my back. He even tried to kiss me in the kitchen. I barely managed to pull away in time. The closer he gets, the more I unravel. He kept asking if I was okay. *Seriously, could he ask anything more stupid?*

To get rid of him, I eventually resorted to laying out fresh running gear on the bed for him, knowing he wouldn't be able to resist the temptation to go for a night run to clear his head.

'I'll be all right on my own,' I had to assure him over and over. 'I could actually use a little me time. I think I'll drive into the city. Do some late-night shopping,' I said, telling a half-truth. 'I'll pick us up some biscuits. We can have them with tea later.'

I play my conversation with Paul over in my head as I drive away from our cottage and down the dark and winding country roads.

It was such a mundane conversation, but it's the first time in days we've actually spoken about something other than constant police updates or what the neighbours are saying now. It's the first time we've made plans for the evening, but I'm certainly not looking forward to it. The idea of sitting in the kitchen having tea and biscuits like a regular couple is torture.

Joining the motorway into the city, I start to panic. I consider turning around at the next exit and going home. My mind is swarmed, thinking about the last time I saw my daughter, about the police, Helen, Paul, biscuits. I scream. My hot breath fogs up the windscreen and I veer towards the hard shoulder, before snapping myself out of it and accelerating to merge with heavy evening traffic like a regular commuter. The street lights shine through the sunroof, casting a dirty yellow shadow into the car. Cars and trucks whizz by in the outside lane and my grip on the wheel tightens as my heart races. I feel so visible. So vulnerable. As if every passing car can see what I've done.

At the shopping centre I park underground, grab some shopping and walk a couple of kilometres into a less than savoury part of the city. My sense of direction isn't the best and as I round corner after corner I begin to worry that I'm completely lost. Finally, a neon blue 'Open' sign flashes in the distance and I recognise the chipper. And more importantly I recognise the grungy flat overhead. *Bingo!*

Nervous, I glance over my shoulder. There are some junkies shooting up in a doorway across the street. I freeze when I notice them, but quickly realise they're oblivious to anything other than the needles in their arms. There's no one else around, no one to see me. I find myself wishing I'd brought a jacket with a hood, and I make a mental note for next time. I hurry around the side of the chipper, pull open the stiff side door and race up the concrete steps two at a time.

The flat door comes into view at the top of the steps. I stop running, catch my breath and slide the key out of my pocket and into the lock.

'Hey, it's me,' I say, the door rattling as I fight with the key in the stiff lock.

'Fuck this thing,' I mumble under my breath.

'Deacon,' I say, pulling the key out and knocking on the door. 'Hey, hello . . . Deacon?'

Footsteps sound in the distance and I freeze, facing the door. Someone is coming up the stairs behind me. My heart pounds furiously as I stare straight ahead, hoping whoever is coming doesn't see my face. The steps grow louder and finally someone brushes behind me and walks past as if I'm invisible. Panic crawls across my skin. I hadn't bargained for another flat up here, or for neighbours. Seconds later, I hear a door nearby close and when I finally turn round the hall is empty, except for a black sack of rubbish slouching against the wall. It's only when I'm alone again that I realise I'm not breathing. I open my mouth and inhale sharply. The smell of frying oil and fish from the chipper below combined with the mould and filth of the ancient hall carpet is repulsive and I close my mouth again quickly.

'Deacon. Open the bloody door,' I shout as I pound my fist against it, loosening some chipped paint, which flakes off and sticks to the fleshy part of my hand under my baby finger.

Finally, the lock rattles on the inside and the door slowly creaks open. Deacon's head appears, unsure, in the gap, but his lips curl into a smile as soon as he realises it's me.

'Shh,' he says, placing his finger to his lips. 'She's asleep. I just got her down.'

'Okay. Okay,' I say, feeling scolded as I hurry inside and close the door behind me.

I press my back against the timber, which is unpainted and rough on this side.

'Who lives down the hall?' I ask between deep, even breaths.

'What?' Deacon's eyebrows wrinkle. 'I don't know. I'm hardly getting to know the neighbours, am I?'

'I'm serious,' I snap. 'Someone lives there. They saw me just now. Jesus Christ.'

'Susan, calm down.' Deacon drags a hand through his greasy hair. 'I doubt they care about you.'

'Maybe not, but with my face all over the bloody news, what if they put two and two together?'

Deacon pushes his shoulders back and stands taller. His stubble is days old and his shirt is half tucked in and half out of a pair of charcoal tracksuit bottoms, but I can tell from the stitching that they used to be black. I haven't seen him look this enfeebled in years.

'You've been on the news?' he says, his voice low and painfully serious.

'Not by choice, obviously,' I snort. 'But it goes without saying that the media are covering the case. Amelia is a missing child, for God's sake.'

Deacon's jaw twitches. 'What are they saying?'

'Haven't you been watching?' I ask, peeling myself away from the door.

He swallows. 'No. I didn't want her to see anything.'

'Of course,' I nod, feeling stupid. 'Good thinking.'

'I can't believe you've spoken to the press,' Deacon says. 'You've always hated journalists. Ever since Adam . . .' He trails off.

'I haven't spoken to them,' I snap. 'But that doesn't stop them reporting. Anyway, Paul thinks we should make an appeal soon. He says people need to see that Amelia is part of a happy family.'

'A happy family,' Deacon snorts. 'What a hypocrite.'

I exhale sharply and roll my eyes. I don't have the patience for another redundant conversation about my husband.

'I brought you some stuff,' I say, changing the subject.

Deacon glances at the bag of groceries I'm carrying.

'Good. Thanks.' He takes the heavy bag from me and turns to walk into the kitchen.

I puff out with relief and twist my hand over to examine where the plastic handles have gnawed away at my fingers. I rub my hand and take some time to look around. The flat is a shithole. The carpet is near threadbare and dotted with cigarette burns, and the brownish-green curtains are so filthy I can't tell what colour they were originally. I chose this place from a listing of cheap, cash-in-hand accommodation advertised on the internet. I was never expecting a palace but how anyone, in good conscience, can charge rent for this dump is beyond me. No wonder the landlord didn't even ask for references.

At least it's surface clean. Deacon has hoovered the carpets and I can smell lemon and bleach; he must have spent hours washing down every surface. There's a blue beer crate turned upside down with a flattened pizza box on top to create a table in the centre of the floor. On top are a packet of crayons and a colouring book open at a half-coloured-in picture of a lion in the jungle. Everything is yellow. The lion, the trees, even the sky.

'Coffee?' Deacon asks when I follow him into the minuscule kitchenette.

I shake my head and begin to pull groceries out of the bag Deacon has set down on the wobbly kitchen table.

'Susan Arnold refusing coffee?' Deacon laughs. 'Well, that's certainly a first.'

I slam Paul's biscuits against the counter and they crunch and break inside the wrapper. 'It's Warner. I'm Susan Warner. You know that. Why is it so hard for you to say it?'

'O-bloody-kay,' Deacon says. 'Jesus, Susan, it was just a joke.'

He snatches the biscuits off the counter, opens them and broken pieces rain like confetti all over the floor. He finds an unbroken one and shoves it in his mouth.

'These are nice,' he says, crumbs spraying from his lips.

'You're disgusting.' I roll my eyes, making a mental note to buy another packet of damn biscuits before I go home.

I open the fridge and shove milk, butter and cheese in. 'I didn't know what you'd need, so I just got some essentials. Stuff to keep you going.'

'There's half a carton of milk still in there.' Deacon points to the fridge. 'And I can't live on toast, Susan. I need proper ingredients, something I can cook with.'

'Since when did you become Gordon Ramsay? How the hell am I supposed to know what you fancy whipping up? I thought you hated cooking.'

Deacon ignores me and opens a larder cupboard behind him. A smell of decay or damp, I can't tell which, wafts out. I begin to cough and back away. He shakes his head and fetches a sweeping brush with a broken handle out of the cupboard. He passes it to me before he stuffs another biscuit in his mouth.

I look at the brush. At the floor. And then at Deacon.

'Eh, you don't expect me to clean this up, do you?'

'It's your mess,' he says, frowning, and I know he's talking about so much more than the crumbs on the floor.

'Fine,' I snap, sweeping up the crumbs. 'But you should be thanking me. I'm bringing you the basics so you don't starve. And I'm doing it with the cops, my husband and the neighbours from hell breathing down my goddam neck.'

Deacon puts the packet of biscuits back on the counter, drags the back of his hand across his lips and wipes away the crumbs. 'I know you're under a lot of pressure, Susan. Don't you think I feel it too? But if you would just let me text you . . .'

'No!' I bark and my teeth snap audibly. 'You can't text me. Don't you fucking dare text, do you hear me?'

'But, Susan, this isn't how it was supposed to go . . .' Deacon says, his arms slipping around my waist.

'I know.' I turn and press my chest against his. 'But it will all be worth it in the end. I promise.'

'I can't do this much longer,' he says. 'I'm climbing the walls with boredom.'

I stiffen and pull away.

'What?' he says.

'Is that why you were at the lake last night?' I ask, turning my back on him so he can't see the flash of temper burning in my cheeks.

'Yes,' Deacon says, and I can't believe he's not even trying to deny it.

'You had one job. One simple little job,' I hiss. 'Throw Amelia's cardigan in the lake and get the hell out of there.'

'And I did,' he says.

'But you went back!'

'She just wanted to see the ducks,' he says, and I can hear him reach for the stupid biscuits again.

'The ducks,' I grunt.

'Relax, Susan. I waited until it was dark. No one saw us.'

'My neighbour saw.' I turn back, swiping the biscuits out of his hand and throwing the packet against the wall behind his head. 'Helen saw you, you fucking idiot.'

'Oh shit,' Deacon says, and instantly glances over his shoulder at the biscuits scattered all around us.

I watch as his attention shifts to the bedroom door behind him. It's slightly ajar and it's dark inside but the light from the sitting room shines through the narrow gap. I want to slap him across the face and tell him that he has no right to look into that room. Not now. Not after he was so reckless.

'That was you and Helen at the lake last night?' Deacon switches to whispering.

'Yes, it was me,' I say, pressing my fingers above my eyes as I try to stay calm and keep my voice low. 'And thank bloody God it was. Could you imagine if it was Paul? Or worse . . .' I gasp as rage chokes me. 'Langton or Connelly. Christ, I can't even imagine the shitstorm. You could have messed up everything.' I raise my arm and hold my thumb and finger millimetres apart as I shake my hand in Deacon's face. 'You were this close. This fucking close to making a mess of everything.'

'Has Helen said anything?' Deacon asks. 'Will she go to the cops?'

'She was drunk,' I say.

'And . . .' His eyes widen, scared.

'And nothing.' I take some deep breaths, calming down. 'She's not going to be a problem.'

'You sure?'

'Of course I'm sure,' I say. 'I have to be sure, don't I? After the bloody mess you made.'

'Okay.' Deacon smiles, but he's still shaking. 'Good. That's good.'

The flash of his slightly crooked teeth irritates the hell out of me, but I smile too and count backwards from five in my head.

'Where did you get the crayons and colouring book?' I ask.

Deacon's smile fades and he doesn't reply.

'And the bleach too?' I ask. 'Where did you get that?'

He still doesn't open his mouth.

'The takeaway pizza?' I growl, my teeth pressed together as I force the words out between them.

Deacon's shuttered eyes watch me with uncomfortable intensity. I'm screaming inside as I stare back at him.

'Jesus, Deacon. How often have you been going out?' I finally explode. 'Where do you go? It's not like you can pop to the local Tesco. And do you take her with you? Or do you leave her here all alone? Oh Christ. I don't even know which is worse.' I drag my hands through my hair as Deacon stares without blinking. What the hell is wrong with him?

'Nearly two weeks.' He finally moves his eyes off me and casts them towards the bedroom door again. 'It's been hard, and this is the first time you've been back since the night I brought her here.'

'It's not easy for me either,' I say. 'I can't be seen, you know that.'

'Would you even be here now, if you hadn't seen me last night?' he snaps back, his voice too loud for the tight space of the kitchen. 'Is that the only reason you're here? To warn me to be more careful? Do you even miss her at all?'

'Don't you dare,' I hiss, keeping my voice much lower than his. 'Don't you dare ask me that. We both knew this was going to be hard.'

'Not this hard, Susan. I never dreamed it would be this hard.'

'Well, that was your mistake,' I say, wondering which of us is more stupid – Deacon for agreeing to help me, or me for considering him capable of helping.

'I think we should stop,' he says. 'I think . . .'

The bedroom door creaks open and there's a sharp squeal of excitement as little legs in pink flannel pyjamas hurry towards me.

'Mammy. You're here,' Amelia shrieks as she throws herself against me.

I crouch down and her warm, chubby arms wrap around my neck. I nuzzle my face against her golden curls and take a deep breath. My heart pinches. Amelia smells like honey and spice and not the summer fruits I was expecting. Deacon must have bought shampoo for her on one of his apparently many shopping trips.

He bends down to Amelia's level. 'What are you doing out of bed, young lady?' he whispers, tilting his head to one side to exaggerate his curiosity. 'Hmm?'

'I heared peoples talking. It's Mammy. My mammy is here.' Amelia's arms grow a little tighter around my neck. 'Is Daddy here too?' she chirps.

'No, sweetie,' I say. 'Daddy's not here.'

Her small body begins to quiver in my arms and she sniffles. 'I want my Daddy,' she whispers, so softly if my face wasn't right next to hers I wouldn't hear her words.

'How about a story?' I ask, scooping her into my arms as I stand up. 'You love stories, don't you? I have a new one all about duckies. Would you like to hear it?'

Amelia nods.

'Good,' I say cheerfully. 'Let's get you back to your special bed and we can snuggle and have story time.'

'It smells funny,' she says, as if it's a secret or she doesn't want to hurt Deacon's feelings.

'C'mon now. I'm sure it can't be that bad,' I say, and I dot a gentle kiss on the top of her head. Deacon puffs out and I can feel his disapproving glare follow us as I carry my daughter back to the bedroom. Amelia is going to keep asking questions and I don't trust him to come up with right answers. I need to hurry up. Move faster. This must end soon, for Amelia's sake.

Chapter Seventeen

Now

I didn't think anything could smell worse than the larder cupboard but the bedroom succeeds. This time I know the smell is definitely damp and I wonder if it's coming from the floor, the walls or both. I flick on the light and stare at the couple of mattresses on the floor. The bedroom is small. Each mattress is pushed against the opposing wall to create a narrow pathway between them. I have to turn sideways and shuffle in the door so I don't stand on either bedding. Not that it would matter much if I did, they're both already disgustingly grubby. I try to put Amelia down, but she wraps her arms tighter around my neck and tucks her legs around my waist so her feet meet behind me.

'C'mon on now,' I say, 'be a good girl and get to bed.'

'I *am* a good girl,' Amelia says, lifting her head from my shoulder to look at me.

'I know you are, sweetheart,' I smile as a wave of guilt washes over me. 'You're the best girl. You're *my* best girl.'

I close my eyes and tighten my grip on her little body. And for a fleeting moment I think about barging through the front door of this horrible flat with my daughter in my arms and never looking back.

'Mammy, you're squashing me,' she complains.

My eyes shoot open and I relax my grip.

'Oh, I'm sorry,' I say, my voice breaking as I try to feign composure. *Just a few more days*, I tell myself. *A few more days.*

'Why are you doing big huffs and puffs?' Amelia giggles. 'Like this . . .' She tucks her chin into her chest and takes a deep breath, holds it for a second and puffs it back out. Her warm, minty breath dances across the air and caresses my face.

'Like that?' I say, my heart aching.

'You're silly, Mammy,' Amelia laughs and kisses my nose.

She laughs again and kisses one cheek, then the other, and finally she kisses my forehead.

'I love you, sweetheart.'

'I love you too,' she smiles. 'Story time now.'

I nod.

She untangles her legs from around my waist and her arms relax around my neck. She slides out of my arms before I'm ready to let her go and scurries on to one of the mattresses.

'Is this your bed?' I ask.

Amelia tucks her feet under her and simultaneously shakes her head. 'My bed is a princess bed,' she explains, eyeing me with uncertainty.

I think of the plastic frame Paul made me buy when we moved Amelia from a cot into a bed last year. It's neon pink and the headboard is shaped like a crown. It doesn't match anything in her bedroom, but Paul insisted our daughter needed a bed fit for royalty. I was hoping we could get rid of it when we moved into the cottage, but Amelia loves the gaudy thing.

'That's Deacon's bed,' she says and points to the mattress across from her. 'I'm having a sleepover at Deacon's house.'

'A sleepover?' I say, the words jarring.

'Yup,' Amelia nods.

'Well, isn't that fun,' I smile.

I've never discussed sleepovers with my nearly three-year-old. Deacon must have offered her that explanation. I forgot how easy it is to settle the mind of a curious little girl. The pressure in my chest eases and I relax slightly. Maybe I could bring over some of her toys next time I visit. I'm certain I can sneak some small things out of the house without Paul noticing.

Suddenly, Amelia rocks on to her knees and bounces back, over and over, throwing her hands in the air. 'Story, story, story,' she demands, clearly losing patience.

'All right, all right,' I smile. 'I really am a silly mammy today, aren't I? Let's get that story started.'

She moves over and makes room for me beside her on the mattress. Deacon's jumper is folded behind her, creating a rather impressive pillow. One of his shirts is balled up at the end of her bed and I guess he's using it to cover her when she falls asleep.

'Here, Mammy,' Amelia smiles excitedly. 'Read this one?'

'Oh, look at that,' I say, as she pulls a hardback storybook out from under Deacon's jumper pillow.

'Deacon buydid it for me,' she explains, running her fingers over the bright cover.

'Did he now?'

'Yup. Yesterday. At the suvermarket.'

'You were at the supermarket?' I say calmly.

Amelia nods. 'To buy stories.'

'Isn't Deacon very kind.' I groan inwardly as I try not to let my frustration show.

'Are you cross, Mammy?' she says, her little body stiffening as her bottom lip begins to quiver.

'Of course not,' I say, taking the book from her.

'But you're making your cross face, like this,' she says, imitating me.

I drape my arm over her shoulder and slide her closer to me, tucking her hip against mine. 'I'm just so excited to start this lovely story,' I say.

Amelia snuggles into me and the heat that radiates from her little body feels gloriously familiar.

'*The Ugly Duckling*,' I begin, reading the cover.

Chapter Eighteen

Now

Deacon pushes open the door of the small bedroom as soon as he hears Amelia's shrieks. The sliver of light shining in through the open door slices into the dark room like a piece missing from a chocolate cake. My eyes squint and adjust to the sudden intrusion of light. Deacon's hair is messy and sticking up and he has no shoes on. I guess he fell asleep in the lounge and Amelia's crying has woken him.

'Shh, shh,' I say, stroking her hair as I try to settle her back to sleep.

Heavy sobs shake her whole body as she cries in her sleep.

'What happened? What's wrong?' he asks.

'Keep your voice down,' I whisper. 'You'll wake her.'

Deacon looks at Amelia asleep in the crook of my arm. 'But she was crying,' he says, concerned.

'It was just a bad dream. She's gone back to sleep.'

'Sounded awful,' he says, running a shaky hand through his hair. 'I thought she was hurt. I've never heard her cry like that before.'

'Well, she's fine,' I whisper. 'Kids have nightmares all the time.'

Deacon shakes his head. 'But she's been sleeping well. She misses you, of course, but she's never woken hysterical like that before. Poor little kiddo. I hate to hear her so upset.'

'I know,' I say, sliding my arm out from behind Amelia and lowering her head back against the pillow.

She tosses and turns for a moment and I hold my breath, thinking she's going to wake up and tell Deacon what just happened, but she settles quickly. She tucks her knees into her chest and her fitful crying seems to ease as she curls herself into a ball. I reach for the shirt on the end of the bed and cover Amelia with it. She snuggles into the soft cotton.

'See? She's fine now,' I say.

Deacon sighs. His worry is palpable. I watch his hand on the door handle, hoping he won't push the door open further and let in more light. Or worse still, come over to check on Amelia. His hand slips off the handle and the hairs on the back of my neck stand on end. I realise my heart is racing.

'C'mon,' he says. 'Let's let her sleep.'

'Can you give me a minute?' I ask, crouching to stroke Amelia's hair. 'I just want a few more minutes with her.'

'Okay. I'll be in the kitchen when you're ready,' he says. 'We need to talk.'

'Sure,' I say, hiding how on edge Deacon's choice of phrase makes me. 'I'll be right behind you.'

He turns and walks away, shaking his head again.

I stand up and creep to the door, pulling it closed after him. I leave just enough light shining into the room to allow me to see what I'm doing. I race back to the mattress and lift the bottom of Deacon's shirt to expose Amelia's foot. My eyes widen and I jump back, horrified. The cut is so much deeper than I meant it to be and blood is trickling down her foot and gathering behind her little toes. I only meant to prick her heel ever so slightly, but it was dark and she kicked just as I pressed the razor against her skin. No wonder she screamed. *My poor baby.*

I keep my eye on the slightly ajar door as I quickly pull out Paul's tie, which I'd tucked into my bra earlier. I specifically chose this white one with the baby-blue pinstripe, which I bought him last Christmas. Not because it's his favourite, although that's an advantage as lots of his clients will have seen him wearing it – I chose it for its light colour and silky fabric that will absorb blood easily.

I scrunch the tie into a ball and dab it against Amelia's heel. She winces and pulls her foot away from me. I hold my breath and wait to see if she cries.

'Shh, shh,' I whisper, stroking her hair some more. 'Good girl. You're a good girl.'

She hums contentedly.

'Susan,' Deacon calls from the kitchen. 'Do you want coffee?'

I hurry to the door and peek out, afraid he'll come to fetch me.

'Coffee would be great. Thank you,' I grin brightly. 'Just give me two more minutes. She's not quite asleep yet,' I lie.

'Okay,' he says, taking the lid off the kettle and sticking it under the tap.

The noise of the water running followed by the clink of cups soothes me and I can feel my pulse slowing. But I know Deacon won't stay distracted for long.

I duck back in and close the door even more, making it almost impossible to see what I'm doing. I really wish I hadn't left my phone in the lounge so I could use its light to guide me. I shuffle between the mattresses and make one last attempt to stop the bleeding. I press the tie forcefully against Amelia's foot, and despite her twisting and turning I don't ease the pressure. Finally, after counting backwards from sixty in my head, I let go. And wait. From what I can see the bleeding has stopped. I wrap Paul's razor in some tissues and put it in my back pocket, then I stuff his bloodstained tie back into my bra.

I cover Amelia's feet with Deacon's shirt. I've no doubt she will complain of discomfort tomorrow, but Deacon will probably assume she's grazed herself on something in the flat. Standing up with shaking legs I run my hands over my clothes, as if straightening out my blouse and jeans can straighten out my conscience too.

I lean over Amelia one last time and kiss her forehead. 'I'm sorry, sweetheart,' I whisper. 'Someday you'll understand. I know you will.'

'Mammy,' she calls with her eyes closed.

'Um-hm.' I wince, praying she doesn't wake up fully.

'I want to go home,' she sobs sleepily, her voice a barely audible whisper.

A single tear trickles down the side of my nose and splashes against her fair skin. 'Soon, baby girl,' I promise. 'We'll go home very soon.'

I listen to her delicate breathing as she falls into a deep sleep. She's beautiful. And I find myself wondering, as I often have before, how a little girl so wonderful and endearing could have been created by a man as vile and repulsive as my husband.

'C'mon, Susan,' Deacon calls again from the kitchen, a little louder this time. 'Coffee's ready.'

'Coming,' I say, pulling open the door and glancing back into the room at my angelic, sleeping toddler. 'I'm coming.'

Chapter Nineteen

THEN

'So that's two Cokes, a strawberry milkshake and the sharing platter,' the waitress says, scribbling our order on her small notepad.

'Yes. Thank you,' Jenny nods, her smile wide and giddy.

I wanted a vanilla milkshake but I don't bother correcting the waitress. I don't feel like talking, or eating. I'm sitting up straight on the uncomfortable red leather diner bench and I'm smiling brightly, and I doubt anyone can tell how furious I am on the inside.

Jenny is nestled against Deacon on the bench opposite me. His arm is draped over her shoulder casually and every now and then they kiss. Her left hand is flat on the table, in case I might for one second take my eyes off the huge engagement ring wrapped around her finger. The round sapphire stone sparkles under the diner lights and it's surrounded by a cluster of diamonds like petals on a flower. It's elegant and beautiful and not at all suited to Jenny's flamboyant personality.

'I just couldn't believe it when he popped the question, you know?' Jenny says, bouncing on the spot. 'It was such a surprise. A wonderful, wonderful surprise.'

'Yes. Definitely a surprise,' I say. 'You've only been going out eight months. It's a whirlwind, that's for sure.'

'This won't change anything.' Jenny leans forward and I think she's going to reach for my hand. I stiffen and drop my hands into my lap. 'We'll still see each other all the time. You'll still have to come round to the flat for Wednesday Wine, and we're still going to take that trip to Ibiza we've talked about.'

'Absolutely,' I say, my eyes shifting to Deacon, wondering if he's going to say something equally as condescending as Jenny.

He doesn't talk. Jenny is talking enough for everyone, as usual.

Our food arrives and I swirl my straw around the thick pink milkshake. I watch as Jenny finally pulls her hand away to reach for some chips and a chicken goujon.

'You'll be my bridesmaid, of course, won't you?' she says, her mouth half full.

She washes chicken down with a large mouthful of Coke. I can see the food work its way down her throat. My skin crawls.

I smile so forcefully my cheeks push up under my eyes. 'Do you even have to ask?'

'Oh good. I was worried,' Jenny says.

'Worried?' I echo.

'Yeah, you know, what with . . .' Jenny begins.

The waitress reappears at our table. 'Oh gosh, I'm so sorry. You asked for vanilla, not strawberry, didn't you?'

'It's fine,' I say, my eyes fixed on Jenny. 'I like strawberry too.'

'No. No, it's not fine,' the waitress continues.

Deacon whispers something into Jenny's ear as the waitress continues to hover around us.

'I said it's fine,' I snap as I try to read Deacon's lips.

'It's my first day. I've been getting things wrong all morning. I'm so nervous,' the waitress babbles, her slender fingers with long, pointed nails reaching for the milkshake.

'I said I like strawberry. Just leave it, okay?' I grunt and wave my hand as if I'm swatting an irritating fly.

She gets a fright and knocks over the glass.

I jump as cold strawberry milkshake splashes across the table and on to my jeans.

'You stupid bitch,' I shout, shivering as the liquid soaks through the denim. 'Look what you've done! I told you to leave it. Why couldn't you have just left it?'

'Susan?' Jenny says, saying my name in a gentle whisper. 'It's okay,' she reassures the waitress as she slides off the bench and stands up. 'It was an accident.'

'I'll get this cleaned up straight away,' the waitress says. She disappears, and I think she's crying.

'Here.' Deacon finally speaks as he gathers some napkins from the dispenser on the table and passes them to me. 'I hope that doesn't leave a stain.'

'What the fuck?' I say, dabbing the napkins against the wet patches on my jeans. 'I told her to leave it.'

'She's new,' Jenny says, as if I wasn't sitting right here when the waitress offered her lame excuse.

'You're right,' I say, suddenly so sweet I'm almost angelic. 'Poor girl. She must be mortified.'

'No real harm done,' Jenny says. 'And hey, it's an excuse to buy some new jeans when we finish here.'

'Always a silver lining,' I say, hating myself for allowing my temper to momentarily shine through so noticeably.

I count backwards from five, smile brightly and make a conscious effort to hide my irritation for the rest of the meal.

We move tables, after being reassured our meal is on the house, and are served by a new waitress. This time I sit beside Deacon and Jenny sits opposite. Every now and then I say something silly and slap his shoulder playfully or press my side against his and giggle like a naughty schoolgirl. Jenny doesn't seem to mind, and more often than not I find her laughing too. The whole experience is painful but I keep up the act.

'So, when is the big day?' I ask, steering the conversation back to the wedding, desperate to know what they were whispering about.

Jenny shifts uncomfortably and her eyes lock with Deacon's.

'Sorry,' I say. 'Have you not talked about that yet? Am I getting ahead of myself? I'm just sooooo excited for you.'

'It's September,' Jenny blurts. 'The twenty-sixth. Susan, I'm sorry but it was the only date the hotel had left this year. If we didn't snap it up we would have to wait until next summer and we just want to be married as soon as possible. Please understand.'

'September twenty-sixth,' I exhale.

Deacon sits statue-like, staring straight ahead, and Jenny fidgets nervously with her nails. The food and drink sit in front of us untouched.

'It's perfect,' I smile finally. 'I mean, I can't think of a better distraction the day before my brother's murderer is released from prison early. Thank you.'

'Oh Susan.' Jenny throws her arms in the air, elated. People at the table behind us turn around to stare. 'You're really okay with this?'

Of course I'm not fucking okay with this, you selfish bitch.

'Yes, yes. It's great news.' I throw my hands in the air too because, well, why not?

'I'm so happy.' Jenny does her usual bouncing on the spot with excitement. 'I was really worried you'd be upset. Wasn't I worried, Deacon?'

'She was,' Deacon says, but he doesn't turn to look at me.

'Well, I'm not. I'm delighted, and you have your fabulous fiancé here to thank for that, Jenny,' I say, stroking my hand up and down Deacon's arm as if I'm stroking a cute puppy.

'Really?' She purses her lips, intrigued.

Deacon shifts and the leather bench squeaks beneath him. I laugh as if he's hilarious.

'I've been struggling these past few months, as you know,' I say.

'I do know,' Jenny sighs. 'That's why I want you to come back to the bereavement group. Everyone misses you. You left so suddenly.'

'I know,' I admit, 'but that's because I have Deacon.'

He slides further away from me on the bench.

'We've been talking, and he's been great,' I beam. 'Encouraging me to open up about Adam. I've even told him things about my mother that I've never told anyone. Not even you, Jenny.'

Her eyes shift from Deacon to the table and back to Deacon. I can tell she's hurt. I keep going.

'And when he told me about Kerri-Ann—'

Jenny cuts across me. 'You told her about your daughter?'

Deacon nods sheepishly.

'That's great,' she chirps. 'Deacon, I'm so glad you're finally able to talk about your little girl.'

My eyes narrow. *Fucking hell, Jenny.* I should have known – she can find the positive in every goddam situation.

'Deacon says I should become a counsellor,' I keep going. 'He thinks I'm a good listener.'

'You are.' Jenny smiles.

'I wasn't sure at first, but I'm just not ready to leave my flat, or campus. All the memories I have of Adam are here. I can't close that door yet, you know?'

Jenny nods.

'It just makes sense to enrol for another year. I know I'll be in a much better place next year. I'll be stronger. I won't still be grieving.'

'I guess . . .' Jenny frowns.

'And Deacon promises that when I qualify he'll be my first client.'

'Really?' Jenny says, her enthusiasm for the idea noticeably waning. 'You never said anything about any of this to me. Either of you.'

'I know,' I shrug. 'But isn't this great? We both have such good news. You with the wedding and me with a career path. I'm so excited, Jenny. Aren't you?'

I glare at Deacon and watch as he squirms.

'It is great,' Jenny says.

She's a terrible liar.

'How long have you two been planning all this?' she asks. 'Deacon?'

'Oh, ages,' I lie.

I'm a much better liar.

'Susan told me about her idea to study to be a counsellor last week, over coffee,' Deacon begins, reaching across the table to hold Jenny's hand. 'I told her to go for it, that's all. It wasn't really my idea, Susan. You're giving me far too much credit.'

'Nonsense,' I say. 'You're my hero, Deacon O'Reilly. You really, really are. I don't know what I would ever do without you. I mean that.'

'Susan, I—' Deacon shakes his head.

'Oh, we just have so much good news to celebrate today, don't we?' I cut across him. 'Milkshakes all round, yeah? My treat.'

I stand up and walk slowly towards the counter, smirking as I hear Jenny raise her voice and begin to fire questions at her new fiancé like emotional torpedoes.

Chapter Twenty

Now

Deacon carries two cups with steam swirling out the top into the lounge and stands in front of the pizza box table. He looks at me but doesn't speak.

'What?' I say.

The way he's looking at me is infuriating. His forehead is wrinkled and his eyes are smouldering.

It takes me a moment to realise he's waiting for me to clear some space on the stupid pizza box table. I gather up Amelia's crayons and close her colouring book, pushing them to one end of the table. Deacon quickly sets the cups down.

'Fuck, that was hot,' he says, shaking the hand that was wrapped around the cup with a broken handle.

I'm about to ask him if he's okay, but he turns away, blowing on his hand to cool it as he walks back into the kitchen. He returns with a carton of milk in one hand and bag of sugar in the other. I don't remember buying sugar for him, so he must have picked some up at the supermarket or, worse still, borrowed some from whoever lives across the hall. *He wouldn't*, I think. I hope! But I hate the feeling of uncertainty that sits in the pit of my stomach.

I watch Deacon splash milk into one cup and leave the other black. He adds sugar to both and stirs roughly, banging the spoon against the inside of the cups.

'Shh,' I warn, his clumsiness worrying me. 'You'll wake her.'

He smacks the spoon against the cardboard table top. It bounces and falls on to the floor, creating another dark stain to join the countless others.

'Deacon, seriously,' I snap, unravelling. 'I've only just got her back to sleep.'

'So you suddenly care about Amelia's sleep?' he says, raising one of the cups to his lips and taking a large gulp.

He pulls a face and quickly puts the cup down. The coffee must have scalded his throat but he doesn't react. He's too angry to focus on anything except me.

'I know you can take care of her when I'm not here,' I say, sweeter than the bag of sugar on the table. 'I trust you with my life, Deacon,' I lie.

'And what about Amelia's life?' he asks. 'What kind of life is it for a little girl, trapped in a dingy flat above a chipper in the dodgiest part of the city?'

'It's temporary,' I say. 'We've been over this.'

'She sits by that window all day . . .' Deacon points to the narrow, rectangular window behind us where street lights shine through the threadbare curtains, casting a dirty orange shadow on the carpet. 'She sits there for hours and hours and just stares out at the people passing by on the street below. I think she's hoping one of them will finally be you or Paul.'

'You let her sit at the window?' I say, horrified. 'What if someone sees her?'

'What the hell do you want me to do? Tie her to a chair? C'mon, Susan. She needs daylight. She needs fresh air. She needs her mother, for God's sake.'

'Well, I'm here now,' I snap.

Deacon snorts. 'It's cruel, Susan. That little girl misses you so much. My heart breaks for her.'

I lift the handleless cup off the table, and although it's too hot to hold I don't put it back down.

'It's just for a few more days,' I say. 'Paul really believes Amelia is dead. It's all going to plan. He's lost all hope. I'm the one saying over and over that she didn't drown. I'm telling him that Amelia is still alive. I'm insisting that she's missing. I'm drip-feeding him the truth and he doesn't believe a word of it.' I pause and an image of Paul's forlorn face as he went out running tonight comes to mind. 'Actually,' I smile, 'it's going even better than I could have imagined.'

'You're saying what?' Deacon's eyes widen. 'Jesus Christ, Susan. Are you mad? What the fuck are you sowing seeds of doubt in his head for?'

'Because why wouldn't I? Anything else wouldn't ring true, now, would it? There's no body, Deacon. Any decent mother is going to cling to hope.'

'But you're giving Paul hope too, then?' Deacon sighs. 'Dragging this out for everyone, especially that little girl.' He points towards the bedroom and I can hear the faintest snores of a sleeping child.

'I have no choice. Paul is stronger than I thought. Breaking him is hard.'

'Jesus, Susan. What are we doing?' He clasps his hands around his head. 'This is madness.'

'It is. It's so mad it's bloody brilliant. Soon we'll be on a ferry to Wales, just the three of us. We'll be a happy family, Deacon. You lost Kerri-Ann, but you'll never lose Amelia. You'll see. This will all be worth it soon.'

'This is what's best for Amelia, isn't it?' Deacon says. 'I mean, we really are doing the right thing here, aren't we?'

'Yes. Of course. You know what Paul's like,' I say, showing a little fear. 'We're protecting Amelia, Deacon. We're the good guys.'

'I think she knows something is wrong,' Deacon says. 'She calls out for her daddy in her sleep sometimes. It breaks my heart.'

'She'll forget,' I say. 'In time, she won't even remember Paul. She's just a baby.'

'It's not too late,' Deacon says. 'I can bring her home. Pretend I found her wandering in the woods near the lake?'

'Wandering the woods for days on end. A two-year-old! Alone. You'd be locked up before you got the chance to ring my doorbell.'

'I could drop her somewhere here in the city, then.' His eyes are wide and bloodshot and I know his mind is racing. 'Or I could leave her in the park. People would recognise her from the news. They'd take her to the police. Bring her to safety.'

'Are you fucking mad?' I say, slamming my cup down on the pizza box table, tiring of his whining.

Coffee splashes over the edge and on to my hand, burning. I ignore how it stings.

'Don't you dare lose your nerve now, do you hear me?' I grab Deacon with both hands, and curl my fingers tight around his arms, my nails digging into his skin. Maybe I even draw blood. I don't look. My eyes are on his.

'If we make one mistake . . .' I begin as I shake Deacon and he sways on the spot like a rag doll. '. . . that's it! Paul gets custody of Amelia while we rot in jail. Is that what you want? You really want me to lose my little girl all because you couldn't keep your shit together? I trusted you, Deacon. I trusted you with everything. Don't mess this up. I'm warning you.'

'Okay, okay,' Deacon says, snapping out of his trance. 'I know how deep we're in, Susan. I'm just scared.'

'It's only a matter of days,' I say. 'I'll pack my bags. I'll tell Paul I want a divorce and we'll be on the ferry to Wales before you know it. After that, maybe Europe. We just have to keep it together for a few more days. You can do that, can't you?'

'A few more days,' Deacon nods and gathers me in his arms.

Chapter Twenty-one

Now

'The body was discovered in shallow water early this morning by a local Ballyown woman walking her dog by the lake. Police have now confirmed that the rumours suggesting the body is that of missing toddler Amelia Warner are false. It is believed to be the body of an adult female. We will have more on this breaking story as it unfolds. And now, over to Marty with the weather.'

I flick off the radio. Sudden eerie silence engulfs my bedroom. I pace the floor, wishing I was wearing shoes. My feet make no sound as my socks sink into the luxurious carpet with each shaky step. I need noise. Something, anything. I'm desperate for a sound other than the deafening drone of my conscience.

Fuck you, Helen. Even dead you're interfering. I throw the remote across the room. It crashes against the wall with a shocking bang and the batteries fall out and roll around the floor. My suitcase is open on the bed with half the contents of my wardrobe thrown in haphazardly. Underneath my blouses and jeans are a few of my favourite dresses belonging to Amelia. I've packed her lemon sundress with a white petal collar that my mother sent her from France for her second birthday, and the turquoise crochet dress that she refuses to wear because 'it's all scratchy', but it's just so pretty and brings out her blue eyes. She has many more pretty dresses that I wish I could pack, but I know Paul will become suspicious if he notices any of her clothes missing.

The doorbell rings unexpectedly and I jump. I snort at myself as I catch my frazzled reflection in the mirror. I quickly zip my suitcase closed and shove it under the bed. I glance over the room, and content that everything looks normal I close the door behind me.

The ringing is incessant, and I expect to find Langton and Connelly on the other side of the door.

So, you murdered your neighbour, Langton will say. *Got any biscuits?* Connelly will add.

I make my way reluctantly down the stairs and take such a deep breath when I reach the bottom step that I make myself light-headed.

Why, no, I haven't seen Helen. Is she missing? I practise over and over in my head, hoping I can squeeze out a few tears. My fingers tremble as I reach for the door handle and I count backwards in my mind. Three . . . two . . . one . . . open.

'Oh. My. God,' I say, letting go of the handle as my hand flies to cover my mouth.

'Hello, Susan. Long time no see.'

'Jenny,' I say, instantly recognising the woman standing on my doorstep.

Her hair is longer now and falls past her shoulders in choppy layers. And her clothes are grown-up and sensible. No more crazy neon colours or wild leopard prints. She's wearing skinny blue jeans, a cream jumper and white runners. But her goofy smile and bright eyes are the same as always.

Jenny folds her arms across her chest and tilts her head to one side. She looks uncomfortable, or perhaps confused. As if she wasn't really sure she would find me on the other side of this door, and now that she has, she has no idea what to do next. Silence weighs heavy between us as we look at each other. She's obviously waiting for me to speak first. It's most unlike her.

All I want to do is close the door in her face and go back upstairs to finish packing. But the first thought that comes into my head spews past my lips rebelliously. 'How did you find me?'

'Your neighbours,' Jenny says. 'I asked about you in the village pub and a man having a pint gave me directions. Simple as that. Could you imagine asking something like that in Dublin? God, they'd look at you like you had three heads, wouldn't they? People round here are so much chattier and friendlier.'

I exhale sharply. 'People around here can't keep their mouths shut. That's true.'

Jenny frowns at my snarky comment. 'He was nice – the man in the pub. Helpful. He even offered to drive me here in case I got lost.'

Great. That's just what I need. Jenny dragging random locals with her for a nosy around.

'Why are you here, Jenny?' I say, reaching for the doorknob again, so I can shut it anytime I need to.

She unfolds her arms and I stiffen, thinking she's going to lunge forward and hug me.

'It's been all over the news about Amelia,' Jenny says, and I can see sympathetic tears gathering in her eyes. 'Susan, I'm so sorry.'

I swallow hard and stare over her shoulder into my garden. It's a beautiful day. A cloudless sky seems to make the summer flowers bloom brighter than usual.

'I would have come sooner,' Jenny continues, 'but I'm ashamed to say I didn't realise Amelia was your little girl, until—' Jenny cuts herself off suddenly.

'Until what?' I say, dragging my eyes reluctantly to meet hers.

'Nothing.' Jenny shrugs, and smiles cautiously. 'I just mean . . .' She takes a deep breath and I've never known her to have to search for words before. She seems such a different person now compared to the overzealous friend I once had. 'All I mean is, I didn't know you'd had a baby. I'm embarrassed it took me so long to realise Amelia was your daughter.'

'Is,' I correct stubbornly.

'Yes. Absolutely.' Jenny blushes, and I can see in her eyes that she thinks I'm mad clinging to the hope that Amelia is still alive.

Perfect.

If someone who once knew me better than I know myself is so convinced Amelia is gone, the rest of the country must be damn well certain. Maybe Deacon and I have really done it. Maybe we've got away with this already.

'I didn't know you'd got married either,' Jenny adds. 'Or moved away from Dublin.'

'We're not living here long,' I say, not sure why I felt the need to add that.

'I guess that's what happens when friends lose touch. They stop knowing what's going on in each other's lives,' Jenny says, craning her neck to see past me into my home.

I'm sure she's looking for an invite inside. That absolutely won't be happening. There's a photograph of Paul and me on our wedding day perched on the hall table. I can't possibly let Jenny see it.

'I must say I was most surprised of all to discover you'd moved to County Cork,' she continues, becoming increasingly chattier and bouncy, and I'm seeing traits of the old Jenny buried beneath the subtle new clothes and hairstyle. 'You were always such a city girl. Is your husband from Cork, is that why you're here?'

'No.' I shake my head. 'He's from Dublin too.'

'Oh really? I thought he might be a farmer or something. I actually went to that big house over there first, thinking that's where you lived.' Jenny turns ninety degrees and points towards Larry and Helen's farmhouse a couple of fields down.

'Why would you go there?' I say.

My pulse is racing. I can feel the pressure of the blood coursing through my veins and pounding in my temples.

'I never imagined you living in a little cottage like this.' Jenny turns back. 'But it's very cute. Different, but cute.'

'Were you talking to anyone at the farmhouse?' I ask, trying to disguise the sudden tremor that's creeping its way into my voice.

'No one answered,' Jenny puffs out. 'A huge house like that and I'm not sure anyone even lives there.'

I don't reply.

'Do you know them?' she asks. 'The people who live there?'

'No,' I say firmly. 'I think you're right. It's abandoned.'

'What a pity.' Jenny sighs as if she's disappointed. 'I bet it's fabulous inside. Or haunted. Maybe it's haunted. Wouldn't that be cool?'

'Jenny, this really isn't a good time,' I say, beginning to close the door.

'Oh God, what am I like?' she says. 'I've come here to support you. To see if there's anything I can do, any way I can help, and all I've done is talk nonsense and upset you. Old habits, I guess. I'll never learn when to shut my mouth, will I?'

'Jenny.' I cut across her as her voice slices through my brain like a hot knife through butter. 'We haven't been friends in a long time. And much as I appreciate you coming all this way, I really would like to be alone. I think maybe you should go.'

The hurt on Jenny's face is intense and for a second I think she's going to cry.

Are you kidding me?

'Susan, I'm sorry,' she says, shoving her foot against the door to stop me from closing it. 'I never should have accused you of sleeping with Deacon.'

'Jenny, this is really not the time . . .'

'Please, Susan. Just listen?' She takes a deep breath. 'I was insecure, as you know. I thought I was losing him to you. And in the end I lost both of you, didn't I? I just need you to know there's not a day goes by that I don't regret it. I miss you. I miss both of you. I just wanted you to know that.'

'Now? You wanted me to know that *now*?'

'Susan . . .'

I raise my hand to warn my old friend not to take a step further. 'My two-year-old daughter is missing. And right now, I don't care about anything or anyone else. I appreciate your apology, but as I said, I really think you should leave.'

'Okay,' Jenny sighs. 'Okay.'

'And stay gone,' I add firmly. 'We're not friends any more!'

'Susan. Susan!' Paul's voice carries towards me, racing through the distance and up the winding laneway to find my ears, but I don't see him.

Oh no. Oh no, no, no. Not now. Please not now!

'They've found a body,' he shouts, coming into view as he rounds the corner before our cottage. 'Turn on the news, Susan. Turn it on now. Quick.'

Paul is out of breath and visibly shaking as he reaches the gate. He rests his hands on his hips and bends in the middle, sucking in huge gulps of air and panting them back out. His bright green shorts expose his long, slender legs and his neon-pink running top has turned cerise from sweat. I know his choice of bold-coloured running gear will pique Jenny's interest, and my chest tightens as I wait for the carnage. I stare at my husband as he slowly pulls himself upright again. I'm properly looking at him for the first time in days, and it takes my breath away to discover he's disturbingly emaciated. I don't understand where he finds the energy to run any more.

'You're back early,' I say, thinking of my suitcase under the bed and how if Jenny hadn't turned up I'd be gone by now. 'Did you not do a full 10k today?'

'They've closed off everywhere around the lake. You can't get near the place.' Paul opens the gate and it squeaks, as always. 'There's cops everywhere. News crew too. And, of course, the usual nosy so-and-sos from the village. I had to turn back.'

'What are they saying?' I ask, shoving my hands into my pockets so Paul and Jenny won't notice them trembling.

'Is this about that body they found this morning?' Jenny says. 'Shocking news. Just shocking. What is wrong with some people?'

'I'm sorry, who are you?' Paul says, and I think he's so shaken he's only just noticed Jenny standing on our doorstep. I can see from his expression that he's assumed she's a reporter. I wish that's all she was.

'This is Jenny,' I say, before she has a chance to speak. 'We were friends in college.'

'Oh.' Paul nods. 'Have we met before?'

'No,' I snap. 'Never.'

My eyes seek out Jenny's and I plead with her to keep silent, something I know she'll struggle to do. Now is not the time to tell Paul she recognises him.

'Well, it's nice to meet you,' he says, extending his hand.

'Yes. You too,' Jenny says, stretching her hand out.

'The body,' I gasp, diving between Jenny and Paul before they have a chance to shake hands. 'Is it Amelia?' I ask, beginning to cry. 'Are they saying it's Amelia?'

Tears come easy. It must be the stress.

Paul shakes his head and gathers me in his arms. 'Oh baby.'

His body is wet and sticky and the feeling of his sweat against my clothes makes my skin crawl, but I cuddle into him as if I need him desperately.

'I think it might be Helen,' he whispers. 'The police say it's a woman. And the rumours have already started, as you can imagine. People are saying Larry killed her.'

'Larry?' I gasp again.

'I know, baby.' Paul reaches his hand up to my hair and presses my face into the crook of his salty neck.

I think I'm going to be sick.

'I'm sorry, Susan,' he says. 'I'm so sorry. I know you and Helen had become friends.'

'I . . . I . . .' I don't know what to say.

'I mean, I know I didn't particularly like the woman,' Paul says, and I hear guilt in his tone for all the terrible things he said about Helen. 'But, Christ. Murdered. I just can't believe it.'

'Who's Larry?' Jenny asks.

Paul lets go of me and turns to face Jenny. I know he's thinking it's an inappropriate question to ask, but I also know he won't be rude and ignore the stranger on his doorstep. He must be wondering how I could be friends with someone so blunt. I often asked myself the same question.

'Our neighbour,' I answer, leaving it at that.

'God, that's terrible,' Jenny says, her eyes on me. 'You think you know people . . .'

I swallow hard.

'Larry seemed like a nice guy,' Paul says, suddenly taking a U-turn on his dislike of our neighbours, obviously for Jenny's benefit. 'A farmer,' he explains. 'He keeps to himself. You know, the quiet type? A bit fond of the drink, mind you. But, then again, so was she. It was just the two of them living in that big old house.'

'Really?' Jenny shakes her head, casting her eyes over her shoulder to stare at Larry and Helen's house. 'It's always the quiet ones you need to keep an eye on, isn't it?'

When she turns back her eyes are narrow and dark, and I realise that she didn't just know me better than anyone else ten years ago . . . she still does.

Oh God. What have I done?

'Excuse me,' Paul says, brushing past Jenny. 'Susan, I'm grabbing a quick shower.'

'Sure,' I nod.

'Jenny, you'll come in, won't you?' he adds.

'I'd love to,' Jenny says.

'Oh good,' I choke.

'I think the cops will be around soon,' Paul continues. 'I'd like to be out of my running gear for once. Save me a ton of bloody questions. Anyone would think going for a jog was a crime.'

'Do you think the police will think the two are connected?' I ask, as Paul steps on to the stairs. 'Helen and Amelia, I mean.'

'Of course,' he smiles. 'Don't you? This could be our first real lead . . .'

'Yeah.' I swallow as an image of my suitcase under my bed flashes before my eyes.

Chapter Twenty-two

THEN

'Hey,' I say, sliding on to the park bench beside Deacon. 'I bought you a coffee. Two sugars, yeah?'

'God, yes,' Deacon smiles. 'Jenny won't let me have sugar. She's on a health buzz.'

'Oh.' I frown and sip my tall Americano. 'How *is* Jenny?' I ask, and I wonder if the sense of sadness and longing is in my voice or if I just sound pissed off.

'Good. Good,' Deacon nods. 'As I say, she's trying to get really healthy. She's gone from vegetarian to vegan.'

'Well,' I snort, 'that's no surprise.'

'I guess,' he sighs.

'Are you vegan too, Deacon?'

'I like to be supportive,' he smiles.

'You also like eggs. And cheese. Jesus. Vegetarian was a big step for you. Now you're vegan. Really?'

'Jenny wants a baby,' Deacon blurts. 'And she wants to be in the best shape.'

'And you want . . .' I say.

'She wants to start trying as soon as we're married.'

'And what do you want?'

He doesn't reply.

'Drink your coffee,' I smile.

Deacon and I don't talk for a while. We sit and people-watch. It's nice. But I find myself getting twitchy as I finish my coffee. I have to ask . . .

'Do you want a baby, Deacon?'

He stands up and walks to a nearby bin. He throws his cup in. He comes back, stretches his arm out to me without a word and I hand him my empty cup. He walks back to the bin. I think that's my answer. Deacon doesn't want a baby.

'Have you told her?' I ask.

'No,' Deacon says, sitting down. 'I don't know how to.'

'What happened to Kerri-Ann?' I ask.

Deacon flinches. The mere mention of his daughter's name rattles him and he begins to fidget.

'Haven't I told you?' He looks at me with such sadness in his eyes my heart aches.

'No. You told me your daughter's name and then changed the subject. You do that every time Kerri-Ann comes up.'

'I do, don't I?' He nods and stares vacantly ahead.

'Deacon?' I say, demanding his attention.

'That coffee was lovely,' he says. 'Just what I needed.'

'You're doing it again,' I scowl. 'Changing the subject.'

His piercing-blue eyes find their way back to me, glistening with tears.

'Don't you want to talk about her?' I ask. 'Don't you want to remember? Tell me about her. Let me in.'

Deacon turns towards me. His eyes drop to the ground and a tangible wave of sadness washes over him and engulfs me too. I really wish we had more coffee because I have a feeling this is finally going to be a long story.

'The sun was shining, not a cloud in the sky,' he says with a pensive smile. 'Kerri-Ann was wearing little pink shorts and a yellow T-shirt. Yellow was her favourite colour. I can see them on her now as clear as day. We took her to the park, Nancy and me. We didn't have much money, you see. We were really just two kids ourselves. But the park is free, you know?'

I nod. I don't chance words and disrupt him, but I do place my hand on his knee.

'It was great. Kerri-Ann was having the time of her life. Flying high on the swing. Crossing the rope bridge. Sliding down the big slide that was really for older kids . . . but Kerri-Ann was such a rebel. There was no stopping her. She got that from Nancy. And Nancy was smiling. All day she was smiling, like it was the best day ever. But then Kerri-Ann fell. She was climbing the ladder to the big slide. I said she was too little but Nancy shot me down. She was halfway up when she lost her grip. She came down on her back. She didn't cry, not for a while anyway. It didn't seem too bad. She didn't even have any cuts or bruises, she was just a bit winded. She even had another go on the swing after. The next morning I heard Nancy screaming from Kerri-Ann's room. She couldn't wake her. At the hospital they said it was a bleed to the brain. Head trauma. Maybe if we'd brought her in sooner they could have helped her. Saved her. But we didn't. We didn't know. Like I said, we were just kids ourselves, really. Six weeks later Nancy killed herself. She took some sleeping pills the doctor had given her.'

'Jesus,' I say. 'Jesus.'

I wish other more comforting words would come out. But they don't.

'And that was it,' Deacon adds. 'I was on my own. No Nancy. No Kerri-Ann. No one.' My heart aches for him. I can't imagine anything more unbearable than losing your wife and child and being completely alone. Deacon doesn't deserve that. No one deserves that.

'Have you told Jenny?' I ask.

'Yeah.' Deacon nods. 'Not the gory details. But she knows.'

'And she still wants a baby?' I say. 'Isn't that a bit selfish?'

'Jenny isn't selfish,' he says, defending his fiancée. 'She's just, well, she's just Jenny.'

'Where does she think you are now?' I ask. 'Certainly not with me.'

'Well, no,' he admits. 'She thinks I'm seeing my counsellor.'

I laugh. 'So does she still think we're having an affair?'

'No.' Deacon blushes.

'Good,' I say. 'Because if I'm going to seduce a nearly married man, I'd like to think it's with more than just my words.'

'Jenny is a really good person,' he says. 'I'm lucky. I mean, I'm really lucky. I didn't think I'd ever be happy again. But I am.'

'Good,' I say again. 'I'm glad. And when you realise that you can talk to whoever you want, maybe you'll be even happier.'

'Susan, I have to go.' He stands up.

'I've my final exams next week,' I say, tugging his arm. 'I'll be qualified then.'

He smiles. 'I'm happy for you, Sue.'

'Thanks,' I smile back. 'I'll be a real counsellor then. You won't have to lie to Jenny any more about us talking. It'll all be official.'

'Yeah,' Deacon exhales. 'Maybe.'

I watch him uncertainly as he walks away.

'Bye, Sue,' he says, glancing back over his shoulder.

Chapter Twenty-three

Now

I close the door behind Jenny and wait for her to say something about Paul, but she doesn't open her mouth. She stands by the door with her hands clasped in front of her and her head held high. Her eyes are all over my home. Sweeping the tiles. Dusting the countertops. Washing over the kitchen. She shakes her head and I wonder when she will realise that she shouldn't be here. The messy college student she was once friends with is nowhere to be found in my flawless cottage.

'Beautiful photos,' Jenny finally says, her eyes settling on the lightning strikes hanging on the wall next to her.

'Yes, they are,' I say unashamedly.

'Are these Adam's work?' she asks, running her fingers across the glass.

I don't answer. I don't need to. She knows.

'The colours are incredibly beautiful,' Jenny adds. 'The white frames really bring out the mood of the sky. Especially this one.' She points to my favourite, an angry purple-red sky with a single fork of lightning caught in the dead centre of the shot.

'The chances of snapping the lightning at the exact moment it strikes are something like a million to one,' I explain.

Jenny gasps, impressed. 'The talent behind these photos blows my mind. They're so good.'

'I always told you they were.'

I hear the noisy electric shower come on overhead and I know Paul will be in there for a long time, running the hot water on his aching legs.

'Can I get you anything?' I ask, hating myself as the clichéd words of a good host slip out, but I'm anxious to steer Jenny away from Adam's photos. 'Tea or coffee?'

'Coffee would be lovely,' Jenny smiles. 'I'm exhausted after the long trek down here.'

I watch as she makes herself comfortable on my couch. She crosses her legs and flops her head on the back of the couch and puffs out a sigh of exhaustion, as if she's just flown in from Australia instead of simply following the motorway from Dublin to Cork. I roll my eyes as Jenny's usual flair for drama pushes my buttons.

'Jenny. What are you doing?' I finally say. 'Why are you *really* here?'

'I told you.' Jenny lifts her head and looks at me with huge eyes. 'I want to help. If I can.'

'Really?' I don't believe a word. 'You came all this way, after all these years, to help me?'

'Isn't that what friends do?' she smiles.

I can't think of anything to say. I have no idea why she's here, but she must know something. I can't suddenly ask her to leave, Paul would ask questions, and besides, if I piss her off God only knows what she'll go down to the local pub and say. Maybe Jenny and I need to be friends again, at least until I figure this out.

'That coffee, Susan?' Jenny bounces, as always.

'Yeah.' I swallow. 'Coming right up.' On my way to the kitchen I hide the photo on the dresser of Paul and me on our wedding day. It's pointless, really, since my husband is upstairs and will come down at any moment to chat with this spectre from my past, who is sitting way too comfortably on my couch.

I take some deep breaths and fill the kettle.

'She's just absolutely gorgeous,' Jenny says, now pacing the open downstairs space and taking in every photo of Amelia dotted around on the walls and cabinets and shelves.

'Thank you,' I say, unsurprised she didn't stay sitting for long.

'She's very like her father, isn't she?' Jenny adds.

Her words sting, and I wonder if she's chosen them on purpose. I'm distracted by the floorboards creaking overhead and I know Paul is out of the shower. The kettle shuts off and I look at the two china cups I've no memory of taking out of the cupboard and placing on the countertop.

I spoon some coffee into the cups. My hand is shaking and I spill boiling water over the edge of one of the cups and scald my fingers. I shove my finger into my mouth and suck, trying to cool it down.

'How long have you been married?' Jenny asks, suddenly appearing behind me.

I'm reaching overhead to put the coffee back in the cupboard when she startles me. I drop the jar and the lid flies off. I watch it roll along the floor, picking up speed before it crashes into the leg of the table and comes to a wobbly stop. Coffee grains scatter across the porcelain tiles.

Jenny laughs awkwardly and bends down to pick up the empty jar. 'Sorry,' she says. 'I didn't mean to give you a fright.'

'Now?' I say. 'Or when you turned up on my doorstep after fifty million years.'

Jenny laughs again.

I open the larder cupboard behind me and fetch the sweeping brush.

'Susan. Stop,' Jenny says.

I begin to sweep the coffee grains into a pile.

'Susan?' she says again.

I walk a little further away and sweep a few stray grains that have made their way under the table.

'Susan, I said stop.' Jenny grabs my arms.

I shake her off as if her touch burns.

'He's your husband?' She finally says the words I've been waiting to hear since she walked through the door, and there's an odd sense of relief in accepting that she recognises Paul. 'Your husband, Susan. I can't believe it.'

I press my finger against my lips and throw my eyes upwards, as if I can see Paul walking around overhead through the ceiling. 'Please, Jenny. Just be quiet. He'll hear you.'

'He doesn't know who you are?' Her eyes widen. 'Oh holy shit.'

'Shh,' I whisper. 'No. No, he doesn't. Of course he bloody doesn't.' I rest the broom against the wall, then hurry towards the patio doors and fiddle with the lock. When the doors finally open, the gust of fresh air hits me like a drag of marijuana.

I take a deep breath, and when Jenny follows me into the garden I lock the doors from the outside behind us.

'Oh Susan, I know you had your issues, but this is beyond messed up. Even for you,' she says, glancing around at the vast green fields that seem to stretch on for miles.

The odd house, cattle shed or stable dare to interrupt the landscape somewhere in the distance but I'm confident no one can hear or see us out here, and for the first time since Jenny arrived unexpectedly I'm not deafened by the sound of my own blood coursing past my ears inside my pounding head.

'Paul Warner,' Jenny says. '*The* Paul Warner.'

'Yes,' I admit.

Jenny grows pale and drags her hand around her face. I eye up the patio furniture.

'Let's sit down.' I point.

'You know, when I saw Amelia's disappearance on the news . . .' Jenny grabs a chair out from under the table and the metal legs squeak and scrape against the patio before she sits down and her weight silences them. '. . . I thought to myself – no! No way. The name Warner is just a coincidence. It couldn't be.'

'Jenny, I can explain,' I say, pulling a chair out.

'No.' Jenny raises her hand to silence me. 'Let me get my head around this for a second. Please.'

Jenny's authority catches me by surprise and I wonder why she wasn't as assertive when she accused me of sleeping with her husband all those years ago. Maybe she's been for counselling, I think, making no effort to hide the smirk that thought splashes across my face.

'Why?' Jenny shakes her head, visibly disgusted. 'Why would you marry him?'

I shrug. 'Because I love him.'

'I don't believe you.' Jenny begins to shake. 'I listened to you telling me over and over how much you hated that man. You were consumed by it. I watched it eat away at you. I watched the hatred hurt you every single day. And what? Suddenly that all went away and was replaced by wonderful, beautiful love? Oh c'mon, Susan. I've never heard such bullshit.'

Jenny stands up suddenly and the chair falls behind her, crashing loudly against the patio. The back cracks a tile as it lands. Jenny doesn't notice. She's pacing in circles with her hands in her hair.

'People change,' I say.

'No one changes, Susan,' Jenny says. 'Not that much.'

'I have,' I protest. 'I've changed so much. You don't know me any more.'

'And has Paul changed?'

'Yes. He's grown up. We both have.'

Jenny snorts. 'Well, no matter how much he's changed, Susan, he's still the man who killed your brother. Nothing will ever change that!'

Chapter Twenty-four

THEN

Dear Susan,

> *A birthday is a special day.*
> *It comes just once a year.*
> *Take the time to laugh and smile,*
> *and give a little cheer.*
>> *Hope you have a wonderful birthday. I can't believe*
> *we're 25 already. Feeling old lol. I miss you. Maybe we*
> *can catch up soon. Please, please get in touch.*
>> *Love you lots, Hon.*
>> *Jenny x*

I snap the card shut and tear it down the middle. I turn it sideways and tear again. I keep going until I rip it into tiny pieces, letting them fall to the ground.

I glance over my shoulder at my calendar. There's a red circle around today's date that I scribbled in permanent marker a couple of weeks ago. As if I could ever forget my own birthday. It's just a regular Tuesday for most people, but I don't have to go to work today. I let them know weeks ago that I'd be taking the day off. No one asked why, and I didn't say. I like it best this way. I hate being reminded by anyone that it's my birthday.

The huge bouquet of flowers Jenny sent sits in the centre of my kitchen table. This bouquet is even bigger and brighter than the one she sent last year. The colourful flowers brighten the room and their fresh scent covers the stench of takeaway pizza and beer from last night. Deep green leaves spill over the edge of the lilac box with cream polka dots that says *Happy Birthday* in swirling gold writing and the purple and yellow fluffy flowers sit proudly on top.

The alarm on my watch beeps and I can't believe I was so distracted by the flowers and Jenny's card that I almost forgot it's time to go to the coffee shop. I lift the bouquet off the table and tuck it under my arm, taking care not to squash the box and spill water all over myself. I press the pedal on the bin with my foot and drop the flowers inside.

Less than an hour later I order a double espresso and take my usual seat by the window in The Sugary Spoon so I can people-watch. I'm way too hot. A coat and scarf was a bad plan today. It was cloudy when I left my flat but it's mild and humid for late October. I couldn't get a parking space outside the café and it's a pedestrian area around the corner, so I had to drive more than a kilometre in the wrong direction to the nearest multi-storey car park and run all the way back so I would be here on time. My back is sticky and I can only imagine what colour my cheeks must be as I feel them burn. But it's worth it when I see Paul walk through the door seconds after I sit down. He goes straight to the counter to order his daily coffee.

I've been following Paul Warner twice weekly for almost a year. On Tuesdays and Thursdays he comes to The Sugary Spoon shortly after midday. I imagine he stops by most other weekdays too, but I'm on a later lunch those days and can't make it down. He works in an accountancy firm around the corner. It's a huge office, a couple of hundred staff by the looks of it. Sometimes he's with a colleague or two when he comes in for coffee. He's alone today.

Paul made it particularly easy to find him. The silly arse attended an alumni ball at the college last Christmas. The college newspaper couldn't resist writing an article on the sizeable donation his firm made to the maths department, as if he was some wonderful philanthropist they were honoured to call a past student. Unsurprisingly, the article left out the part where Paul graduated behind bars while serving a sentence for manslaughter. It would seem the little details aren't important when you're throwing money around. You can clearly buy yourself a clean reputation these days.

'An Americano and a croissant to go, please,' Paul says, as I crane my neck to listen.

'Anything else?' the girl behind the counter asks routinely.

'No,' Paul smiles. 'That's everything. Thank you.'

'That's four euro and eighty cents, please,' the girl says.

Paul passes her a fiver and tells her she can keep the change. She rolls her eyes and I cover my mouth with my hand to hide my snigger.

After just a couple of months following Paul I decided he must be one of the most boring men alive. Tuesday is black coffee and croissant day. Thursday is cappuccino and a Danish. Every now and then he will mix up Tuesday's order with Thursday's or vice versa, but nothing as adventurous as ordering a cappuccino with a croissant. Paul owns three suits, four shirts and three ties. At least he mixes his outfits up more often than his coffee order. Although someone should really tell him to stop wearing the red tie with the yellow shirt. It's fuck ugly. Every day he walks to and from work. No surprise there. His driving ban lasts another year. His rent must be crazy in the posh part of the city centre, so I can only imagine he's earning a lot as an accountant in that fancy firm. I can barely afford my tiny flat around the corner from campus, since a lot of my counselling work is still voluntary while I try to expand my experience.

'Thank you.' Paul's familiar voice cuts into my thoughts.

I watch him reach up to take the brown paper bag the girl behind the counter passes him in one hand, and he takes his coffee in the other.

'There's milk and sugar over there.' The girl points to the usual spot as if Paul isn't in here every day.

Feeling light-headed from the heat and a little shaky from my double espresso, I stand up and try to time it so I reach the door at exactly the same moment as Paul. It's actually rather tricky as he takes longer than I expect, trying to get the lid back on his coffee cup after adding such a tiny drop of milk I wonder why he even bothered.

Finally, he's moving and I pick up pace as I swerve around tables and chairs and pass the counter. I'm practically power walking as he opens the door and I lunge forward so my arm collides against his as we squeeze through the gap at the same time.

'Oh my God, I'm so sorry,' I say as I watch his coffee cup fly out of his hand.

Scalding coffee rains down on his grey suit jacket. Ironically, I like this jacket best out of all of his suits.

Paul takes his jacket off quickly, but the coffee has soaked right through to his shirt.

'Here, let me help you.' I pull some tissues out of my bag and begin to dab at his shirt. 'I'm so embarrassed,' I say. 'That was all my fault. I was rushing for my bus and I just didn't see you there.'

'It's fine,' Paul says, pulling away from me.

Clearly my dabbing is making him uncomfortable. I stop and pass him some fresh tissues instead.

'Can I buy you another coffee?' I ask.

He shakes his head. 'Thank you. But I really need to get back to work.'

'I could pay for your dry-cleaning, maybe?' I suggest, curling a strand of hair around my finger. 'Would that help?'

'No. It's fine, really,' Paul says and he's not even looking at me. 'It was just an accident. Don't worry about it.'

'I feel awful,' I continue.

'Well, don't.' He finally looks at me and his big blue eyes are round and kind. 'Accidents happen all the time. Don't beat yourself up over it.'

'Thank you for being so understanding, eh . . .' I extend my hand.

'Paul,' he says, shaking my hand.

'Nice to meet you, Paul,' I say. 'I'm Susan. Maybe I'll see you again sometime.'

'Yeah, maybe,' he says, slipping on his wet jacket and walking away.

Chapter Twenty-five

THEN

Wednesday drags by. On the one hand I'm relieved it's no longer my birthday, but on the other I don't want to be at work listening to people drone on about their boring lives and minor problems that they blow out of proportion. The only one with a real problem is me. But that's all getting sorted out now. I have a plan.

At five minutes past twelve there is a knock on my office door. I lift my head from filling in some boring paperwork after my last client.

'C'mon in, Deacon,' I say, expecting him for his midday, midweek session.

The door creaks open and Deacon's head appears around the door first.

'What's behind your back?' I ask, standing up and walking around to the front of my desk.

'I know you hate birthdays,' he says, blushing.

Deacon has a present behind his back. I can see the top of a bottle of wine peek out on one side, and the corner of a box of chocolates juts out on the other.

I shake my head. Deacon wouldn't remember my birthday. He's terrible with dates – he can't remember his own daughter's anniversary or the date he and Jenny got married. He considers it an achievement if he guesses the month correctly. *Jenny must have told him.* I sigh, disappointed that they're obviously keeping in touch.

'But I couldn't resist bringing you a little something,' he continues. 'It's almost lunchtime. What do you say we have a little birthday drink?'

Deacon pulls the wine and chocolates out from behind his back and brushes past me to set them down on my desk.

'I can't.' I try to smile, masking my frustration. 'I've back to back clients this afternoon.'

'Surely one glass won't hurt?' he says.

'I'll tell you what,' I say, sitting behind my desk again, 'why don't you come round to my flat later? We can open it then. I'll even cook dinner.'

I can fill Deacon with wine and fill his head some more with how terrible a father he was. There's only so far we can get in our sessions before he starts to pull back. It's easier to get inside his head when he's drunk. It does mean I have to have dinner with the boring bastard at least twice a month, but it'll all be worth it when the time comes to call on Deacon for help. By then, I'll have him so convinced we're two broken kindred spirits he'll practically be begging me to do away with Paul.

'No.' He shakes his head and catches me by surprise. 'I'll cook. There's something not right about you cooking dinner on your birthday.'

I smile and nod. 'My birthday was yesterday.' I can see I've burst his bubble.

'I knew that,' he says. 'But I don't see you on Tuesdays. Can't we do a post-birthday dinner?'

'Sounds good,' I smile.

He takes a seat and we begin our session as usual. I wait until we're halfway through to ask the question that's been burning a hole in my mind like acid since Deacon wished me happy birthday.

'How's Jenny?' I finally blurt, completely out of context as Deacon was telling me about his childhood collie and how losing her was his first experience of death.

'Erm,' he swallows. 'Okay, I guess. We signed the divorce papers on Friday.'

'Oh Deacon. I'm sorry,' I lie. 'That must have been hard.'

'Yeah,' he sighs. 'I didn't think it would ever really happen, you know. I always thought we could fix things.'

'Yeah,' I nod. 'I know.'

He turns and stares out the window, becoming emotional.

'But you're still in touch, that's good,' I say.

'We're not,' he whispers, and I'm glad he's not looking at me because I'm sure my anger at being lied to flashes across my face.

'Can we talk about something else?' he says, turning back to face me.

'Of course, Deacon.' I concentrate hard to keep my voice low and level. 'This is your session. Whatever you want to talk about is okay.'

'Can *you* talk?' he asks.

I shake my head, unsure what he means.

'About anything,' he adds. 'Just talk, please. And I can just sit here and listen. Please, Susan?'

'Okay. It's not very professional, but . . .'

'Screw professional,' he snorts. 'We were friends long before you were a *professional*.'

I laugh at his wiggling fingers creating air quotes. I begin talking. At first, it's incoherent babbling, as always. I say something about the weather. Then about the traffic on the way to work this morning. I know I don't really have his attention as he stares out the window again. I notice a tear trickle down his cheek. I don't mention the flowers Jenny sent. I never tell Deacon about Jenny's constant efforts to throw me an olive branch. I've no doubt he still loves her. Painting her in a positive light wouldn't do me any favours, but equally I can't lambast her and risk losing even a fraction of his trust.

I continue to ramble on about mundane things, and just as I'm losing his attention again, I add, 'And then I bumped into Paul.' I pause and wait.

'Paul?' Deacon crooks his ear, still facing away from me.

'Yes. Paul,' I say, so softly my breath tickles my lips. 'Paul Warner. At a coffee shop in town.'

He turns round. His eyes are wide.

I continue, treading carefully. There's a very fine line between making sure Deacon feels like my closest friend and sharing a detail too far. I'm not entirely sure where the balance lies just yet. I watch him carefully as I speak.

'I spilled coffee all over him.'

'You threw coffee at him?' Deacon squeaks in a high pitch that really doesn't suit him.

'Oh no,' I giggle, as if I'm terribly embarrassed. 'It was an accident. I bumped into him coming out the door of the shop.'

'Did he know who you were?' He stands up, beginning to look uncomfortable.

'No,' I admit. 'He has no idea I even exist.'

'Good. That's the way to keep it. It was just a freak meeting. Don't let it upset you. I'm sure you'll never have to see him again.'

'It didn't upset me,' I smile brightly, standing up too. 'I think I've finally made my peace with the past,' I lie. The words knot in my gut, but I keep smiling until my jaw aches. 'You're right. Learning to forgive is the only way I can ever be truly happy.'

'That's great news, Susan,' he says. 'I'm really glad you've reached that point.'

'Have you ever thought about becoming a counsellor, Deacon?' I laugh, as he walks towards the door and I follow him. 'You really have a gift for making people happy.'

I can't believe I just quoted some sort of Hallmark card, but he buys into the cringey bullshit and he's grinning as if I've just made his day. *Bleurgh*. I turn my wrist and look at my watch.

Deacon pauses on reaching the door and kisses me on the cheek. It catches me by surprise.

'I'll see you tonight,' he says.

'Um,' I grin, my mind already at the coffee shop as I usher him out the door. 'Yeah. Can't wait.'

I close the door behind him and hurry over to the window and wait until I see him walk by on the street below before I pull out a metallic blue gift bag from under my desk. I reach both hands inside and carefully scoop out the smart white shirt I bought yesterday with money I really don't have to spare. The lady in the shop assured me that I could return it if it didn't fit. She didn't say it but she seemed to assume I was buying it for a boyfriend or husband. She never would have guessed the expensive cotton shirt is a gift for the man who murdered my brother. The man I stalk as a hobby.

I slide the shirt back into the bag and place Deacon's box of chocolates and wine on top. Beaming with excitement, I take a pen out of the top drawer of my desk and pull off a sheet of headed notepaper from the pad next to my phone. I'm tempted to circle the address or to underline my phone number printed below the company logo, but I credit Paul with enough intelligence to follow the not-so-subtle trail to find me. I click the top of my pen repeatedly as I struggle to think up something not too gushing but hopefully sweet enough to pique his interest.

> *Dear Paul,*
>
> *I'm so sorry for spilling your coffee yesterday. Please accept this gift as a token of my sincere apology. Now it seems I need to find somewhere else to buy my coffee because I really can't show my mortified face in The Sugary Spoon again.*
>
> *Best wishes,*
>
> *Susan*
>
> *P.S. It was very nice bumping into you.*

I dab some perfume on to the corners of the paper. The scent isn't actually mine; a client left it behind last week, but it's floral and fruity and will do nicely. Folding the page in the middle, I take care to make sure the perfume is dry and the ink doesn't smudge. I squirt some perfume on to the shirt too. I want to be damn sure that the first time Paul wears his new, overpriced shirt he's reminded of the note and my apology. I work the silky blue handles of the gift bag into a neat bow, taking care to avoid the neck of the wine bottle that protrudes annoyingly. My schedule is clear for the rest of the afternoon, and if I hurry I will make it on time to drop Paul's gift into the coffee shop before lunch.

The first of my two buses into the city arrives on time, but I get caught waiting on the second for at least ten minutes. It's a frustrating blip in my plan and by the time I reach The Sugary Spoon I only have minutes to spare.

'Hi there,' I say, approaching the counter, thankful there's no queue ahead of the lunchtime rush.

'Hello,' the girl from yesterday says.

She doesn't recognise me, I can tell from her eyes.

'I was here yesterday,' I begin, the words getting caught up in my mouth as I become awkward and fidgety.

I think about placing the same order as always and chickening out of my plan for Paul. It is crazy, after all. But I glance over the barista's shoulder at the day's specials scribbled on a blackboard behind her.

Need to zap some energy into your day? Try our Lightning Bolt Americano.

Realistically, I know it's a dubious marketing attempt to sell a double espresso and some boiled water, but I can't seem to get past their choice of phrase. *Lightning bolt.* Maybe it's a sign from Adam? It's probably not, but either way I don't care. I've made my decision. Today is the day.

The girl behind the counter is staring at me blankly and I slowly realise I haven't spoken in a minute or so.

'Sorry,' I wince. 'This is all a little awkward. As I said, I was here yesterday and, well . . .'

'I remember you,' she says, smiling warmly. 'Don't worry about it. You're not the first person to spill a coffee.'

'Oh gosh.' I blush genuinely. 'I'm so embarrassed.'

'Don't be. It's cool. That guy comes in here all the time. He's really nice, I don't think he'll hold it against you. Now, what can I get you?'

'Actually,' I say, instantly irritated that she seems to think Paul is some sort of good guy, 'I was hoping to leave something with you.'

I produce the gift bag from behind my back. The barista's eyes widen and her smile grows.

'An apology,' she says, and I'm grateful I don't have to explain.

'I ruined his shirt,' I admit.

'Okay, cool.' She reaches her arm over the counter and I pass the bag to her. 'This is definitely a first. I like your style. And I don't blame you . . .' She winks. 'He's hot.'

I shake my head, uncomfortable. 'No, really. It's not like that. I just want him to know how sorry I am.'

'Sure. Yeah. Sure,' she says. 'If you say so.'

I stare her down, but a stupid smug smile is plastered across her face.

'He'll be here in a few minutes,' she grins. 'If you wait . . .'

'No,' I say firmly. 'I have to get back to work.'

The barista shrugs.

'Thank you,' I add, before turning my back and walking out the door.

I curse myself for not ordering a takeaway coffee as I perch on a bench across the street and watch Paul walk into The Sugary Spoon moments later.

Chapter Twenty-six

Now

Paul comes downstairs in jeans and a loose T-shirt that used to fit him more snugly. Jenny's eyes crawl all over him.

'You okay?' I ask, as Paul pauses at the bottom of the stairs.

'Yeah,' he says. 'Fine.'

'Langton called,' I say as he makes his way into the kitchen past Jenny and me.

He pours himself a large glass of water and guzzles it in one go.

'She said she'd call by this afternoon, if that's okay,' I say a little louder, so Paul can hear me over the tap he's left running.

'Sure,' he nods. 'I mean, why the hell not?'

'She's trying to help,' I say.

Paul slams his glass against the granite countertop. Mercifully it doesn't break. 'Nah,' he grunts, turning off the tap. 'She's just getting paid.'

'I don't think anyone goes into that profession unless they really care,' Jenny says.

A glass smashes in the kitchen.

'Excuse me, Jenny,' I say, jumping off the couch to follow the noise.

I find Paul crouched on his hunkers, cleaning up broken glass with his bare hands.

'Wow,' I say.

Blood trickles down the knuckles on his right hand where he's cut himself.

'What are you doing?' I ask softly.

Paul flops from his hunkers on to his bottom and sits among the shards of glass.

'I don't know, Susan.' He swallows. 'I just don't bloody know any more.'

'Show me?' I say, turning his hand over to examine the gash on his finger.

I raise his hand to my lips and take his finger in my mouth, running my tongue gently over the cut.

'There,' I say, lowering his hand. 'All better.'

Paul is still and calm and I cradle him in my arms the way I some-times do with Amelia when she has an upset tummy or has had a bad dream.

'Hey,' Jenny says, standing in the space where the living area meets the kitchen, clearly uncomfortable to come any further. 'I'm going to take off. Give you two some space. Maybe we could talk more later, Susan?'

I know by the way she looks at me that her *maybe* means definitely. I haven't wriggled out of this yet.

'No. I'll go,' Paul says, scrambling to his feet. 'You two should catch up. I'll get out of your way and go for a walk.'

'But you're just back from a run,' I say.

'A half run,' he says. 'Really, it's fine. I need the fresh air anyway.'

As usual, Paul can't seem to cope with being in our home for long without Amelia. Or with me. I'm not sure which.

I watch as Jenny and Paul seem to pass each other in slow motion as she walks into the kitchen and he walks out. He stops suddenly and turns round.

'I *do* know you,' he says, and I can see the spark of relief at finally placing Jenny, which had obviously been irritating him. 'We were in college together. Professor Flynn's economics class. Room 398, wasn't it?'

'No. Sorry.' Jenny twitches and I can tell she's hiding something. 'Not me.'

'Really, I could have sworn . . .' Paul says, his eyes shifting to seek out mine.

The hairs on the back of my neck stand to attention like obedient soldiers as the painfully familiar room number repeats in my mind. For three years I sat in the front row of room 396, directly across the hall. When I leaned forward in my chair I could see through the pane of glass in the door of 396 and straight into 398, where Adam would sit in the same spot and we'd pull faces at each other and try to make the other laugh to pass the time.

Paul raises his hand dismissively. 'Sorry. I'm terrible with names and faces.'

'Oh yeah,' Jenny laughs sheepishly. 'Me too.'

'Are you going for your walk?' I ask.

'And that is Susan's way of letting me know I've made this awkward,' Paul says. 'I better head on. Let you two catch up some more.'

'Well, it was nice meeting you,' Jenny says.

'Okay, bye,' I say, walking towards the door with Paul. My heart feels as though it might beat through my chest as I usher him out.

'No, hang on,' he says, turning as he reaches for the handle, an unfamiliar expression knotting his brow. 'Trinity College. You came to my party. That's where I know you from. You've changed a bit.' He points at Jenny. 'You weren't feeling well, and I held your hair back – you're the girl who was sick in the fountain.'

'I most certainly am not,' Jenny says and folds her arms.

My palms begin to sweat as I play the night of the party over in my head. The whole college was talking about it for weeks, even more than they talked about the trial. Jenny made a show of herself, and she suffered a three-day hangover from hell as a result. Her sudden fidgeting with the button on her blouse tells me she remembers it as clearly as I do.

'Paul. Really?' I frown, my heart beating so furiously it's painful. 'Don't you think this is a little inappropriate? You're making Jenny uncomfortable, for God's sake.'

The party plays on a loop in my mind now and I can't make it stop. Jenny had heard about some popular third-year student's party in the campus bar. She begged me to take her. I only intended to stay for a couple of drinks, but the music was good and it was the first time I'd been out since Adam died. I got drunk pretty quickly – not as quickly as Jenny, of course. Everyone was talking about the host and how he was about to go on trial for killing another student.

'You've nothing to worry about, bro,' some drunk guy said. 'You've the best lawyers on your side.'

'Yeah, man. You'll get off. And rightly so,' someone even drunker added.

'Have you heard about the dead guy's sister?' a third, somewhat more sober guy asked. 'Apparently she's hot as shit. And she goes here. She's probably looking for a shoulder to cry on.'

'Nah. Not my type,' Paul laughed. 'Too much emotional baggage.'

'Dude,' all three of his friends chimed as if he was hysterical.

'Here's to freedom,' Paul said, raising his glass like a cocky bastard. 'Cheers.'

They all clinked glasses.

I watched them intently for ages. Listening to more of their bullshit. I was so confident they were wrong. I trusted the system. I was certain Paul would get the punishment he deserved. But you know what they say? If you want a job done right, you have to do it yourself. And here we are . . .

'I didn't go to Trinity,' Jenny says, and I hold my breath. Her mother died when she was in the sixth year and she dropped out of school just weeks before she was due to sit her Leaving Certificate. It's a sore subject for her and I hope to God she's not going to share any of it with Paul.

'Where *did* you go, then?' he says, and I can sense his patience is running out.

'UCD, with me,' I lie effortlessly.

'Oh,' Paul nods. 'Of course. Can't be you then, Jenny.'

'We were quiet girls and we didn't go to parties. We studied hard, got our degrees, then lost touch over the years,' she says, trying much too hard and I can see the flash of disbelief in Paul's eyes.

Suddenly, the doorbell rings, and I've never been so grateful to hear it.

'Thank you,' I mouth towards Jenny as Paul turns away to open the door.

Jenny doesn't answer me; she barely even looks at me, and I wonder why she's stayed quieter now than she ever has in her life. And I know for sure she wants something. I'm just not sure what.

'Langton . . . Connelly . . .' Paul grunts as the door swings open.

Chapter Twenty-seven

Now

'I can't believe they've arrested Larry,' Paul says, pacing our living room. 'It'll probably make the news later. They said that, didn't they?'

'Yes,' I nod. 'They did.'

I'm not really listening to him. I'm so agitated my chest is tight and every breath burns my lungs. Jenny excused herself shortly after Langton and Connelly's arrival. That was more than an hour ago. She didn't say where she was going or if she would be back, and I didn't want to be seen to care too much and arouse Paul's suspicion. But I haven't stopped thinking about her. *Did she go home? Or did she go back to the pub?* I've no doubt half the village are in the pub gossiping about poor Helen's demise over a pint or a mid-afternoon glass of wine.

It's so sad, someone will say.

I know. Poor woman, someone else will add. *Another glass of wine? Oh yes. Please.*

Jenny could end up talking to anyone. Or everyone. She's not exactly known for keeping her mouth shut. God only knows what she'll say about me. Or worse, about Paul. It doesn't bear thinking about.

Paul continues talking and pacing from one side of the kitchen to the other. He stops occasionally to catch his breath and shake his head, exhausted from disbelief. I barely heard a word Langton and Connelly said, and I'm relying on Paul to drip-feed their advice back to me now as I zone in and out.

'I think I have some photos on my phone,' he says, catching my attention with such an out of context statement. 'I took some at the barbecue. Mostly of Amelia, obviously, but I did get some of our neighbours enjoying themselves too. I'm sure I have one or two nice ones of Helen.'

'Photos?' I ask. 'Why are you thinking about this now?'

'Well, I'm just thinking . . . reporters are going to want a photo of Helen, aren't they?' Paul says.

I shrug. 'I guess.'

He paces faster, his mind obviously racing.

'Usually they ask the husband, don't they?' he says. 'But, well . . .'

'Helen and Larry have three sons, Paul,' I tell my husband. 'I don't think it's our place to interfere.'

'Yeah. You're right,' he says. 'I'm just trying to help. I feel so damn useless.'

'I know,' I say. 'But I'm sure if the reporters, or the Guards for that matter, want to know anything about Helen, they'll speak to her family. It really is nothing to do with us.'

Paul stops pacing suddenly and wraps his arms around me, pulling me close to him. I flinch. I wasn't expecting his hug.

'How did this happen?' he says. 'How the hell did all this happen?'

I wrap my arms around his waist. 'Shh,' I say. 'Shh. Shh.'

'I can't turn on the bloody radio or telly without hearing Amelia's name. And now Helen's too,' Paul says. 'The place is heaving with reporters and camera crews and cops. It's like living on a fucking film set. Except it's real. Everything is real.'

Langton and Connelly spoke to us about the media shitstorm Helen's death will bring our way. They said the police haven't mentioned Helen and Amelia in the same statements to the media, but that won't stop them making the connection. Reporters will be dying for a quote, they warned. In the absence of any leads they'll probably just print something said by some overzealous local know-it-all. Langton told us not to be surprised if tomorrow's front pages feature a picture of Helen on one side and Amelia on the other, along with some sort of emotional or distressing headline: 'Lake Lives Lost' or 'Local Lake, National Horror'. I can see the tacky phrasing in bold print already.

My mind wanders to my half-packed suitcase under my bed.

'Do you think things have calmed down in the village?' I say. 'Maybe you could try going for a run now.'

'No.' Paul shakes his head. 'I'm not feeling it.'

'You sure?' I prod. 'Could be good for your head.'

'No,' Paul repeats. 'My head is a mess. I keep connecting the dots. Larry, the barbecue, Amelia, and now Helen. I was so focused on god-dam Deacon I didn't see what was happening right under my nose.'

'They brought Larry in for questioning, Paul,' I say. 'That's not the same as saying he's guilty. I told you Helen was drunk and falling all over the place. Who's to say anyone is responsible? This could all be a tragic accident, you know.'

'An accident,' he grunts, and I can feel his heart beating furiously against my cheek as I cuddle into his chest. 'This is no bloody accident. It's a matter of time, Susan. Just a matter of time until they charge the monster responsible.'

Paul breaks away from me and walks into the living area. He folds his arms and faces the window. I follow him and stand alongside him to stare outside too. I know this view by heart, but something about the rural landscape takes my breath away now. Grassy fields stretch out endlessly, divided into haphazard squares by wild hedging like a patchwork quilt of emerald and teal. The bright blue sky is punctuated by the odd fluffy white cloud. Directly across the road from our cottage are eight or nine black and white cows huddled with their heads low, munching on grass – completing the picture of a lazy summer's day in the countryside. It's hard to imagine just metres beyond our line of vision is the chaos the discovery of Helen's body has brought to the unassuming village of Ballyown.

'I can't believe it, you know,' Paul sighs. 'Larry was here with Helen. In our home. We invited him in. I thought he was a nice guy.'

He begins pacing again. I can see the built-up anxiety he hasn't run off this morning is torturing him.

'No you didn't,' I correct. 'You said he was a bit of an arsehole.'

'Yeah.' Paul breathes out and lowers himself to sit on the bottom step of the stairs. 'A normal arsehole though. Like a pain in the arse neighbour. Not a psychopathic arsehole who commits murder.'

Paul's words hurt. The feeling surprises me.

I look at my husband crouched on the stairs. His slender legs are too long and cumbersome for the bottom step. With his feet on the ground, his knees come halfway up his chest. It can't be comfortable, but he sits like a statue. I don't even know if he's breathing. I glance at the photos on the wall and remember the day Adam took them. I remember how everything changed after that day. Especially me. And I allow Paul's words to trickle off me, just as the rain ran down my window that afternoon. I'm not a psychopath, I tell myself. I'm just a little broken.

Chapter Twenty-eight

Now

Paul falls asleep on the couch sometime in the afternoon, with the help of some sleeping pills the local doctor prescribed for us both after Amelia went missing. Paul has been going through his like Smarties. Two to be taken ten minutes before bed, every night. I don't have any trouble sleeping. And Paul has been too emotionally fucked up to notice that I've been crushing my share into his water when he gets back from running, timing how long he'll sleep. The most he naps for during the day is an hour, even with the damn pills. I've had to put up with him moaning about his headaches most evenings, probably the result of a double dose every day, but his incessant grumbling will be worth it soon.

I wait until I can hear snoring before I creep up the stairs. My fingers are trembling as I lock our bedroom door behind me to finish packing. I drop gently to my knees and fish under the bed for the handle of my suitcase. I smile as my fingers curl around the soft leather. *Nearly there.* I pull but the damn thing seems to be caught on something. I tug harder, determined. Finally, it releases and I tumble backwards, falling on to my bottom with a loud thud. The suitcase follows me, crashing against my chest as it spills Amelia's and my clothes all around me. I don't move, holding my breath and waiting to hear if the noise has woken Paul. My heart is beating so loudly I'm not sure I'd hear him walk up the stairs over the noise of my pulse, banging like a tiny hammer against my temple from the inside out. I stay very still and wait. *Nothing.* The house is eerily silent. I hurry to my feet and gather all the clothes and stuff them into the suitcase as quickly as I can.

I dash across the room and open the sturdy oak window box that I bought and refurbished a couple of weeks ago. I lift out the folded ivory flannel blankets to find Paul's favourite running shirt at the bottom of the box. Exactly where I hid it. I can smell it before I even pick it up. It reeks of old sweat dried into the lining. I grab the nearest blanket and wrap the shirt in it. It masks some of the smell. I hurry back to the suitcase and lay the blanket on top of the clothes, folding the ends back over itself like an envelope so Paul's shirt won't touch any of mine or Amelia's things.

The suitcase is heavier than I was expecting and as I hoist it on to the bed I notice the huge tear in the side that dragging it out from under the bed must have caused. *Dammit.* It's gone right through the outer casing, but the lining is still intact. It should hold for now, I decide. I don't have time to pack another suitcase. I can work something out later.

There's a notepad on my bedside table but no pen. My lipstick is there, next to my reading lamp. I pop off the lid. There's something oddly satisfying about choosing Paul's favourite shade, which I've never liked.

I'm leaving you, I write in thick, chalky red lipstick. I try to sign my name but the lipstick snaps and all I manage is S U and a streak that flies off the side of the page. I snort and find myself wishing that my name began with F.

I close my suitcase and notice Paul's running clothes are draped over the end of the bed. Inspired, I kick off my shoes, shuffle out of my skinny jeans and unbutton my blouse. I pull on Paul's running pants first. I'm surprised at how snugly they fit. Just like wearing a pair of my own leggings. They're much too long but the soft material rolls up easily. His running shirt isn't as good a fit. The shoulders are ridiculously broad and it's longer than some of my dresses, but I tuck the bottom into the waistband of the pants. Lastly, I fetch his tattered baseball cap. I've tried to replace it numerous times. Whenever I was stuck for a birthday present idea or something for our anniversary. I bought him caps in an array of colours over the years. But he's too attached to this one to embrace change. He says it's his lucky charm and he's never run a race without it.

It used to be dark green – the stitching still is, but the rest is a washed-out mint now. I gather my hair on top of my head and pull the cap on. The inside is rough like sandpaper against the top of my forehead and I don't even want to think of all the years of perspiration this cap has suffered. *Gross!* I turn round and my breath catches in the back of my throat when I stare at my reflection in the mirror. I'm a miniature version of my husband. It's actually uncanny. I'm shorter and curvier, obviously, but it's fascinating how an outfit can transform you.

I reach for my suitcase again and take a deep, satisfied breath as my fingers curl around the handle. I'm just twenty-eight steps, including the stairs, away from the front door. I've counted them many times since we moved in. But the next step feels more significant than ever. I tiptoe towards my bedroom door and press my ear against it. My legs tremble as I listen to . . . nothing. Silence hangs in the air. Testing me. Warning me not to make a sound as I leave.

I turn the key and it groans in the lock like a nail scratching against steel. The painfully sharp noise pinches inside my head. I drop my suitcase and cover my ears, wondering how I got here. How I became this person. *This monster.* The moment passes, and I scramble for my suitcase again – if I pick it up quickly enough, the noise it made when it collided with the floor will be erased and I won't have made a mistake. I won't. I'm not Sue Arnold any more, I remind myself. She died the day of her twenty-first birthday. I'm Susan Warner now, and she doesn't get things wrong.

Calmer, more together, I listen for Paul one more time. Nothing. I wonder if three pills was too many this time. I didn't think about adding one extra for good measure, it just sort of happened. I guess I was nervous.

Drawn to attention by a noise from downstairs, I open the door and walk out on to the landing. I stare over the banister at the man I've had to call my husband for the last four years. My tiny cottage seems to grow to enormity as I watch Paul from a distance as he snores and groans and turns over.

Please don't fall off the couch. Please don't fall off the couch.

Within seconds his restlessness settles, and his loud snoring occupies the air. It climbs the stairs, scales the banister and reaches out to touch me. To poke me, to slap me, to pinch me. As if even in his sleep Paul is still stamping his mark on me.

Chapter Twenty-nine

Now

I don't remember the journey down the stairs. Did I run or tiptoe? Was the suitcase heavy and did it bang against the steps? Did I put it down as I opened the front door or did I keep it close to me, ready to charge through as soon as I saw daylight?

I know I definitely didn't look back. I didn't glance around the beautiful cottage I had painstakingly transformed – I knew all along it never truly belonged to me. I didn't look back at my husband as he lay ungainly on the couch – I knew he never belonged to me either. I do, however, remember pausing to take one last look at Adam's photos hanging in my hall. They have always belonged to me. Always. It hurts my heart to leave them behind, but as reality slowly dawns on my husband I know those photos will serve as a painful reminder of everything he has done. And he will see why I did the things I have done. I know Adam would be proud of me. I am proud of myself, I think, as I get into Paul's car and start the engine.

Rain wasn't forecast but delicate drops splash against the windscreen as I turn the corner on the narrow country road, leaving behind my cottage, my husband and the life I pretended to live. I don't turn on the wipers. I let the rain patter against the glass, and for a few blissful seconds I lose myself in the purr of the engine and the lull of the rain and I forget about the last few days. The last few years!

Suddenly, the day darkens as if Mother Nature takes a dramatic mood swing. Large, angry clouds rush in overhead and a loud clap of thunder rattles the sky as if two of the more aggressive clouds have collided. Torrential rain erupts, creating almost instant puddles on the side of the road. I set the wipers to their fastest, but they struggle to keep up. The windscreen begins to fog up as my hot breath hits the glass that's suddenly cold on the other side. I can barely see where I'm going. I slow down. God, I haven't seen rain like this in years. Not since . . . No! I'm not thinking about that now.

I swerve right, just missing a woman walking along the edge of the road. I slam my foot on the brake and curse the silly bitch under my breath. I roll the window down on her side as soon as I glimpse her face between the drops.

'Jesus Christ, Jenny,' I say, as the rain blows in through the window. 'What in the name of God are you doing out here?'

'The rain came out of nowhere,' she says, pulling her blouse away from her skin to show me she's soaked through.

'Where are you going? Why are you out here walking? This road is full of blind spots. I nearly didn't see you.'

'I was going to walk back to your house,' she says. 'I thought we could talk some more.'

'There's nothing more to say really.' I shake my head and my foot hovers over the accelerator.

'Are they your husband's clothes?' Jenny points a shaking finger at me, obviously recognising Paul's running gear from earlier.

'No,' I lie breezily. 'We wear matching outfits sometimes. Paul thinks it's romantic. Silly idea, really. Bit embarrassing now that you mention it.'

'Right. Sorry,' Jenny says, sounding unsure as she drags the back of her arm across her face to wipe the rain away.

A Jeep drives towards us, slowing down as it passes. The driver waves. I can't make out who it is, but it's definitely someone local and they certainly seem to know me. Or they recognise Paul's car. The rain is still blinding but I hope they take note of the driver in running gear and cap. Paul. I'm every inch Paul.

'Get in,' I say, unlocking the doors reluctantly; I don't want anyone else to see me talking to Jenny.

She opens the passenger door and gets in. I can only imagine how Paul would react if he saw her drenched arse press into his ivory leather seat.

'Jesus, it's cats and dogs out there, isn't it?' she says, and I'm relieved we're back to talking about the weather.

I shift in my seat and the leather squeaks beneath me. Paul's long running top tucked into my pants is bulky and uncomfortable around my waist. I shift back again, trying to get comfortable. Jenny's eyes are crawling all over me, like tiny, irritating insects biting my skin. I can feel frustration grow inside me, filling me up until I think it might spill over. I want to scream at her for coming back into my life. She's ruining everything.

'Jenny, this isn't going to work,' I say.

'Sorry?' Jenny tilts her head.

'Us.' I point at her and drag my finger back across the air to me. 'I can't be friends right now. The timing . . .'

'But isn't this when you need a friend most?' Jenny asks.

'Maybe in a few months when I'm in a better place I can call you. We could meet for coffee or something. Let's see how it goes, yeah?'

'Susan, I really think—'

My phone begins ringing. She cuts off mid-sentence and waits, watching me. My phone dances as it vibrates in the drinks holder under the radio, twisting and turning as if it's determined to flash its screen at Jenny. She remains silent, expecting me to answer.

I see Deacon's number flashing on the screen. But not his name – *thank God*. I don't have his number saved in my contacts, in case Paul ever went through my phone. Besides, I don't need it saved. I know Deacon's number off by heart. He's had the same number for years. Thankfully, Jenny doesn't seem to recognise it. Or she's not paying close enough attention. Finally, my phone rings out, but as I'm about to breathe a sigh of relief the ringing starts again. *For fuck's sake, Deacon.*

'Aren't you going to answer?' Jenny says. 'Seems like someone is pretty determined to get hold of you.'

The ringing is loud and demanding as it carries through the surround sound of the car speakers. I've forgotten to turn off the Bluetooth. I can't answer and have Deacon's voice fill the car.

'It's just Paul,' I lie. 'He'll call back.'

'But what if he has news from the Guards,' Jenny says. 'About your neighbour . . . or . . . about . . .'

'Well,' I smile while shaking my head, 'then he'll definitely call back.'

Another car approaches. This driver is more cautious. Crawling towards us. They honk their horn, demanding I move the nose of my car back on to my side of the road.

The ringing finally stops, but Jenny's voice instantly fills the silent void and I think my brain might explode. 'There's a farm gate up here.' Jenny leans forward and taps her nail against the windscreen. 'It's a field of horses. I was watching them for a while before the rain started. There's room to pull in off the road.'

I know the spot Jenny's talking about. Amelia loves to pat the horses and feed them grass when curiosity brings them as far as the gate, but I've no intention of pulling in and having a chat. Jenny is insane.

Honk. Honk. Honk. The approaching driver is losing patience. The phone begins to ring for a third time as Jenny continues talking about the damn horses. The combination of sounds scrapes against my mind like a rusty nail, and finally I snap.

'Enough!' I shout, pounding my fists against the steering wheel. 'That's enough.'

Jenny closes her mouth and stares at me with wide eyes. My phone seems to obey too and the ringing stops. But the driver in the oncoming car won't be silenced. *Honk. Honk. Honk.*

Jenny reaches across and her hand finds mine. She gently curls her fingers around my clenched fist.

'Shh,' she whispers. 'Deep breath. It'll be okay. It'll all be okay.'

Hoooonnnnnkkkkk.

Jesus Christ.

I shake Jenny's hand off mine and inhale deeply before I calmly re-grip the steering wheel at ten and two. I tap the accelerator gently and the car rolls forward. It picks up more speed than I intend as we descend a hill. Turning the wheel sharply, the car straightens and lines itself back up on the right side of the road. My breath catches in the back of my throat when I recognise the driver of the other car. *Larry.* The police must have released him. *Oh Jesus Christ.* I'm running out of time.

'Jenny, I have to go.' I cough to mask my panic. 'There's somewhere I need to be. Urgently.'

'Where?' she asks, raising her eyebrows, enthused with irritating curiosity.

'Excuse me?' I snap as I stop the car to let her out.

Jenny giggles. It's by far the most irritating noise to come out of her since she sat in the car. 'I don't mean to pry . . .' she says, embarrassed. 'Sorry, that must have sounded very rude. I mean, are you going into Cork city? I could really use a lift.'

'No,' I say firmly.

'Oh. I'll just get out in the village then.'

'Haven't you just come from the village?' I ask, hoping she'll mention if she got talking to anyone.

'No. I just went for a walk. It's lovely around here, very quiet and peaceful.'

I smile, relieved that she hasn't bumped into any of my nosy neighbours.

'Where's the best place to grab a taxi back to the city?' Jenny asks.

'A taxi?'

I roll my eyes and wonder if Jenny is serious. Ballyown village consists of two pubs, a corner shop and the post office. That's it. Where the hell she thinks she's going to hail a cab among the green fields is a mystery.

'Where is your car?' I ask.

'I came by train. And then a nice taxi driver dropped me off here,' she says, and I can see she's slowly realising how stupid she's been. 'I didn't think about getting back. I didn't realise it would be so remote out here.'

Jenny's hopes of us rekindling our friendship were even higher than I imagined. *Wow!* She must have thought I'd invite her in as a guest in my home. Or at least chauffeur her back to the train station like a good friend after we'd spent the afternoon catching up. *Poor deluded cow.* And it kills me that I'll have to indulge her fairy-tale notion, for a little while at least. I can't very well drive away and leave her roaming around Ballyown after I've gone.

'C'mon.' I try to sound breezy as I flash a huge smile. 'I'll take care of you.'

Chapter Thirty

THEN

My degree took four years to complete. I've worked hard to earn the pieces of paper that confirm I know my shit, and I'm exhausted after four long years of study. Yet the relief of finally finishing and moving on doesn't come.

Unsurprisingly, my mother fails to show up at my graduation. It's three days later before she calls. I allow two missed calls and a grovelling voicemail before I finally answer. She tells me that she has arranged to have my certificates framed and that they will arrive by courier soon.

'I hope you like them, sweetheart,' she says, and I swear I can hear her smiling. 'Be sure to let me know when they arrive safely, won't you?'

'Thank you,' I say, while imagining shoving the frames under my bed or tossing them into the back of the wardrobe, never to see them again.

'I'm so sorry I couldn't be there, Sue,' she says. 'You do understand, don't you?'

'Yes. Yes, of course I do,' I lie.

She goes on to reiterate for the umpteenth time how it would be too emotionally distressing to set foot on the university grounds where Adam was knocked down. 'It would bring it all back, Sue,' she says.

I wonder if she realises that I spend as much time on campus as possible since Adam died, and only leave to return to my little flat right around the corner. *It doesn't matter.*

The conversation drifts towards evening walks in vineyards and descriptions of the new friends my mother is making among the expat community in Provence. I shake my head in disbelief at her wonderful life that seems a million miles from the hell I'm living. My mother is moving on, maybe even healing. I wonder if it's possible to resent anyone more than I resent her right now. And then I remember Paul. I hate him!

'Goodbye, sweetheart,' my mother says. 'I'll call again soon.'

I hang up.

I skip the graduation after-party, and blow off the week in Spain that I've been planning with my classmates since before Christmas. They tell me how disappointed they are and that we'll catch up soon. It'll never happen, I know that. We'll drift our separate ways now that college is over, but we'll still text awkwardly from time to time and make plans that none of us will keep, until we eventually fade out of each other's lives.

I'm content to settle for DVD box set marathons, popcorn and endless days of unwashed hair and lounging around in my jammies. Of course, Jenny remains a steadfast friend and drops by every so often. She tries to pretend they're casual visits because she has no better plans but I can see the concern for me in her eyes. It's sweet, really. And wasted. Jenny fills me in on the mundane aspects of day-to-day married life. Things like how complicated the paperwork for a mortgage application is. And what vegetables are on special offer in the local Tesco. She never tells me that after a year of trying she can't fall pregnant and that it's eating her up inside. She never tells me that the pressure is putting a strain on her marriage. She never tells me that she's jealous of how close Deacon and I have become. And she absolutely never tells me that she's gone from politely asking him not to spend time with me to expressly forbidding him from seeing me. But she doesn't have to, Deacon has already confided in me when we meet in secret.

Most of the summer goes by this way. I shower when I just can't cope with how greasy my hair is, or when I can't remember the last time I changed my socks. Without Adam here to nag me I rarely clean and there's a funny smell coming from the kitchen. I suspect there's mould growing on an uneaten crust in one of the takeaway pizza boxes stacked in the corner. I keep meaning to throw them out. Jenny's mentioned the smell a couple of times, and I've caught her in the kitchen trying to wash up when she thinks I'm distracted and engrossed in something on the telly. The last time she called over she actually brought rubber gloves, antibacterial spray and disposable cloths. I didn't even bother to pretend to be embarrassed. I wasn't. It's not that I enjoy living in squalor. *Who would?* I just don't care enough about living at all to actively do something about the mess.

I reach lower days over the summer. There are days on end of eating beans on toast for breakfast, lunch and dinner. The dishes are stacked in the sink to toppling point and I rarely watch telly, I prefer simply staring into space. One particularly low afternoon, a light knock on my door catches my attention. I don't answer. I know who's on the other side and I'm in no mood to deal with Jenny today. I also know she won't give up. The knocking grows louder and I turn up the television. There's something on the news about a hit and run in West Kerry. A teenage boy is critically injured and the Gardaí are looking for witnesses. I shake my head and stand up.

'Poor bastard,' I say towards the telly, as if anyone can hear me.

The door rattles as Jenny's knocking grows increasingly more aggressive.

'All right, all right,' I grumble. 'I'm coming. Hold your horses.'

I unlock the door and pull the handle down. I let it swing open by itself. I'm about to drag my moping arse back to the couch when I'm caught off guard by the state of Jenny standing in front of me. The apples of her cheeks are red and swollen and punctuated with long streaks of black mascara. More mascara clumps her eyelashes together where she's obviously been rubbing her eyes. Her shoulders are shaking and she can barely draw her breath.

'Shh,' I whisper as I drape my arm over her shoulder and usher her inside.

My other hand drags the door behind us closed with a loud bang.

I switch off the television and we sit on the couch for a long time. The only sound is the odd sniffle and sob from Jenny.

'Deacon doesn't want children,' she finally manages to cry between exhausted breaths.

'Not ever?' I say, surprised he finally told her.

'Not ever,' she sobs.

I don't say anything more. What is there to say? There's no point telling her it will be all right. It clearly won't.

Finally, when Jenny is all cried out she lifts her head off my shoulder and looks me in the eye. 'Look at us,' she says, and I hear a sudden anger in her voice. 'Look at the state of us.'

'The state of us?' I echo.

'What's happened to us, Susan? We didn't deserve this life.'

I look into the eyes of my friend, who I've never known as anything other than much too loud and needy. I look around at the revolting filth of my flat. I think about my close to non-existent relationship with my mother and about how different it would all be if Adam was still here.

'No one deserves this life, Jenny,' I say.

She drops her head back on to my shoulder and I hold her while she cries herself to sleep. When she's lightly snoring I slip out from under her, pop her head on a cushion and cover her with a blanket.

Jenny won't ever know it but her simple sentence has offered me more clarity than all the time in a bereavement group ever could. I set about cleaning up. My flat, my career, my future. Because Jenny is so very right. No one deserves this life – except Paul Warner. He deserves so much more than he got. *And everyone should get what they deserve.*

Chapter Thirty-one

THEN

By the time September comes, Deacon and Jenny's marriage is at rock bottom. And when they finally separate Jenny becomes as prominent in my life as before. It takes some time, but she slowly returns to her usual loud, bubbly self. Clearly marriage never suited her. Deacon also reverts to his old ways. He's quiet, pensive and lets Jenny walk all over him when it comes to taking the house and half of everything he's worth. I'm surprised by how much I resent her for it, but I never let on.

The irony of being the most together out of the three of us isn't wasted on me, and it reinforces my focus on the future as I plan ahead.

I didn't make a conscious decision to remain a student. It seemed to happen organically. My only disappointment is that I spent the entire summer torturing myself when the answer should have been there all along. Logically, when it comes to studying my next subject, four years feels like the appropriate benchmark. I won't have the privilege of lectures to support me this time, but that will balance out without the distraction of student nights out and binge drinking. There'll be no textbooks or tests this time. A crash course in revenge is very much independent work. I intend to get an A.

The first thing I do is buy myself a calendar and some coloured markers. Cheap ones from the Euro Shop in bright colours. I hang the calendar in the kitchenette next to the cooker, so I can see it often, and I keep the markers on top of the microwave nearby. I did the exact same thing four years ago when Adam and I started college. The calendar was Adam's suggestion. He thought it might help me become organised. It didn't work because I never actually bothered to fill that one in. This time, however, I'm much more dedicated to my studies from the get-go. I enjoy filling in the square boxes with tasks. I start with light blue: Monday, every week – call Mam and make small talk for fifteen to twenty minutes, before hanging up and feeling shit about the conversation until next week. Green marker is next. These days are more haphazard: cinema or drinks with friends – seem normal and be seen in public with friends! Orange is 'find a job' day. Rent is crippling me, especially since I'm now paying Adam's share too and my grant money is quickly running out. Yellow is my least favourite colour, but there are only four markers in the packet, so my choice was limited. It seems to make ironic sense that yellow marks 'clean the flat' day. If only Adam could see the place now. It's spotless and there's a subtle hint of fig and sandalwood from the scented candles I regularly pick up on special offer in the Euro Shop. I've even managed to get the hair dye stain out of the sitting room carpet with a mix of baking soda and vinegar.

I save the red marker for last. Red is for 'Paul' days. There is a lot of red on the calendar.

There is one task I don't mark on the calendar. No colour would ever be strong enough to highlight such a momentous milestone. Besides, I don't just box up all of Adam's things in an afternoon as if he's moving out. It happens organically over time. Sometimes I calmly drop some of his stuff into the cardboard box I've placed in the centre of his bed and get on with the rest of my day. Other times I put something of his in, only to fetch it back out immediately, taking out two or three other items along with it. Things I have no recollection of adding in the first place. I cry for a while, holding his stuff close to me. Later, when I'm exhausted and all cried out, I put them all back in the box. This happens a lot.

Finally, one day as I'm teaching myself to tolerate the bitter taste of chilled white wine from a crystal glass with my pinkie raised like a lady, my eyes wander around the flat and I realise that I've boxed up the last of Adam's things. I drop the glass. Wine splashes halfway up the height of the cupboards but I ignore the mess and hurry into Adam's room.

I don't look inside the box before I close it and use a whole roll of sticky tape to secure the lid. I pick up the box. It's cumbersome and my arms can't seem to settle on where to hold – underneath or around the sides. Finally, I slide one arm under and the other shifts from the side to the top and back every so often to keep the box tucked against my chest. It's certainly much bigger in my arms than it looked on the bed and I need to tilt my head towards the ceiling so I can see over the top. I don't bother to change out of my jeans, which have a large, sticky stain streaked down the leg from the wine, before I leave my flat and walk to the post office around the corner.

By the time I reach the post office my back is sore and I have a crick in my neck. It's hard to pull open the door and keep hold of the box but I manage. Inside is much smaller than I expected. It's narrow and cramped like the kitchenette in my flat. It smells of cardboard and deep, musty perfume. A lady sits behind thick glass at the far end and I let the door close behind me before I shuffle towards her.

'Hello,' she says, sliding the security glass all the way back as she eyes up my large box.

I set the box down on the countertop; unsurprisingly, it won't fit through the gap in the glass. My eyes begin to water and my chest is tight. The post office seems to be shrinking.

'Not to worry,' the lady says, standing up from her swivel chair to open a glass door I didn't notice before now at the side of her cubicle. 'I can take it in this way,' she explains as she walks around to me. 'Umph,' she groans, lifting the box into her arms and settling it on her hip as if it is a small child. 'This is going to be an expensive one to ship, I'm afraid. Is it going far?' the woman behind the counter says.

'Provence,' I say.

'Oh, a beautiful place,' she says. 'Do you visit often?'

My eyes are burning now but I can't blink and send tears trickling down my cheeks. I don't want to admit I've never been to France.

The lady shuffles back behind the counter, carrying the box expertly. I watch as her long, polished, red nails fan each side of the cardboard. The hairs on the back of my neck stand like hundreds of sharp, pointed splinters against my skin and an uneasy shiver runs from my head to my toes as she continues to touch the box that sums up my brother's life. I think I hate this woman. This friendly, helpful woman with chubby fingers and long nails taking my brother's memories away from me. I imagine lunging forward and wrapping my hands tightly around her neck and shaking her until she lets go.

A queue is forming behind me. There's a man with a letter in his hand. I can feel his hot breath puff out of him and climb across the air to fall on to the back of my head. My skin crawls. Behind him there's a woman with a little boy swinging around her leg. He's screeching and demanding ice cream.

The woman behind the counter is asking me questions. The man is huffing and puffing. The mother is pointing her finger and talking to the little boy, who is now shouting and running around. The tiny post office is hot and stuffy and so full of noise, and the inside of my head is hot and stuffy and so full of noise.

I run my hands through my hair and take some deep breaths. They don't help. It's getting louder and louder. My face is burning. My eyes are stinging. The noise is pounding inside my head like a hammer attacking my skull from the inside out.

'Shh,' I hiss through gritted teeth. 'That's enough now. Enough.'

The little boy stops running. He tilts his head back and looks up at me with piggy eyes. I wonder if he's about to cry. I don't expect him to jam his hands on to his little hips and stick his tongue out at me before running towards his mother to hide safely behind her leg.

'Ice cream. Ice cream. Ice cream,' he chants.

'Stop it,' I snap, turning around and bending down to his level. I wag an angry finger. 'You're a bold boy,' I scowl. 'You don't deserve ice cream.'

The mother scoops her son into her arms and her startled eyes peer at me over his shoulder.

'Jesus. Relax, love,' the man behind me says. 'That was a bit uncalled for.'

The loud, annoying child begins to cry and nuzzles his head into the crook of his mother's neck. His sobbing is shrill and pierces my brain.

I take a deep breath and smile apologetically. My face stings with embarrassment. I don't know where the anger came from. I've never lashed out at a child before. I want to be calm and say something reassuring or polite but temper still swells inside me like the sea after a storm and I'm afraid to open my mouth in case more venomous words spill out. I'm breathing heavily and I'm twitching. I don't doubt it's noticeable. The mother takes a step back. And another. Her eyes locked on mine. I stare back. She's trying to be assertive and stand her ground but as she takes a third step back before turning to face the door I know I've scared her.

'Sweetie, c'mon,' she says, cuddling her son and rubbing her hand up and down his back as if he's an infant with colic. 'Let's go get some ice cream. Did that crazy girl scare you? Did she, huh?'

'Let me get that for you,' the man says, hurrying towards the door to pull it open for her.

The man, the mother and the little boy stand outside the glass door and chat. The little boy is running around again but at least I can't hear him screaming any more. The man and the mother point back inside and shake their heads. They're talking about me. *I shouldn't have come here. Not today. Not ever. This was a mistake.*

'Well, thank goodness for that,' the lady behind the counter finally says, breaking the overwhelming silence. 'The little shit, God forgive my language, and his mother come in here twice a week and he's always running around and shouting. He's as bold as brass, he is. I'm glad someone finally gave him a talking-to. Heaven knows his mother never would. How she puts up with that awful behaviour I'll never know.'

'That's why I'm never having kids,' I say.

The lady laughs, but I wasn't joking. I can't think of anything I would hate more than becoming a mother.

'Ah, give it time,' she smiles. 'Someday you'll meet a lovely fellow and babies will be all you can think about.'

I scrunch my nose in response. 'How much for airmail?'

She places the box on a large weighing scale. Her face is expressionless as she leans forward and squints, trying to read the numbers.

'How much?' I ask again, twitching. I'm behind on this month's rent and I haven't done a food shop in a week.

The lady leaves the box and walks out from behind the counter.

'Are you all right?' she says, placing her hand on my shoulder.

I wince and back away. My hand reaches for my shoulder and I rub it as if she's hurt me.

'Sorry,' she blushes, realising she's made me uncomfortable. 'It's just . . .' She pauses, finding the right words. '. . . you seem a little pale. Do you need to sit down?'

'Is this going to take much longer?' I say.

She walks back behind the counter and doesn't make eye contact again. I like it better this way.

I hand over the last note in my wallet and watch as she takes the brown, square box that sums up my brother's life and stacks it among some smaller boxes ready for collection.

'It should arrive in Provence in two to three days,' she says despondently.

'Thank you,' I say, blinking away tears.

Chapter Thirty-two

THEN

Returning home to a flat with no trace of Adam is harder than I imagined it would be. The door seems to whisper his name as it creaks open. Stepping inside, the walls shrink and wrap around me like Adam's strong arms holding me. I flop on to the couch, exhausted. I grab a cushion and tuck it against my chest as I bring my knees up and rock back and forth. I take slow, deep breaths, trying to soothe my aching heart, but it doesn't help. The cushion smells so distinctively like my brother, probably from all the times he fell asleep on the couch after a night out and slept with his face mashed into the fluffy fabric. Finally, the tears that I've been holding back all day fall heavy and fast down my cheeks, and it feels good to let them flow. I fall in and out of fitful sleep. Sometimes I topple to one side and wake up with my neck twisted in an uncomfortable direction or find my arm has gone numb for the weight of my body flopping on top of it and pinning it against the couch. Other times the cushion has fallen out of my grasp. I quickly retrieve it and inhale sharply like a junkie needing her fix.

I don't leave my flat for two weeks after that. I run out of food after the first four days, but I don't feel hunger for another ten. By the time I finally leave the flat I'm half a stone lighter, possibly anaemic and most certainly no longer me.

By the time my birthday rolls around I've gone through a few calendars. I worked as a waitress and barmaid before finally finding work in my own field as a bereavement counsellor for a small charity. My weekly calls with my mother gradually became monthly, then biannual, then they fizzled out completely last year. I've made new friends and lost old ones.

Losing Jenny as a friend stung more than I expected it to. We were two peas in a pod when we first met. Both so consumed with grief and so broken. But gradually Jenny began to heal; she started to say things like 'time helps' or 'it gets easier' and other equally unhelpful bullshit. She was no good to me any more. I had to move my attention to Deacon. Jenny blames me for stealing her husband away from her. It irritates me that she doesn't see that it's all her fault. She has no one to blame but herself.

Thankfully, one thing remained constant: my study of Paul Warner. For ages I kept note of what coffee he drank. What he ate for lunch. Who he ate lunch with. Smart girls, always. He liked to surround himself with educated, intelligent women. He had male friends too. Some very attractive in their dapper suits. But Paul still stood out among them as better-looking, and I hated him even more for it.

I took lots of photos, with the only thing of Adam's I kept – his camera. It took me a while to figure out its multitude of buttons and settings, but the zoom lenses proved immensely useful.

Sometimes I'd follow Paul home after work. Sometimes I wouldn't bother. Sometimes I'd sit alone in a restaurant a few tables away as he ate a romantic dinner with a date. If he took her back to his apartment, he was unknowingly bringing me and Adam's camera too. Usually he would draw the curtains, and what he and his date got up to would be left to the confines of my imagination. Occasionally, however, he'd be so caught up in the passion of the moment that he'd forget to close the curtains, and I'd watch as he made love to some girl from his office or someone he'd met in The Sugary Spoon. Those intimate moments were when I'd study him most closely. I'd lie on my bed and scrutinise the photos for hours. I'd learn every little move that triggered a smile. How he liked nails dragged gently across his chest. Or how a tiny bite on his bottom lip almost always made him orgasm. When I was finally satisfied that I knew Paul Warner better than he knew himself, all that was left was for him to meet his perfect match. Me.

Change was never going to be easy. I'd spent twenty-one years sure of who I was and where I belonged. I was a twin sister. A loving daughter. A good friend. A confident tomboy. And I loved being me. When I was little I'd climb trees with my brother for hours on end. Sometimes we'd fall and there would be tears. Adam's. Never mine. I wasn't a crier. My mother would tend to his grazed knees and elbows lovingly, and then tell me to be more careful. She'd warn me that my brother wasn't as tough as me and that I needed to take care of him. I would nod and promise that I would. Then she'd smile and gather us into her arms, hug us tight and tell us that she loved us equally, no matter what. I would later learn that statement wasn't entirely true, but at the time I loved to hear the happiness in her voice and I loved her warm hugs.

Adam's death brought uncertainty and strain to my relationship with my mother. Maybe it was inevitable that I would change. But not like this. Reinventing myself to fit a certain mould was undeniably more difficult than I'd anticipated. But I was determined to become someone Paul Warner would notice.

However, I slowly embraced the new me. It turned out I quite liked her. Smart, tailored clothes that aren't as expensive as they look suited me. They showed off my petite frame and didn't swamp me the way baggy jeans and black T-shirts with the name of my favourite heavy metal band printed across the front used to. It broke my heart to cut my long, straight hair into a sensible bob, but it instantly made me look smarter. Older too, but that wasn't really a negative. My drastic makeover piqued interest from some friends, but it wasn't unreasonable to think that it was the right time in my life to put my formative years behind me and embrace a new, more mature look. I even received the odd compliment, which was nice – but unnecessary.

Trying to match the confidence of my look with my personality took a little more work. And taking an interest in boring stuff like politics, current affairs and cookery nearly killed me. But I knew it was all necessary. Looking the part would only get me so far. When I managed to catch Paul's attention I would need something to talk to him about.

It was obvious early on that he was a perfectionist. His choice of career as an accountant was my first clue. And his impeccable manners. His pleases and thank yous were always on point ordering his coffee, and he'd never miss an opportunity to hold the door open for an elderly lady or a mother pushing a buggy. He was sporty too. I could tell. His suits hugged his body perfectly. His car was the only deviation I could find from his sensible lifestyle. He drove a grossly overpriced coupé. Complete with a flashy grid, loud exhaust and leather interior. On the days when I had doubts, the days when I felt my plan was too extreme or too cruel, I would look at his flashy car parked outside his apartment or office or the coffee shop and I would think about how unfair it is that not only is Paul behind the wheel of a car again, but he is living a life of luxury that most people can only dream of. And I would decide that my plan wasn't nearly cruel enough.

Although I spent years wishing Paul Warner dead, I'm never going to kill him. He doesn't deserve the peace that comes with death – that's far too lenient a sentence for what he's done. Paul needs to go to hell for his sins. No judge in a courtroom will send him there, but I will.

I know hell, I've been there. I'm still there. Hell is waking up in the middle of the night exhausted but unable to sleep because the pain of your broken heart keeps you awake. Hell is profound loneliness in a room full of people because the only person you want there is dead. Hell is no more hugs, no more giggles, no more anything. Hell is what Paul Warner inflicted upon me when he ran my brother over. Hell is missing the person you love most in the world and knowing they will never come back. Paul needs to lose the most important person in his life. And that person needs to be me.

Chapter Thirty-three

Now

The village is pretty today. The heavy rain has eased off and the sky is clearing. The wet road shimmers under the shining sun like a beautiful watercolour painting. It would make a stunning postcard, and I think if Adam was here he would jump out of the car with his camera and happily snap panoramic shots.

People are starting to emerge from the shelter of houses and the pub. It's fascinating to watch the little village come to life again after the rain.

'Just let me out anywhere along here,' Jenny says, tapping her nail against the window to point at the footpath.

One of my elderly neighbours passes by. Her boisterous dog drags her forward as she struggles to keep hold of his lead.

'Afternoon, Paul,' I hear her shout as she passes.

Jenny laughs. 'Did that old lady just think you were Paul?'

I smile, delighted. 'I guess so.'

'Susan, you really need to get some decent running gear,' Jenny says. 'You and Paul are like twins.'

My smile flatlines.

'Oh Susan.' Jenny twists in her seat to turn towards me. 'I'm really sorry. I didn't mean to mention twins. I just wasn't thinking.'

'It's okay,' I say. 'I know it was just a joke.'

She blushes. 'But it wasn't funny.'

'It's fine, honestly, Jenny. Just because Adam and I were twins doesn't mean you can't make a harmless joke.'

'Okay,' she nods, unsure.

'As I told you earlier, I've changed. Grown up. I still miss Adam. Every day. But I'm not as sensitive as I used to be.'

'Good,' Jenny says. 'That's good. Time heals, I suppose.'

I want to open the door and shove her out face first. But instead I nod and drive on, mumbling something about maturity.

Within a minute or so we've passed through the village and come out the other side on to a road as winding and narrow as the one I live on.

'Oh Susan,' Jenny says, staring out the window at the vast green fields and tall trees. 'I think we've gone too far. I needed to get out back there. I'll never hail a taxi out here.'

'I told you I'd take care of you,' I say.

Her breath quickens and for a moment I think she's afraid of me. I ease my foot off the accelerator and allow the car to slow a little.

'You do want me to take care of you, don't you?' I ask.

She nods.

I press down on the accelerator again and we pick up speed. Jenny is unusually quiet, and I think it's slowly dawning on her that she really doesn't know me any more. I think she's realising that maybe she never knew me at all.

Minutes of silence later we come to a crossroads and merge with a main road. Jenny seems to relax as cars whizz by and we're not as isolated and alone.

'Why didn't you tell me you remembered Paul from that party?' I ask, as a huge truck rattles past us in the outside lane.

Jenny squirms. 'I didn't think I did, not really.'

I snort and my grip on the steering wheel tightens until my knuckles whiten. 'Well, it certainly seemed to ring a bell earlier. Your cheeks were bright red when he mentioned the fountain,' I say through gritted teeth. 'You told me you were so drunk you couldn't remember a thing from that night.'

'I *was* drunk.' She shrugs.

'In all the time I confided in you about how much I hated him, how much he ruined my life, it never once came into your head to say, "Oh, remember that time I was his vomit buddy at a party?"'

'It was a chance encounter, Susan,' Jenny says. 'You know that. I didn't know the terrible things he'd been saying about Adam. About you, until you told me. I didn't even remember what he looked like until I saw him at the courthouse on the day of his conviction.'

'Well, he remembers you,' I snap. 'Great. That's just fucking great.'

'Susan, I'm sorry. I should have told you,' Jenny says.

'Yes,' I snap. 'You should have.'

'But I didn't know he'd be a constant in your life. You have to admit it's strange how it worked out. You ending up married to a guy you despised a few years back. It's fascinating, really,' Jenny snorts, and I'm almost certain she's being sarcastic. 'I mean, I forgot him, but you vowed to spend the rest of your life with him.'

Silence falls over us and the only sound is the purr of the engine as Paul's car glides along the motorway.

'Let's just hope he doesn't do any digging and discover how we *really* met,' I say, the past playing over in my mind. 'And Deacon too. Fuck, this is such a mess.'

'Deacon?' Jenny's voice is shrill and hurts my already aching brain. 'What does Deacon have to do with anything?'

'Nothing,' I back-pedal, cursing myself for thinking out loud. 'He has nothing to do with anything. Just that we all used to be friends because Adam died, that's all.'

'Susan?' Jenny says, turning to glare at me.

I can sense her disapproving expression from the corner of my eye but I don't take my concentration off the road.

'Susan.' Jenny's voice wobbles as a slow, creeping realisation obviously dawns on her. 'Susan, what have you done?'

Chapter Thirty-four

Now

Jenny is worryingly pensive for the rest of the journey, and by the time we reach the city half an hour later I suspect she's twitchy and no doubt riddled with questions. There's ample parking outside the train station, but I can't pull in and risk being spotted by a security camera. All my good work dressing up as Paul and being noticed by my neighbours would be undone by my face getting caught on camera now. I pass the station and head for a narrow side street. I leave the engine running as I pull up next to the footpath.

'We're here,' I say firmly, demanding Jenny's attention.

'Why have we stopped here?' she asks, staring out the window.

'So you can get out. Goodbye, Jenny.'

'But the train station is way back there.' She looks confused.

'I'm going this way,' I lie. 'I told you I had somewhere I need to be.' She reaches for the door handle.

'Susan . . . I just . . .' she begins, her voice cracking and laced with emotion. 'I really did just want to help.'

'I know,' I say, believing her.

'But so much has changed,' she says, shaking her head. 'Especially you. Your house, this car, your life, it just doesn't seem to fit the person I knew.'

My phone begins ringing again. I reach forward but my seatbelt objects. Jenny's fingers get there first, and I hold my breath as she glances at the screen. A sparkle of recognition dances in her eyes. She knows it's Deacon's number. *Dammit.*

'Please,' I say, stretching out my hand.

Jenny inhales sharply and places the phone in my hand.

I hit the reject button and throw the phone into the door pocket on my side of the car. Jenny watches me with her jaw gaping.

'There's a train in ten minutes,' I say. 'I checked the timetable.'

'Who was calling you?' she asks.

'There isn't another train for over an hour. If you miss this one you'll have to wait around on the platform.'

'Is it Deacon?' she asks.

'Why bother asking a question you already know the answer to?'

'Are you sleeping with him?' Jenny says, her voice cracking as she tries to assert herself.

'Oh for fuck's sake, not this bullshit again,' I groan.

'Well, how else do you explain your weird behaviour since I got here? You're so jumpy and stressed out. You clearly don't want me anywhere near Paul in case I open my big mouth and expose you.'

Jenny has misconstrued the situation so badly it's laughable. And to think I was actually worried that she had me figured out. I guess that's laughable too.

'Just tell me, Susan.' Tears stream down her cheeks and I realise she's never got over Deacon. She's still in love with him. *If only he knew.*

I smirk. I don't mean to, it just sort of happens when I remember how easy it is to manipulate Jenny. She might dress better nowadays and appear a little more reserved and less boisterous but she's still the same insecure girl I met at the bereavement group all those years ago.

'Oh God.' Her hand covers her mouth. 'You're not even going to deny it any more, are you? I swear, Susan, if you tell me you've slept with him, I'll never forgive you. You'll never see me again. Missing child or no missing child, I can't be a part of this.'

'Yes,' I say firmly. 'I am sleeping with Deacon.'

Jenny gulps and I can almost see the vicious lie slice her heart in half.

'I knew it.' She begins to cry. 'I *always* knew it, really. I tried to tell myself I was crazy, but I could see the hold you had over Deacon. You could ask him to do anything for you and he would do it. Anything.'

'What can I say, Jenny?' I throw my hands in the air in mock surrender.

She can't bring herself to look at me and I watch with bated breath as her fingers reach for the door handle again. I can't believe I didn't think of this simple solution to get rid of her sooner.

'All these years,' she cries, her grip on the handle tightening. 'Have you been together all this time?'

I don't know what to say. She's obviously built up this story in her head and I don't want to deviate from whatever she's convinced herself of and set her off asking more questions. She might never get out of the damn car.

'Susan, answer me,' she snaps, her voice much too loud for the confines of Paul's compact car.

'Jenny, you really need to go home now,' I say. 'And take the memories of the person I was with you. I'm not that girl any more, and I never will be again. You need to go home and never come back. Do you understand?'

'Is that a threat?'

'No.' I glare at her through impatient eyes. 'That's me asking nicely.'

'I can't believe you,' she sniffs as she wipes her teary eyes with the back of her hand. 'You're not even going to try to defend yourself.'

I pull a face.

'Or apologise,' she shouts.

'I'm sorry,' I say. 'Now will you please get out?'

'Don't.' Jenny points a finger at me. 'Don't you dare bloody say that unless you mean it.'

I groan inwardly. I don't have time for this drama.

'You know what?' Jenny says. 'It's Paul I feel sorry for. He has no idea who he's married to, does he?'

My mind is racing. Jenny is scratching at the surface of the truth but her judgement is so clouded by her failed marriage.

'I can see your suitcase in the back of the car, Susan,' Jenny says.

I glance over my shoulder at the suitcase with a huge tear in the side. One of Amelia's bright dresses is poking out. My heart races.

'I'm not stupid, I know you're leaving Paul,' she says. 'What I don't understand is why you married him in the first place. But I'm going to find out, Susan. Mark my words.'

A growl forms somewhere in the back of my throat and explodes past my lips. It's animalistic and scrapes my throat as it passes. 'Jenny. No. Please, please. I'm begging you. Go home. Please go home.'

'No, Susan,' she says confidently. 'You can't get rid of me this time.'

'Oh Jenny,' I say, a tear finding its way to the corner of my eye. 'I really wish you hadn't said that.'

Chapter Thirty-five

Now

The smell of greasy chip oil and battered fish is repulsive as I hurry up the concrete steps leading to the dingy flat.

'Deacon,' I shout from the corridor, not caring if the guy in the flat across the way hears me. 'We have to go. We have to get out of here.'

My voice carries across the corridor and bounces off the wall and comes back to hit me like a slap across the face.

'Open the door. Open the door,' I say, breathless as I reach the top step.

I pound my fist against the door. It rattles and a shard of timber flakes free and drills into the fleshy part at the base of my palm. The pain is sharp and sudden and makes me angrier. I pound harder.

'Open the fucking door, Deacon,' I shout.

Finally, the door creaks open and Deacon's head appears in the gap.

'Where have you been?' he asks.

'Dealing with your ex-wife,' I snap, barging inside and almost knocking him over.

'Jenny?' he gasps, closing the door behind me. 'Where is she? Is she here? Oh God, that's all we need. I told you this was too risky. I knew we'd never get away with it. What does she know?'

'Nothing,' I say.

Deacon clasps his hands on top of his head as he exhales sharply. 'You know she'll just keep digging until she finds something. Fuck, this is a mess. I knew we should have left sooner. I told you. I bloody told you, didn't I?'

'Deacon,' I snap. 'Get a grip. I've taken care of everything.'

'Everything except Amelia.' He drops his hands by his sides and his worried eyes glance towards the bedroom. 'She's sick.'

'Okay, we'll get her some ibuprofen on the way to the ferry,' I say. 'But we need to get going now. Paul is going to come looking for us soon.'

'What?' Deacon shakes his head. 'We can't take her on a boat now. She's burning up. She needs a doctor. I've been trying to call you all day, but you wouldn't answer.'

'I know,' I say. 'Jenny recognised your number on my phone. I told you not to call.'

'I didn't know what else to do.'

'You shouldn't have called,' I say, cracking under the pressure.

'Deeeeeccccaaaan,' Amelia begins to cry. 'Deeeeeeccccccaaaaan.'

I try to ignore the sting in my gut hearing my little girl cry out to Deacon the way she would usually call to me when she's feeling unwell. I barge past him and hurry into the bedroom.

The curtains are drawn on the poky window, but daylight still brightens the room. Amelia is lying in the centre of the mattress. She's barely moving. Her fair skin is tinged greyish blue and her eyes are closed. Her angelic face is flushed and beads of perspiration gather on her forehead like morning dew on the grass. And her long, curly hair is damp and matted against her head.

'Christ,' I say, hurrying over to her. 'Oh Amelia.'

I scoop her into my arms and her tiny body rests against my chest like a furnace.

'What happened?' I ask, whipping my neck around to glare at Deacon. 'How did you let her get so sick? I trusted you.'

Amelia groans and cries.

'It's all right, sweetheart,' I say. 'Mammy's here now. It's all right.'

I hurry into the lounge and lay her on the couch. Her eyes remain closed and her crying is faint and whisper-like.

'We need to call an ambulance,' Deacon says, holding his phone in his hand.

'Don't you dare,' I growl.

'But, Susan, look at her,' Deacon says. 'Aren't you worried?'

'Worried?' I repeat, instantly taking offence at his question. 'Of course I'm bloody worried. I'm exhausted and scared, and Jenny showing up out of the blue has thrown me completely. But we can't lose our nerve now. Not after coming this far.'

Amelia whimpers again and Deacon rushes into the kitchen, runs a cloth under the tap and hurries back.

'Here, place this on her forehead,' he says.

I press the cool, damp cloth against Amelia's clammy skin. I recognise the pattern on the cloth. It's the sleeve of the T-shirt Deacon was wearing yesterday. He must have ripped it up to make cloths.

Amelia flinches under the coolness of the fabric but she settles quickly.

'It should cool her,' Deacon says. 'I've been trying to bring her fever down as best I can all night, but she's just getting sicker and sicker.'

Deacon's phone is still in his hand and I know his fingers are hovering over 999.

'I want to go home,' Amelia murmurs, and the five simple words leave her exhausted and drained.

'It's not too late,' Deacon says. 'We can take her to the hospital. I'll take full responsibility. I'll say I snatched her or something.'

'Will you listen to yourself?' I snap. 'It doesn't work like that and you know it. As soon as you walk through those hospital doors you'd be arrested. Paul would get Amelia back and live happily ever after and all of this would have been for nothing. For nothing, Deacon. Are you listening to me?'

Deacon shakes his head and he's scaring me. I can usually control him with carefully selected words and firm logic, but fear has a much stronger grip on him now than I do. I see the way he looks at Amelia. He never looked at Jenny that way. Or me. I imagine this is the way he looked at his daughter. It's a look of unconditional love, and I slowly realise that Jenny and I never even came close to the way he loves Kerri-Ann or Amelia.

Amelia twists ever so slightly and I catch a glimpse of her foot out of the corner of my eye. Her heel is red and swollen and greenish-yellow pus is building up around the cut I inflicted. Guilt washes over me.

Oh my God, what have I done?

'It's an infection,' I say. 'Look.' I point to Amelia's foot.

Deacon moves closer. He touches her ankle and tries to turn her heel towards him for a better look, but she screams and pulls away.

'Oh Jesus.' He jumps back. 'What happened? I don't understand. She was fine. How could she have hurt herself that badly?'

Deacon straightens and a sudden cloud of darkness gathers in his expression. His eyes narrow and he glares at me.

'What did you do?' he hisses.

'Nothing,' I lie. 'She must have taken a fall. Kids fall all the time, don't they?'

'She hasn't fallen.' Deacon's expression grows darker. 'I haven't let her out of my sight . . .' He pauses and stares me down. 'Except when she was with you.'

I've never seen him so assertive. It's really rather attractive.

'Calm down,' I say. 'Panicking isn't going to help anyone. Least of all Amelia. Stay here and keep cooling her with damp cloths. I'm going to go and get something from the pharmacy to bring her fever down. She'll be right as rain in a couple of hours. Trust me. Kids bounce back so quickly, it's nothing to worry about.'

Deacon doesn't reply but his glare burns into me.

'Be packed and ready to leave as soon as I get back,' I say. 'We *are* catching that ferry.'

Chapter Thirty-six

Now

Knock. Knock. Knock.

Someone's at the door of the flat. I physically jump.

'Who the hell is that?' I whip my neck round, hoping to find a clue in Deacon's face, as if he can see through the door any better than me.

Deacon shakes his head, his eyes wide and unsure.

Knock. Knock. Knock.

A shiver trickles down my spine.

'Susan, I know you're in there.' Jenny's voice carries through the flat door.

Fuck!

Deacon scoops Amelia into his arms, already a step ahead of me.

'Get her out of here,' I whisper.

He hurries to the bedroom.

'Susan, I'm not kidding around,' Jenny shouts. 'Open this door right now or so help me God . . .'

I take a deep breath, count backwards from three and open the door just as Jenny is about to knock again.

'You followed me,' I say.

I'm seething that she didn't get on the train, but I'm even more disappointed with myself for not being more careful and noticing that she was following me.

'Taxis are a lot easier to come by in the city,' she says, clicking her fingers for effect. 'I know when you have something to hide, Susan.'

Oh Jenny.

'I told you the truth,' I say. 'What more do you want?'

'I want to know why.'

'Why what?' My heart begins to race as I hear Deacon or Amelia move about in the bedroom behind me.

I shake my head. Jenny is making this difficult. I knew she would have questions, but I really thought she would piss off back to Dublin to think about everything I said outside the train station and stew over it for a few days at least. Like a normal person. And Deacon, Amelia and I would be long gone by the time she came back looking for answers. I should have known better. I should have known Jenny better. Her overzealous personality was never going to allow time for reason or calm thinking. I made a huge mistake letting her get out of the car.

'Where is he?' Jenny shouts, her expression ignited with temper.

'Who?' My pulse races. *Paul?*

'Who?' Jenny mimics. 'Don't give me that "I don't know what you're talking about" bullshit.'

I fold my arms as I look her up and down. She's practically my mirror image. Slender jeans, a tailored blouse and she's even cut her hair into a sensible long bob that really doesn't suit her. We were so similar in our younger years too. We liked the same bands, wore the same oversized baggy T-shirts and slouchy jeans that hung off our hips and made us look like we hadn't washed in weeks. I can't believe I never noticed before how Jenny copies me. She really should have picked a better role model. And I wonder if I ever really knew Jenny at all – was she just some desperate, lonely girl so needy and alone that she became my clone?

'I think you've made a mistake,' I say, beginning to close the door, but she sticks her foot in the gap and glares at me with her hands on her hips.

'Oh no, Susan,' she says. 'You're the one who's made mistakes. Several, in fact. I was prepared to let all the other crazy shit slide.'

I throw an expression her way that asks 'what crazy shit?', though I'm certain she is going to tell me anyway.

'Marrying the man who killed your brother is madness. Having a kid with him is batshit crazy. But sleeping with my husband is just too fucking much, Susan. It's too much. You've gone too far this time. You really, really have.'

'Ex-husband,' I snap.

Of all the things I could have said in that moment, I wish I had come up with anything other than that knee-jerk comment. Jenny screams so loudly it rings in my ears and she charges forward, pushing the door back all the way until the handle slams against the wall behind with a loud thump.

'Deacon,' she shouts. 'Come out, you bastard, I know you're in here somewhere.'

I don't dare glance towards Amelia's bedroom.

'Jenny, calm down, please. You're scaring me,' I lie.

Jenny paces the lounge.

'Deacon, you can't ignore me forever,' she shouts. 'I'm going to find you. The least you can do is come out and make this less embarrassing for all of us.'

I take a deep breath as Deacon appears from the bedroom, pulling the door closed behind him before Jenny has a chance to see inside.

'Jenny, it's not what you think,' he says.

She grunts. 'You're running away.'

'No one is running anywhere,' I say.

'Susan, don't patronise me.' She squares up to me as Deacon remains statue-like, guarding the bedroom door. 'I saw your suitcase in the car. You're hardly going on holiday now, are you?'

'Jenny, please. Calm down,' he says, taking a couple of steps forward. I twitch nervously as the bedroom door creaks open ever so slightly.

'Are you going to tell me you're having an affair?' Jenny asks.

Deacon glares at me and I know he's wondering what the hell I've said.

'You know . . .' Jenny starts pacing again and I breathe a sigh of relief as she creates some distance between us. '. . . I almost believed Susan's bullshit. I'd spent years convincing myself there was something between you two.'

'Jenny . . .' Deacon begins.

'Shut up and listen,' she shouts, coming to an abrupt stop as she folds her arms furiously across her chest. 'I was prepared to accept you and Susan had something that we just never did.' Jenny points at Deacon and then slices her finger through the air to drill her nail into her chest. 'She always had this weird, controlling hold over you that I just never had. And I let it drive me mad. For years I let it eat away at me and I always thought Susan was a better, prettier, more interesting person than me.'

'Jenny . . .' Deacon tries again.

'Shut up,' she shouts. 'I'm not finished.'

'Say what you have to say, Jenny,' I finally say. 'It's the least you deserve.'

'Well, aren't you gracious,' Jenny sighs. 'But, you see, Susan, gracious isn't really you, is it? Your confession that you were sleeping with my husband . . . sorry, ex-husband, as you so kindly reminded me, didn't ring true. It's just too simple. Too neat a bow to tie up all the loose ends of your life.'

'So, what are you saying?' I snort. 'You're annoyed now because I'm *not* sleeping with Deacon?'

'Oh Susan, stop it,' Jenny snorts. 'You're not as smart as you think you are.'

'Jenny, Susan and I are not sleeping together,' Deacon says calmly. 'We never were. Ever.'

'That's not what Susan says,' Jenny smirks.

Deacon glances my way and shakes his head.

'Deacon.' I swallow, his name feeling cumbersome in my mouth. 'I can explain.'

'No need,' he says, raising his hand and warning me to stop. 'Jenny is doing a perfectly good job.'

'I know you're not having an affair,' Jenny says. 'I realise that now.'

'Good,' Deacon sighs, visibly relieved.

'Your relationship is a hell of a lot more twisted than that,' Jenny says, shaking her head. 'You know, Susan, I really was going to get the train. I was going to leave you alone once and for all, but I suddenly remembered the photos of the lightning strikes hanging in your hall. I thought about how your face lit up when you talked about them. There was so much pride in your eyes when you finally had a chance to showcase Adam's talent. And I knew then, I knew that you could never ever forgive Paul. Never.'

Jenny takes my breath away, and for a moment I stand staring at her with my mouth gaping and tears glistening in my eyes.

'Go on, Jenny,' Deacon encourages.

My eyes shift to him and I see something unsettling in the way he's looking at Jenny. I think he's relieved she's actually on to us. As if his conscience has reached breaking point and he can finally confess what we've done. And I'm powerless to stop him.

'I know you didn't just stop hating Paul as much for taking Adam away from you,' Jenny says. 'I know you hate him more than ever. And I don't even blame you for it.'

'Then, what do you blame me for?' I ask.

'For taking Deacon away from me . . .'

'But, Jenny, I haven't,' I say. 'He's standing right here.'

'Because you brought him here,' she shouts. 'And that's what I don't understand. Why?'

'Because he's my friend,' I admit, maybe to myself more than to her.

'But why here? Why now? And for what?' Jenny asks. 'Some shitty flat in Cork city? You're clearly hiding here, but from who? Paul?'

Deacon shakes his head. 'Jenny, it's complicated.'

'Why did you marry Paul, Susan?' she asks. 'You don't love him. You couldn't possibly.'

She can only figure out so much. I'm still safe. And there's still time to leave.

'Maaaaammmmyyy.' A whimper carries through the slightly ajar bedroom door. 'I want my maaaaammmmyyyy.'

Blood courses furiously through my veins. I can feel the sudden swell of pressure inside my brain as if a dam has burst its banks. I hold my breath and wait. Maybe Jenny didn't hear Amelia. Maybe she was too distracted with temper . . .

'Maammmyyy,' Amelia cries again, a little louder this time.

And Deacon cracks. I see it in his face before he even turns towards the sound of Amelia's sobbing. It's in that moment, that one rebellious turn of Deacon's body, that I know I've lost. I always thought he would put me first. And he did, for a long time. Even above his wife. But he has a new priority – Amelia. It's all over.

'Shh, sweetheart, shhh,' Deacon says, charging towards the bedroom and fecklessly throwing the door wide open. 'I'm here. It's okay. You're not alone. I'm here.'

Jenny's hand is across her mouth. She's shaking her head and I can see her joining the dots.

Oh my God. Oh my God.

'Jenny, please,' I say, grabbing her other hand. Her skin is clammy and I realise she's scared. 'Let me explain . . .'

Her eyes burn into me as she jerks her arm back roughly. I lose my balance and stumble backwards.

Hot, sharp pain explodes in the back of my head as I knock the pizza box off the blue beer crate and a shard of broken plastic drills its way into my skull. I instinctively reach up and warm, sticky blood trickles on to my fingers.

'You bitch,' I hiss as I watch Jenny standing over me. 'You fucking bitch.'

'I'm sorry,' she says, her eyes wide with disbelief. 'I didn't mean to hurt you.'

My vision blurs as the searing pain swamps my thoughts.

'You're bleeding,' Jenny says, her voice shaking. 'It looks bad. Oh God, Susan. I'm so sorry.'

She takes a step forward and I try to grab her ankle to drag her to the ground with me, but she jumps back, screeching.

'It's okay. It's okay.' Deacon's voice creeps from the bedroom.

'Who's he talking to?' Jenny asks, her eyes burning into me.

Her curiosity is drawing her towards Deacon, but she's scared, it's obvious from how slowly she moves. But I don't understand why. She must know it's Amelia. So what is she afraid of? Does she think I've hurt Amelia? Does Jenny really believe I'm such a monster I could harm my own child? The realisation stings. What Jenny thinks of me should be irrelevant, but I find it's not and my feelings are hurt.

'Oh Amelia,' Deacon says. 'You're too hot. You're much too hot.'

'Noooo,' I screech as Jenny turns towards the bedroom.

I pull myself to my feet. My legs are shaking and I'm light-headed. 'Don't,' I warn her. 'Don't you dare take another step.'

Jenny ignores me and runs into the bedroom.

'Oh my God,' she says. 'I don't believe it.'

I try to hurry after her but my legs are heavy and I can feel blood trickling down the back of my neck.

'Oh my God,' Jenny repeats. 'What's wrong with her? What have you done? Have you hurt her?'

'God, no. Of course not,' Deacon splutters defensively as he sits crouched on the mattress with Amelia in his arms. 'I've taken care of her. Good care of her, I promise. I would never hurt her. Not in a million years.'

'Look at her,' Jenny says, close to tears. 'She's so pale. Is she dying? Oh God. Oh God.'

'Don't be fucking ridiculous,' I bark, finally reaching the bedroom door. 'She's just sick. Kids get sick all the time. I was on my way to get her medication when you arrived.'

'Oh Susan,' Jenny says, disgusted. 'What have you done?'

'Nothing,' I growl, pushing her out of my way so I can garner a better view of Amelia.

Her skin is blotchier than before and her lips are a terrifying blueish purple.

'It's not too late,' Deacon says. 'We can get her to hospital. Jenny can help, can't you, Jen?'

'I . . . I . . .' she stutters.

'Enough,' I shout. 'Enough.'

Amelia begins to cry and Deacon gathers her frail body closer to his chest.

'Everything has changed. Amelia is sick. She has to come first, Susan,' he says. 'You must know that.'

'Paul needs to pay for what he's done,' I say.

'But Amelia doesn't,' Deacon says. 'She's just a baby, Susan, and she needs help.'

Jenny slowly backs away. I'm so distracted by my daughter's worryingly pale complexion that I don't notice Jenny leaving until she's right by the flat door.

'Where the fuck do you think you're going?' I shout after her.

'Susan, let her go,' Deacon says. 'We've much more important things to worry about.'

'She's going straight to the Guards,' I panic. 'You do realise that, don't you? We're fucked. We're completely fucked.'

'Shh, princess. Shh,' he says, stroking Amelia's hair calmly, as if the whole world isn't imploding around us. 'Don't be scared. There's nothing to be scared about.'

'Have you gone completely mad?' I growl, turning to run. 'I'm going to catch her before it's too late.'

'Susan, no . . .' Deacon pleads. 'Don't do this . . . Don't do anything you'll regret.'

I can hear Jenny running down the concrete stairwell. *It's not too late. I can catch her.* I have to catch her.

'Take care of her,' I say as I turn my back on Deacon and Amelia.

I press my hand against the back of my head. The bleeding has stopped. My legs slip for a moment and lose grip as I charge so fast after Jenny I almost topple over.

'Susssaaaannnn, nooooo,' Deacon screams, his voice chasing me out the door and down the stairwell.

I don't look back. At Deacon. At the flat. At my little girl.

Chapter Thirty-seven

Now

The rickety door at the bottom of the concrete steps is closed and Jenny pulls instead of pushes. I gasp inwardly. Her simple misjudgement buys me valuable seconds and I'm catching up with her as I charge down the stairs.

'Wait, Jenny, please,' I puff, short of breath. 'I just want to talk.'

I'm right behind her when she finally pushes on the door and spills out on to the street. The sudden burst of sunlight dazzles me and I lose my footing and stumble on the bottom two steps, going over on my ankle.

'Jenny, you bitch,' I hiss, shaking off pain.

The door slams closed. I lunge forward and press both hands flat on the frosted glass in the centre and push much harder than I need to. It swings back and I burst on to the street. I glance left and right, grinning with satisfaction when I spot her almost immediately.

'Jenny, please?' I shout as she runs down the street towards the main body of the city. 'Wait up. Please wait up.'

A woman with a double buggy strolls towards us, taking up most of the footpath. She makes no effort to move over. Jenny swerves around her, dodging passing traffic. Jenny's back on the path within seconds and picking up speed. The woman trundles towards me.

'*Twinkle . . . twinkle little star,*' I hear her sing, out of tune.

My eyes focus on Jenny as the woman continues walking towards me, oblivious.

'*Up above the sky so bright,*' she continues.

The footpath narrows ahead to allow room for the traffic to widen from two to three lanes of fast-moving cars. There isn't room for the woman and her buggy to pass me without pinning me to the wall. I can tell she's expecting me to move into a shop doorway and allow room for her to pass. It's unspoken etiquette and she continues singing and walking, obviously expecting me to oblige. But I can't afford the lost time. I keep running.

'Stupid bitch,' I grunt, reaching the woman and her young children. I kick the front of the buggy out of my way. The woman gasps and struggles to keep hold of the handle as the buggy jerks and the front wheels flop off the path. An approaching car stops suddenly. The squeal of brakes is piercing and sudden, and the smell of burning rubber as tyres skid on tarmac wafts into the air. A child screams and car horns honk. Jenny takes advantage of the sudden commotion and darts across the road in front of the stopped cars.

'Did you see what that woman just did?' Someone runs out of a nearby shop to assist the mother with the buggy. 'Crazy. Just crazy.'

Their shock slides off me as if I'm impenetrable. Perhaps in the moment of adrenaline and fear, I am. My eyes shift from them and on to Jenny. Traffic is moving again and I can't cross the road. I run faster than ever. Charging ahead, parallel to Jenny. We glance over our shoulders at each other, only tossing our eyes at the path ahead every couple of seconds to keep track of where we're going. I'm gaining on Jenny. As soon as the traffic stops, I'll have her. But suddenly the bitch rounds a corner. I can't see her. My chest is tight, and my breath is laboured. Each inhale drags too much oxygen into my burning lungs. I feel like my whole upper body might explode under the pressure.

I charge to the end of the road, running faster than ever. The lights change, and a generic green man beckons me obliviously across the road. Reaching the far side, I press my hand against cool pebble-dashed plaster and take a second to gather myself. I'm panting desperately, and my heart is pounding. Beads of perspiration that cling to my hairline begin to trickle down my forehead and run into my eyes. I drag a shaking arm across my eyes and with fresh vision look up. Jenny's back comes into view instantly in the distance. I'm desperate to catch my breath, but Jenny isn't giving up. If anything, she's getting faster and gaining distance. I pick up the chase as she turns another corner. And another. It's a maze of sharp, sudden rights and unexpected left turns. My calves are on fire but I push on, determined. I've never been in this part of the city and I don't recognise any of the streets or buildings. There are no more shops, just large, industrial warehouses, and there are no more people walking the streets. If I've no idea where we are then Jenny must be completely lost too. I suddenly realise that I don't know how to find my way back to Deacon and Amelia. But that doesn't matter right now. Nothing matters except catching Jenny.

She whips around another corner, and when I follow my eyes light up and I come to a confident stop. It's a dead end. The narrow laneway leads to the docks. It's dull and chilly down here. I creep forward slowly. Jenny darts left. And then right. She's cornered. And she knows it. I take another step. My foot hits something and I glance at the ground. A rusty old pipe stares up at me. It's long and thin and useful. I bend down and pick it up. All the while Jenny's knowing eyes are pleading with me not to.

'Oh Jenny,' I say. 'Tut. Tut. Tut.'

'Susan, please,' she says. 'Let's talk. You said you wanted to talk.'

I step forward, closing the gap between us. The buildings on each side are storeys high and banish the sun. There is no light to break up the long tarmac path leading to the sea. No more side streets, no more exits. There is nowhere left for her to run except into the water behind her.

'Oh Jenny,' I say, edging closer with one hand confidently on my hip and the other wrapped tightly around the metal pipe. 'Why couldn't you have just gone home? I asked you to go home. I tried to protect you. I really, really did.'

Chapter Thirty-eight

Then

The smell of disinfectant hits me like a slap across the face as soon as the hospital doors slide open. Reception comes into view straight away, spanning almost the entire left side of the spacious lobby. But I don't hurry over. I don't know why. Maybe I need a moment to catch my breath. Or maybe I'm desperate for some time to mull over what I'm going to say. I just can't believe that I'm really here, that this is really happening. An hour ago I was straightening my hair and slipping into killer high heels, and now I'm standing inside the main doors of A&E in my little black dress, with mascara smudged around my eyes. I look at my mother standing beside me. I try to catch her attention, but her glassy eyes are vacant as if her body is present but her mind is somewhere else entirely. I take a deep, painfully sharp breath, link my mother's arm and take a reluctant step towards the reception desk.

'C'mon, Mam,' I say.

There are two young girls behind reception. One is on the phone and the other is sitting painting her nails. Neither look my way when I approach. I stand for a moment, statue-like, and wait. It's noisy. A TV is on in the waiting area to my right and patients litter the corridors that span like tree branches at either side. Some people moan and groan. Some sit quietly in solitude and some talk confidently into mobile phones despite all the posters dotted around prohibiting the use of phones. Two paramedics whizz by with a patient on a stretcher. The patient is crying loudly in obvious pain and he rolls to one side and throws up just as they pass by. I jump back as vomit splashes the glazed cream tiles next to my feet. The paramedics burst through nearby double doors into an even busier area and my eyes can't help but follow them until the doors close and my focus is brought back to reception.

'Excuse me,' I finally say, followed by an awkward cough to clear my dry throat. The younger of the two girls lowers the delicate brush into the bottle of nail varnish and secures it with a quick twist. The smell of drying nail varnish is distinct, and I cough again. The girl slowly drags her eyes away from her fingers to meet my stare and I'm almost certain I hear her grunt inwardly.

'Yes,' she says.

'I . . . I . . .' I swallow.

My mother's fingers grip my arm and her nails bite into my skin as her grip is tight and desperate. She's hurting me, although she's completely unaware. She's heavy too, like a huge leech needing to be carried. I want her to take charge of the conversation. I want her to lead. To be the parent. I need her to shield me from this nightmare but she's nothing more than a quivering mess.

My mother looks amazing. Her fair hair is sleek and falls in thick, layered waves around her face. Her make-up is pristine except for the long, narrow charcoal lines of mascara that trickle down her cheeks. She is dressed for the party, like me, although her crimson pencil dress is more conservative and mature. I'm sure to the girl on reception we look perfectly normal – too normal. We don't belong among the injured, with bloodied body parts or broken limbs, among the stressed-out parents waiting with a child in pyjamas, among the drunks and drug addicts. But I can feel my mother swaying as if her legs just won't hold her up much longer and her body shaking with angry tearless sobs.

'Can I help you?' the receptionist says.

'My brother . . .' I pause. 'They asked us to come in . . . they said there was an accident . . .' I trail off.

'A car crash?' the receptionist says, her shoulders round, and I notice a spark of recognition in her concerned smile.

She's been waiting for us, I can tell. Her eyes fill with sadness as she slides her chair back and stands up. She catches the attention of the other girl on the phone and they share some mutual nodding. The girl on the phone's eyes shift to me and she smiles at me gently.

'My brother wasn't in a car. He was walking.' I shake my head, desperate for her to tell us this is all a big mistake. They've called the wrong people. We're not the family they're looking for. 'He doesn't drive,' I continue. 'He doesn't even have a car.'

The girl walks out from behind her desk and drapes her arm over my mother's shoulder. 'This way please,' she says.

It feels odd, the three of us tangled up together like a human caterpillar with so many legs. I unlink my mother. She doesn't seem to notice I've suddenly lagged and she walks ahead with the receptionist's arms steering her.

We walk through the doors next to reception where I watched the paramedics take their patient moments ago. *Adam must be this way*, I think, *maybe the same paramedics brought him in*. The main hub of A&E doesn't seem as chaotic as moments before and I breathe a sigh of relief as I desperately try to gather my thoughts. Hideous floral curtains punctuate various cubicles. Some curtains are drawn. Some are open. Some patients are alone. Some are with medics. It's all very stereotypical and expected. This isn't somewhere bad things happen. This is somewhere people come to get better. Like that time Adam fractured his arm during the interschools hurling final when we were eleven. Mrs Clancy, our fifth-class teacher, chastised Adam for being so reckless, but looking back I guess she was just put out that the team captain would be out of action for six weeks until his cast came off. Although Adam didn't attend this exact hospital as a child, the layout and environment are familiar. But the feelings now are frighteningly unfamiliar. Back then, I was excited to visit my fearless brother and tease him about his injury. *This time . . . well, this time . . .*

The receptionist steers us away from the curtains. Adam isn't behind any of them! Not this time. She leads us down a corridor, away from familiarity. Away from the doctors and nurses and patients. The stench of disinfectant is more potent than ever down here and the artificial light compensating for lack of windows is insanely bright. I squint. My high heels clip clop as I trail behind my mother and the receptionist. We stop midway down the clinical corridor and the receptionist opens a door that seems to appear out of nowhere. It squeaks in protest at being awakened and swings back to reveal cool cream walls, soft grey furniture – a three-seater couch and a couple of armchairs with brightly coloured cushions. *Christ it's miserable.*

'Okay,' the receptionist smiles, her voice wilting and delicate like the last petal on a rose ready to fall off at any moment. 'If you'd like to take a seat, one of the doctors will be with you soon.'

'Can we see Adam?' my mother asks, finally finding her voice.

'Please, if you just take a seat . . .' the receptionist repeats.

'I want to see my son,' my mother protests.

'Please, Mrs Arnold. I'm sure the doctor won't be long.'

'Mrs Arnold,' I say. 'We didn't introduce ourselves.'

'I . . .' The receptionist's cheeks flush but the rest of her face is ghastly pale.

'His ID,' I swallow. 'You know our name because of Adam's ID, don't you? You found his student card on him. Or his bank card. Probably his passport. He was buying booze. He always uses his passport to prove his age in the off-licence.'

The receptionist nods. I can't tell if it's a *yes, I'm listening* or *yes, you're right*. I keep talking.

'It's our birthday today,' I say, fighting back tears. 'Adam only went out to pick up his suit. He wasn't supposed to be long. He wasn't even supposed to stop at any shops but I asked him to pick up some champagne. It was my idea. You see, we're twenty-one today, so it's kind of a big deal.'

'You're both twenty-one today?' the receptionist says and she can't keep it together any more. A single tear escapes and trickles down the side of her nose. She catches it impressively quickly with the flick of her fingers.

'Twins,' my mother says. 'My beautiful, special twins.'

I shake my head. 'But not any more,' I sigh knowingly.

Chapter Thirty-nine

Now

Christ, my legs hurt. I must have walked a million miles. Thank God for Google Maps or I'd never have found my way from the docks to Paul's car. I'm still painfully unfamiliar with this city.

Even when I reach the car park I'm so frazzled I walk around several storeys trying to remember where I parked the damn car. I find myself pointing the car keys left and right, clicking over and over, hoping for the familiar *beep-beep* and flash of orange lights. Eventually, Paul's car comes into view. I check that no one is around before I walk over to it.

A double click on the middle button of the car keys unlocks the doors. The car beeps and plays a three-note melody. It spits the same spritely tune when you start the ignition and when you turn it off again. It's an overpriced car trying too hard, but I've never noticed how irritating it is before now. I snort at the car's arrogance, open the passenger door and duck inside. I don't bother to let the seat down. I simply climb over, stomping my dirty shoes all over Paul's pristine ivory leather. I get into the back seat, and grateful for the tinted windows I quickly strip off Paul's running gear and slip on my blouse and jeans. I glance around the silent car park before I open the door and hop out.

I hurry around to the back of the car, hyper-aware that I can't afford to be seen. I stare into the abyss of the boot. Dull black felt lines the boring square space, in bleak contrast to the shiny, expensive leather that kits out the rest of the interior. The boot is clearly the basement of the car, the lesser level, the dump!

My heart is beating furiously and my palms are sweating but I can't rush and risk making sloppy mistakes. I've spent years planning this moment, and it has to be perfect.

I place the running gear and baseball cap in the boot, next to the blood-spattered white tie with the baby-blue pinstripe. *His favourite*, his colleagues will hopefully say, if the tie gets a mention on the news. *His wife bought it for him and he wore it all the time – he was such a lovely man, I just can't believe it*, someone else will add. I'm sure Paul's arrest will come as a shock to the public, at first. Young father, clever businessman, friend, sportsman, blah blah blah. But as the media dig into his past the truth will slowly dawn on people. That Paul Warner is an evil murderer. Adam's name will be in all the papers again. *Paul's First Victim*, they might say, or hopefully something punchier. Adam will be remembered, and Paul will finally get the punishment he deserves. His life will be ruined. I will be long gone with Amelia, and he will finally know what it's like to have the person you love most in the world snatched from you. Paul will finally know what it's like to be me.

I wish I could add the metal pipe that Jenny recently became so well acquainted with, but my fingerprints are all over it, so it had to make its way to the seafloor, along with Jenny and the cavity block I secured around her ankle. Seriously, the stuff they leave lying around the docks is dangerous. *Someone needs to look into that!*

Finally, I reach for the overhanging boot door and the bracelet around my wrist catches my eye. I freeze and glance over my shoulder then quickly whip my head back to glance over the other side. I'm alone. It's eerily silent, apart from the furious beating of my heart that seems to echo deafeningly loud inside my head. I close my eyes, exhale sharply and count backwards from three. Steadier, I open my eyes again and concentrate on the bracelet. It's such a pretty thing. Strands of platinum and rose gold twist around each other like a fine rope, and the subtle diamantés dotted evenly all the way around sparkle as they catch the overhead light. It's no doubt expensive and smacks of extravagant taste. I first noticed Helen wearing it at the barbecue. I'd admired it and she explained it was Larry's mother's. It was later, when we became friends, that she told me that she hated the damned thing and the only reason she wore it was to remind her that her mother-in-law was dead.

'If you like it so much, you should have it,' Helen said.

I blushed and mumbled something about how I couldn't possibly.

'Nonsense,' Helen said, and then she took it off and gave it to me. 'I've a box full of more like it at home. Larry's mother left me all her jewellery. Ironic since the old bitch wouldn't even let me borrow so much as a pair of earrings when she was alive.'

I've been wearing it ever since. Tears prick the corners of my eyes, but I shake my head and blink them away. I have no time for guilt.

Helen's death was a regrettable spur of the moment thing, I never had a chance to make a plan or think it through. I'd been so desperate to get rid of her body before someone saw me that gathering evidence was the last thing on my mind.

I concentrate on the bracelet's clasp. It's finicky and delicate and I'm struggling as my hands shake nervously. Worried about the time I'm wasting, I tug at it and the bracelet flies off my hand, catching the skin of my knuckle.

I scan the boot, trying to see where the bracelet landed as blood bubbles to the surface of my scratched fingers. It's not a lot. A minor graze, really. But it's enough to have splattered the bracelet with my DNA. *Dammit.* I hadn't planned on adding my blood to the mix of evidence in Paul's boot, but Helen's stupid bracelet has left me with no choice. I pause for a moment and think. Faking my own death could prove useful. Paul won't come looking for a dead wife.

Searching for the bracelet, I duck and lean into the boot. If any-body comes along now they'll almost certainly approach to ask if I'm okay. My heart beats even faster.

'Got it, Helen,' I say, triumphant as if she's beside me and would want to know.

I'm so pleased this is all working out for you, Susan. You're doing such a great job framing Paul for murder. You know I'm happy to help, I imagine her say. *Oh Helen. I'm sorry. I'm so, so sorry.*

Straightening up, I shove the bracelet under Paul's running clothes and suck my stinging fingers. I leave the boot open as I scramble into the back of the car and pull Paul's stinking jersey out of my suitcase. I reach into my hair and scratch at the scab forming on the back of my head. It stings as it starts to bleed again and I dab the jersey against it. There's no way the police will miss my DNA now, I think, content that this sudden change of plan is inspired. I toss the jersey into the boot.

In a day or two, when I'm nowhere to be found, the police are bound to interrogate Paul. It's not unreasonable to assume that after murdering our neighbour and my best friend, Paul turned on me.

'Local Man Murders Wife and Child', the headline will say. I hope I can get the articles online. Maybe I'll print them off and have them framed. By morning Amelia and I won't be in the country and the only trace of us will be our DNA in the boot of my husband's car. It's working out better than I ever imagined. Of course, not for Jenny or Helen, but I'm sure they'd understand. If they knew Paul as well as I did, they would.

Finally, I slam the boot and it snaps shut with a loud bang that rattles the whole car. The damn thing sticks halfway down so I have to tug hard to get any sort of traction going. I keep telling Paul it needs WD-40 or something sprayed on its hinges to loosen them, but Paul won't hear of it. He mumbles something about bringing it in for a check-up, as if it's a puppy visiting the vet. Sometimes I wonder if he loves this stupid car more than me. But never more than Amelia. My God, that man loves that child. He'll be devastated to lose her.

I turn around and glance over the silent car park one last time. Almost every space is full. Old cars, new ones. Large ones, compact ones. Cars of every colour occupy the entire floor. Paul's car is simply another inconspicuous vehicle. It could hide here, unnoticed, indefinitely. Unless, of course, someone drops a hint.

Chapter Forty

Now

The familiar smell of grease and batter wafting from the chipper below Deacon's flat makes me feel as queasy as ever. The door is wide open, but that doesn't stop the floor to ceiling glass shop front fogging up around the edges. Inside is busier than usual. There's a long line of mismatched, hungry people. But it's the overweight man with an abundance of tattoos that draws my attention. He sits inside the window with a brown paper bag of chips on his knee and a burger in his hand.

A toddler with a tight haircut and a grubby face runs around the small space shouting, 'nee-naw, nee-naw'. The little boy is loud and boisterous, and I can hear his squeaky voice through the thin glass.

'Look at me, Da,' he shouts. 'I'm a policeman.'

'Stop that. Stop that now,' the man says, as he picks up a newspaper next to him, rolls it and swats at his son as if the little boy is an irritating fly.

'Na nana nana nah!' The little boy sticks out his tongue and taunts his father.

The father drops the newspaper on the chipper floor and wags his finger. 'Wait till I get my hands on ya, ya little shit. I'll wring your bleedin' neck, I will.' He takes a bite of his burger.

I look away and shake my head, disgusted. Some people really don't deserve children, I think, so glad that Amelia and I have a much healthier relationship.

I pull my shoulders up to my ears, take a deep breath and let them flop down as I exhale. A huge smile spreads across my face as I take another couple of steps, ready to find Amelia and Deacon and start over.

My breath catches when I find the side door leading up to the flat is open. I wonder if it's been like that for hours. Maybe I left it open when I chased after Jenny. Or maybe that good-for-nothing neighbour leaves it open every time he goes out.

I walk inside. And a sense of unease clings to me like a shadow I can't shake off. My exhausted legs are feeling the burn as I take the steps two at a time.

'Hey,' I shout, reaching the top step. 'Sorry I took so long. I just had . . .'

The door is wide open and fresh air blasts through from an open window. I can hear the traffic on the road below. I charge inside, my legs suddenly quick and nimble.

'Deacon,' I shout.

The flimsy curtains on the open window flap wildly in the draught and I bound over to close it. But the sudden quiet is worse than the traffic.

'Deacon, where are you?' I race into the kitchen. 'Where the hell are you?'

I fling open a cupboard. It's bare. I open the next one. Nothing. I whizz from one to another and another. Finally, I stumble across one containing minimal rations. Coffee, a couple of slices of stale bread and some sugar. My heart sinks. Maybe Deacon really wasn't getting out and about as much as I foolishly accused him of.

I turn towards the bedroom. A sinking feeling weighs me down.

'Amelia,' I cry out, breathless. 'Amelia, honey, it's Mammy. Are you here, darling? Mammy's here now.'

I run with my hand instinctively pressed against my chest, protecting my heart. I charge straight through the lounge, crashing into the stupid crate and pizza box table. Amelia's colouring pencils rain down like long, slender sticks of rainbow confetti.

'Ouch, fuck!' I wince, hopping on the spot as a throbbing ache attacks my shin.

It's noisy, for a moment. But when the colours settle on the floor, silence once again engulfs the room. The only sound is my deep breathing.

I run, hurrying into the bedroom. The mattresses sit waiting at either side of the room. Empty!

'Deacon,' I scream, clasping my hands and pressing them down on top of my head. 'Deacon? Please. Where are you?'

I spin around. And around. And finally, exhausted, I flop on to the mattress where just hours ago I held my little girl in my arms. I tuck my arms close to my chest, close my eyes and rock back and forth. I've no idea how long passes. Minutes, hours. Weak and broken, I open my eyes. Tears sting and my vision is blurry, but I notice the drawing that was hidden under Amelia's pillow.

I toss the pillow aside and with shaking fingers I pick up the piece of colourful paper. I smile as I count the bright yellow duckies.

'One . . . two . . . three,' I count out loud.

And the stream. Amelia has chosen dark blue to mark out a long stream that stretches from one side of the page to the other. There's a house too, with one side longer than the other and with a crooked front door and only one window. But I recognise the red door. It's our cottage. There are some stick people too. A mammy. A daddy. And a little girl. There's a fourth, unexpected stick figure. Wobbly black circles frame his eyes. Glasses! It's Deacon. Amelia has drawn Deacon as someone important in her life – equal to Paul and me, and I don't know whether to be happy or sad.

I kiss the beautiful picture, fold it and stuff it into my bra.

'Christ, Deacon. What have you done?' I say.

I blitz through the flat with a Tesco plastic bag I found in the kitchen. I toss in any evidence that proves Deacon or Amelia were ever here. I chuck in Amelia's crayons and colouring book. I tear up the pizza box and throw that in too. The crate is much too large, but I make a mental note to toss it into the hall. I gather up the minimal food from the cupboards and the fridge. I double-check that all the windows are closed and that there's nothing left in the bathroom or bedroom, and with a deep breath I walk out of the flat and close the door behind me.

I plan to turn a few corners and walk a couple of streets away before tossing the bag in a bin. Then I'll call Deacon. And if he doesn't answer . . .

Chapter Forty-one

Now

'Paul,' I gasp as I see my husband at the bottom of the stairs. 'What are you doing here?'

'Shouldn't I be asking you that question?' he says, taking the concrete steps two at a time.

'I . . . I . . .' I can't think.

'Who lives here?' Paul says. 'Is it Deacon? Is that who you're leaving me for? A desperate loser living above a chipper. Nice, Susan. Real classy. But that's you all over, isn't it?'

I'm exhausted and all I can think about is my phone in my pocket and how much I want to call Deacon and find out what the hell he's doing.

'What's this?' Paul says, snatching the bag of rubbish out of my hand. 'Been shopping, have you? Going to cook a fancy meal for two? Or is a greasy takeaway more his style, eh?'

'It's just rubbish, Paul.'

He casts his gaze around the dreary corridor. 'Our daughter is missing and here you are taking out your boyfriend's rubbish.' He rips open the plastic bag. 'You make me sick, Susan. You really—'

My back arches like a startled cat as the expression on his face changes from hurt to suspicion. 'What are these?' he says, pulling out some of Amelia's crayons. I didn't notice earlier that the yellow one is much shorter than the others; worn from use. Paul opens his hand and the crayons tumble on to the steps. 'And this?' He reaches into the bag and pulls out the colouring book.

My back straightens as I get ready to run.

Paul flicks the book open, and I make a dash for it. But I don't get far. He grabs a fistful of my hair and throws me against the wall.

He turns the open colouring book around for me to see. 'Look,' he says, pointing. 'Yellow. Nearly everything is yellow.'

I drop my eyes to the ground. I can imagine the realisation hitting him, and I can't bear to see it in his face.

'What have you done, Susan?'

'Paul, listen, you don't understand—'

His hand is suddenly around my neck, his long, slender fingers crushing my efforts to catch my breath. The cold wall behind my back grates against my spine.

I look up. My eyes are wide and bulging, just like Paul's as he stares back at me.

'What have you done, Susan?' he repeats, shaking me. 'Tell me.'

I can't answer. I'm silently pleading with him to release his grip before I pass out.

Paul loosens his fingers, but he doesn't let go. An animalistic grunt bursts out of my open mouth as I desperately gather air into my lungs. Breathing is uncomfortable and minimal but I'm not dying. For that, I'm grateful.

The repulsive smell of batter and frying oil that I've become familiar with rushes in with each laboured breath.

'Chips,' I say, my voice raspy.

'What?' Paul's fingers twitch.

'I smell them.' I drag more reluctant air in – it rattles in my restricted throat.

'And?' Paul grunts, losing patience.

'I was worried that she wasn't eating properly,' I say. 'But they could have gotten takeaway anytime. And she loves chips, doesn't she? Especially with ketchup.'

'Amelia?' Paul exhales our daughter's name as if the syllables are the air he breathes. His heart is breaking as he adds up the clues, not really believing what he's realising.

'He wanted me to think I was a bad mother, you see?' I say, adding my own clues. 'He tried to say I was neglecting her. Don't you see? Oh God, he was playing me at my own game all along.'

'What are you talking about?' Paul's grip tightens again. 'Where is Amelia? If you've hurt her, so help me God,' Paul warns.

I raise my knee and try to kick him in the groin, but I'm dizzy and light-headed and I miss. Paul snorts and shakes his head.

'Don't do that again,' he hisses.

I wave my arms to surrender. Paul doesn't take his eyes off me, they twitch from side to side, searching mine for answers.

'Tell me,' he shouts.

He smacks the back of my skull against the wall, warning me to give him my full attention.

I move my lips but I can't tell if sound comes out because the ringing in my ears is too loud after the bang.

Like before, Paul's hand slackens, and I gulp, desperate to breathe. I don't care that I sound repulsive or greedy as I guzzle oxygen.

Paul is physically shaking. I can feel it in his hand around my throat and I can see it as stray strands of his floppy hair sway as they dangle into his fiery eyes. I wonder if this is how Helen and Jenny felt shortly before they died. I wonder what they saw in my eyes. *Rage, fear, desperation.* Maybe all of it. I certainly see all of it in Paul's.

Paul reduces his question to a single guttural word. 'Where?'

Breathless, I can't manage a sound but I flick my eyes upwards. He follows the hint and quickly shifts his gaze to the flat door at the top of the stairs. He releases me and charges, ready to take the stairs two at a time.

I scream and grab the back of his jacket, tugging as hard as I can. I let go and watch as he falls down the stairs. But he only stumbles back a couple of steps and quickly regains his balance.

'You won't find her,' I gasp. 'She's not there.'

'She's not here?' Paul points towards the flat door, pinning me against the wall with his other hand. This time his strength is against my chest, crushing me until I feel as if my ribs will snap and puncture my heart. 'Oh, I forgot, she's in the bottom of the lake, not hidden away in this vile shithole colouring pictures.'

The pain in my chest is intense, and I can't manage any words. But it doesn't matter, there's nothing I can say to appease him now. We've reached the crux of this thing and all I can do is see it through for as long as he lets me live. He's stronger than I ever realised.

'She's been here, in the city . . . all along.' His eyes glass over and for a second I think he'll let me go as he breaks down and cries.

I'm wrong.

His free hand curls into a fist and I close my eyes and hold my breath. I open them again when I hear him pound the wall next to my face. He punches the wall over and over.

'Paul, please,' I beg, certain the next punch will be in my face.

'My office is just a couple of streets away,' he says. 'Is that why you chose this place? To taunt me. To have Amelia so close all this time but I didn't know it?'

No. I chose the dingy flat above the chipper because it was cheap, available at short notice and the landlord asked no questions. Street names in Cork city mean nothing to me. I had no idea Paul's office was nearby. If anything, had I known the location was so close to Paul's office I'd have chosen differently. The last thing I needed was bumping into my husband.

'At least tell me you didn't leave her alone? She's just a baby, for Christ's sake. No. No, you wouldn't,' Paul says, shaking his head as he answers his own question. 'Even *you* wouldn't do that.'

My eyes cloud over. It's hard to see. *I would never hurt Amelia – I mean, not intentionally.* I think of her little foot and how she yelped when I cut it. I think of her chubby arms around my neck and her pleading with me to take her home. I think of her whimpers as she cried herself to sleep the last time I saw her. But mostly I think of where she might be now.

Paul's face reddens and he gasps. '*Him*. You left her with him, didn't you?'

Hot, salty tears that I can't hold back any longer trickle down my cheeks.

'Deacon?' Paul spits.

I nod.

'I knew it,' Paul shouts. 'I fucking knew it.'

'Paul, stop,' I shout back. 'You knew nothing.'

'You all right there, love?' a man's voice interrupts us.

I recognise him as his head appears in the doorway. It's the tattooed man from the chipper. He's noticeably drunk now, swaying on the footpath as he tries to navigate his way through the door but his shoulder collides with the frame. He has a six-pack of cheap beer tucked under his arm and his toddler son is holding his hand as he stands listlessly beside him. The child is silent now and desperately in need of sleep.

'The missus can't decide if she wants burger or nuggets,' Paul yells in an accent I've never heard him use before.

'Good luck, mate,' the drunk man shouts back, his accent matching Paul's. 'Rather you than me. That's the beauty of divorce, I say.'

Paul leans in and places his lips next to my ear. I can feel the heat of his breath against my skin.

'Nah,' Paul says. 'Marriage is way too much fun, eh, Sue?'

Chapter Forty-two

Now

'Sue?' I swallow, the air slow and cumbersome as it scratches its way down my aching throat.

'Well, that is what your friends call you, isn't it?' Paul says.

I don't reply.

'Sue, Sue, Sue. It has a nice ring to it. It suits you,' Paul continues.

'Please stop,' I say. 'Don't call me that.'

Paul finally releases the pressure against my chest and pushes me to the side as if he's discarding rubbish. My hip collides with the edge of a step, shooting pain up my spine. My knees follow, scraping against the cold concrete stairs as my hands instinctively stretch out to hit the ground before my face. Paul steps forward and I look up at the face of a man who so obviously hates me as much as I despise him.

'I've called Connelly and Langton,' he says. 'Did I ever tell you how much I like Langton? She's fantastic, isn't she? She can read people so well. Sniff out bullshit at a hundred paces.' Paul watches me, waiting for a reaction. I won't give him one. He's made his thoughts on Langton and Connelly expressly clear. He's not going to intimidate me by making out they're suddenly best buddies.

'They're coming here? To this exact address that you had no idea existed until you followed me?' I snort, struggling to my feet while rubbing my stinging palms.

Paul laughs. 'You know, next time you want to leave me and disappear without a trace you should probably turn off the GPS on your phone.'

I never have my location on; it eats the battery. But Paul is watching me with such unwavering confidence I second-guess myself. My fingers slip into my pocket. I'm desperate to pull out my phone and check if he turned it on at some point.

'Check it, if you don't believe me,' he says. Beads of perspiration gather on my hairline and I drag my hand across my brow to catch them. I hate that Paul notices me flinch with uncertainty. I wonder when he could have turned it on. Certainly before I was at the docks with Jenny. Maybe even before I was at the lake with Helen. I imagine Google recording my every fucking move for the last few days. *Christ!*

'Everything okay, Sue?' Paul says. 'You're a little pale.'

'What is it you think Langton and Connelly are going to find, Paul?' I ask, trying to keep the tremor out of my voice that would let him know I'm afraid of his answer.

'You,' he says confidently.

'Me.' I tap my chest, feeling the bruising starting already where Paul's hand crushed me. 'Langton and Connelly are going to find me doing what exactly?'

'Wasting police time. Kidnapping. Conspiring to fuck over your husband.'

That's all you've got? I think as a smile settles across my lips and the frustration in Paul's eyes pulls it even wider.

'I won't be made a fool of, Susan,' Paul says. 'You've no idea what I'm capable of if I'm pushed too far. And I don't think you want to find out.'

'Touché, my love,' I smirk. 'Touché.'

Sudden pain explodes across my cheek as the punch I expected earlier knocks me off my feet and sends me tumbling down the stairs. Winded, I lie in a crumbled heap on the cold floor just inside the door. I can feel something warm and wet behind my head and I know I'm bleeding again. My vision is blurry but I can still see Paul charge up the stairs, and I know I need to be on my feet and far away when he discovers the flat really is empty.

Chapter Forty-three

Now

On the street the daylight seems brighter than usual and there's ringing in my ears. I'm unsteady on my feet as I take one final look at the window of the flat. It's ambiguous and dull, like the one Adam and I shared in college. I doubt anyone would imagine that for the last few days the poky flat hid a beautiful little girl from the world. I try to run but my legs can barely move. My whole body begs me to curl into a ball and cry.

I duck into the doorway of the nearest shop. 'Value Fruit and Veg' or something like that it says overhead. There's an elderly man behind the counter and a middle-aged woman at the far side. They chat as he weighs her potatoes. Paul can't hurt me in here, I think. Not in front of these people.

I take my phone out of my jeans pocket. A hairline crack runs across the screen. It must have happened when Paul pushed me. I check my GPS. *On!* I gasp. *The bastard tracked me.* I'm shaking as I plead with myself to calm down and prioritise. Nothing matters now except calling Deacon and getting the hell out of here. I dial his number and wait.

His phone rings out. I swear loudly and hit redial.

'Deacon, for fuck's sake answer your phone!' I grunt when I reach voicemail.

I dial again. A light smattering of traffic passes by and I find myself glaring in the window of each passing car, wondering if my daughter is inside one. *I know she's not.*

Hello. You've reached Deacon O'Reilly. I'm sorry I missed your call, but if you'd like to leave a message I'll get back to you shortly. Beep!

'Deacon.' I exhale. 'Please. Please answer. You're not at the flat and Paul knows what's going on. He followed me. He's called the cops. It's all such a mess. I need you. I know I said never to call but it's different now. I need you. Answer the damn phone. Please, Deacon. Please.'

I hang up and stare at my screen. My wallpaper is a photo of Amelia taken on her second birthday. Her hair was shorter then, and curlier too. Her smile is as bright as her eyes and I stare at her beautiful face as the realisation of what I've done sinks in.

Amelia is missing. The police are looking for her. The papers are printing her photo. Locals are searching for her. Because Amelia is missing. She's really, truly missing now and it's all my fault.

I reach into my bra and pull out her picture. Tears swell in the corner of my eyes. The sun rounds a building across the street and shines down a narrow laneway to warm my face. I'm about to close my eyes, savouring the warmth, when I notice the sunlight shining through Amelia's picture to reveal words written on the back that I hadn't noticed before.

I flip the page over quickly. There's a number. 'Call this' is scribbled in almost illegible handwriting. My heart skips a beat.

The man behind the counter laughs and the woman cackles as I make my way to the back of the shop. I slide between a shelf of bananas and a staff door as I punch the number into my phone.

Deacon's voice croaks against my ear after a single ring. 'Hello.'

'Oh God, Deacon. It's you. Thank God.'

'You called.' He sounds surprised. Maybe he thought I wouldn't find his note.

'You took her,' I say.

'Yes.'

'Without telling me.' I can feel my voice become clipped and loud. The laughter at the front of the shop has stopped and they're back to talking quietly. I lower my voice. 'You shouldn't have done that.'

Deacon doesn't reply.

'Where are you?'

'Where are *you*?' he echoes.

'The fruit and veg shop beside the chipper. I went to the flat, but you weren't there.'

'You came back?' And there's no hiding the surprise in his voice this time. Maybe he really wasn't expecting me to call. *What the fuck?*

'Of course I came back. You have my daughter.'

Deacon falls silent again.

'We have a plan, don't we?' I say, my palms growing sweaty.

'Do we?'

'Yes,' I snap, forgetting to be quiet.

The woman at the front of the shop turns round. I press my back against the wall and hold my breath until she turns away. I think she's getting ready to leave. It'll just be me and the man behind the counter then, and he'll no doubt try to serve me.

'Deacon, please? I don't have much time. Paul will be finished searching the flat soon.'

'Paul is there?' he asks, concerned.

'He followed me. I don't know how. I was careful, I swear. But he knows.'

'Fuck, this is a mess.' Deacon's voice cracks.

'No. We can still fix this. There's time. Everything will be okay if you just tell me where you are.'

'I can't,' he says.

'What?'

'You heard me. I said no.'

'Deacon, what are you doing? I trusted you.'

'You trusted me to take care of Amelia, Susan, and that's exactly what I'm doing.'

'She's my child. You can't replace Kerri-Ann with Amelia.'

'Where's Jenny?' Deacon asks, and I can hear the tears that stick in his throat because he already knows the answer.

'I don't know,' I lie.

'Oh Susan,' he sighs, and I'm certain he's crying. 'I tried so hard to help you.'

'You did help me,' I say, trying to get inside his head the way I usually can. 'I would never have been able to do this without you.'

'Don't say that . . . Jenny and your neighbour. Don't say I helped you.'

'No,' I back-pedal, 'that's not what I mean. Deacon, please, you're scaring me.'

'I always knew you would stop at nothing to hurt Paul. I knew that you would walk all over me or Jenny or anyone who got in your way. But I thought you'd draw the line at Amelia. I never thought you'd hurt her.'

'I didn't mean to. You have to believe me. It was just supposed to be a little nip.'

'I lost one little girl, Susan. I won't lose another.'

'No one is asking you to, Deacon,' I say, feeling his walls break down. I'm getting through to him. 'You're coming with us, remember? Just the three of us.'

'It's just the two of us now, Susan,' Deacon says before the line goes dead.

I hit redial and wait. No answer. I try again. Nothing.

'You bastard,' I cry. 'You can't do this. You can't fucking do this.'

'Excuse me?' the lady at the counter says, turning to glare at me with disapproving eyes for a second time in as many minutes.

'Oh fuck off,' I shout back, marching past the aisle of vegetables and back out on to the street.

My phone beeps and I stop in the middle of the footpath to read it. Suddenly, I don't care who sees me.

My old fone in top drawer in kitchen.

If u left msgs. Delete em.

Get sum help Sue. U need it!

D x

I read the text again, but my hands are trembling so much the words are shaking and it's hard to make sense of them. My eyes scramble to the last part. *Help?* I don't need help. I need Paul to go to hell. This is all his fault. I lost Adam because of him, and now he's cost me Amelia too.

Chapter Forty-four

Now

I march up the stairs to the flat with an energy I didn't have moments ago. Anger and heartbreak battle for a space inside me. I'm not afraid when I find Paul sitting on the grubby couch in the lounge. His elbows are resting on his knees and his back is arched like a question mark as he holds his head in his hands. I can't believe he's the same man who pinned me to the wall a few minutes ago.

'I told you you wouldn't find her,' I say, turning towards the kitchen.

I open the top drawer and, as promised, Deacon's phone is resting face up, waiting for me.

'Five missed calls – all from me,' I say, picking up the phone and throwing it to the floor.

It bounces on the lino but it doesn't shatter. I bend down, infused with rage, and smash it repeatedly against the edge of the countertop. I think I'm screaming. It's hard to tell if the noise is just inside my head or if it's coming out of me. Finally, pieces of glass, metal and plastic scatter everywhere.

I slide my phone out of my pocket and run my finger over the hairline crack Paul inflicted earlier. A surge of electricity shoots up my spine and I bash my phone against the edge of the countertop too. I count backwards out loud from ten.

'Ten . . . nine . . . eight . . .' This time I'm certain I'm shouting as the numbers burst past my lips, louder with every hostile clatter of my phone against the countertop.

My phone is sturdier and more stubborn than Deacon's, and I laugh sheepishly, realising I've forgotten to remove the cover. I slide off the sparkly pink and purple glitter cover that reads *Follow Your Dreams, They Know The Way.* The irony is sharp and unexpected as it drills through my chest.

'Fuck you, Deacon,' I shout. 'Fuck you!'

I raise my arm above my head and bring my phone down with one final, fatal blow. It shatters impressively.

'There,' I say. 'Let's see Google spy on me now.'

Paul finally stands up. His gaze locks on me, his pupils terrifyingly dilated.

'You think the cops won't come because you've smashed up your phone, Susan?' he snorts.

I offer a loud, exaggerated laugh as if my husband is the funniest man alive. 'No,' I say firmly. 'I think the cops won't come because you're going to call them and tell them you've made a terrible mistake.'

It's Paul's turn to laugh.

'You're going to tell them that I left you, which is true, and that you were so upset and emotional that you lashed out. You know it's wrong and you're embarrassed . . . blah, blah, yada yada yada. Feel free to improvise.' I smile.

Paul glares venomously.

'They'll understand,' I explain calmly. 'A missing child . . . emotions are running high, add my infidelity into the mix and you were bound to lose it.'

'An affair?' Paul laughs again but this time it's more of a throaty grunt. 'You seriously expect the cops, or me for that matter, to believe that you were sleeping with that waste of space client of yours?'

My head hurts. I guess I underestimated Paul's ability to see through bullshit. I press my fingers into my temples.

'I don't give a shit what you believe, Paul. Just make it convincing when you phone the cops,' I warn.

'And why would I do that?'

My eyes narrow and I stare at my husband. 'Because . . .' I take a long, exaggerated breath, enjoying how he hangs on my every word. '. . . you'll never see Amelia again if you don't.'

'I have to say, Susan, this dominatrix thing you've got going on is incredibly sexy,' Paul grins. 'Why couldn't you have been more like this in the bedroom? Instead of that boring missionary crap.'

'Don't be disgusting,' I snap.

'Okay, Susan,' Paul smiles, disturbingly cooperative. He's making me nervous again. 'I'll oblige. Just for you.'

He takes his phone out of his pocket and hits a button on his speed dial. A female voice answers, but I can't hear what she says. Paul walks away, taking the call into the bedroom and closing the door behind him. I'm about to open the door when he re-emerges.

'So, really,' he says, 'there's no need to send anyone. Susan isn't here. I guess she's left me, and probably the country. She talks about Thailand a lot. Maybe she's gone there.' Paul's voice breaks and I think he's crying.

Christ, he's good.

'I'm so sorry for the confusion,' he adds. 'I can only apologise again.'

He hangs up.

'Thailand?' I snort. 'When the fuck have I ever mentioned Thailand?'

'You haven't,' he shrugs. 'But it's far away and people go missing there all the time. I thought it would be easiest.'

My eyes narrow and I realise Paul wasn't sitting waiting on the couch like a broken and distraught father. He was waiting for me to come back.

'And by easiest, I mean easiest for me,' he says. 'With you out of the picture Amelia only has one guardian. *Moi.*' He points smugly at himself.

'You'll have to find her first,' I say.

'But I thought you'd have guessed by now – I'm a dab hand at finding people, Sue!' Paul smirks, sliding his phone confidently back into his pocket.

'What the hell is that supposed to mean?' I snap.

He produces a small grey rucksack. He must have been wearing it earlier when he pinned me against the wall, but I was so desperate for air I wasn't paying attention.

He unzips it slowly; the crackle hangs in the air. Finally, he places Adam's lightning strikes, minus their frames, on top of the blue crate. I stare at the photos, confused.

Paul doesn't speak. And I don't know what he wants me to say.

At last he cracks. 'Aren't you going to say something?'

'Like what?' I ask, unable to take my eyes off the photographs. 'I have no idea what's going on here, Paul.'

'Susan, you're much too modest,' he grins. 'I bet you know a lot more than you're letting on, don't you?'

I'm still like a statue, despite trembling inside.

'You know,' he says, picking up one of the photos, 'I've never really liked these.'

He catches the top and I look on breathless as he rips the beautiful photograph clean down the middle. I gasp. He places one half on top of the other and tears again. And my chest aches as if he's tearing the chambers of my heart. He drops the photo on the floor and the pieces scatter.

He reaches for the second photo.

'No. Please,' I shout, lunging forward and snatching the photo up before Paul touches it.

'You're no art buff,' Paul smiles. 'But I guess you know better than I do how valuable these little bits of paper are.'

I stop breathing as I instinctively cradle the photograph against my chest. Paul's eyes are all over me, trying to crack my façade, but I don't budge. I won't offer him the satisfaction.

'Sentimental value, I mean . . .' he says, his voice low and raspy as if he's high on the pleasure of this act of destruction.

In that moment – with the single sentence that took no more than a second to say – I hate Paul more than ever. I flinch. He notices and his smile grows dazzlingly wide. I don't dare blink and send tears trickling down my flushed cheeks.

He folds his arms. 'I'm sure Adam would be glad to know you have them, wouldn't he?'

'Adam,' I echo, my brother's name sending a shiver down my spine.

'He was talented, I'll give him that.'

'Yes.' I swallow, defeated.

'Twins, weren't you?' Paul says. 'Only, it's hard to believe. Sorry, Susan.' Paul shakes his head. 'You're nothing alike, are you?'

I'm not breathing. I'm not even sure my heart is beating.

'I always hoped we'd have twins, Sue. I did. I must admit I was disappointed that Amelia was a singleton. Twins just look so cute in their photos, don't they? And I crossed my fingers that when we tried again we'd have twins. A boy and a girl. We could even have called them Adam and Susan, if you wanted to. I mean, I'm not a complete arsehole, I know that would be important to you.'

I can't speak. It's as if Paul's sharp words are a knife that has severed my vocal cords.

'There's just something so special about the bond between twins, isn't there?' His eyes dance with enthusiasm.

'Don't,' I warn.

'Did you know Langton is a twin?'

I swallow.

'Oh, you didn't. Well, she is. And she knows you are . . . sorry . . . were! It came up in one of her pointless questions. I wondered why she always waited until you were out of the room to drill me about my past. I think she was actually trying to spare your emotions – she must have assumed you were too stupid to really know the man you married. Can you believe that?'

'How long have you known?' I ask, bile burning the back of my throat.

Paul jumps into the air and dances around the room before turning to stop suddenly and stare at me. 'Always,' he says. 'All bloody ways, Sue. I made it my business to get to know the sister . . . the damaged goods, the casualty.'

'You're sick,' I spit.

'Thank you. No more fucked up than your good self,' he says, 'Oh, c'mon, Susan. Don't you think I would have taken the time to find out about Adam's family?'

'Why?'

'For the very same reason you were obsessed with me. Revenge. We really are a pair of kindred spirits, aren't we?'

'You were drunk,' I try to justify. 'Adam was a victim. Wrong place, wrong time. How can you blame anyone but yourself. Jesus.'

'Ah, see.' Paul smiles at me sickeningly sweetly. 'This is why I married you, because you're just too damn innocent and adorable, no matter how hard you try.'

I take a step back, drowning in my own thoughts.

'Didn't you know Adam was after a big story?' Paul asks.

Of course, I knew. Adam told me the college president was humping her favourite students in the canteen after hours. It was a guaranteed honours degree if you made her come. First class was only guaranteed if you could make her scream.

'You know what they say,' Paul grunts, 'ambition is a killer.'

'You were one of her boys,' I say, hating myself for admitting my surprise at this twist. 'I bet you really liked her.'

'Not really,' Paul shrugs. 'I guess Adam and I were alike that way. We both wanted the grade and we realised you had to work hard, and I mean real hard . . .'

'Adam wouldn't sleep with her. Not for a story. He wouldn't do that.'

'God, you really did think your brother was perfect, didn't you? You poor deluded bitch. How do you think Adam knew so much about her? Didn't you know your beloved brother was top of her list of booty calls? His undercover antics would stop at nothing. He'd have Professor Mahon screaming his name twice weekly if he thought his article would make the national papers.'

'I don't believe you. You're only saying this because he's not here to defend himself.'

'But Adam took it too far. He was all about exposing Margaret. He didn't care that he was exposing all of us too. He was ruining people's lives. All he wanted was photos and evidence.'

'And he got them,' I grin.

The lightning strikes finally make sense. Paul snatched the film from Adam's camera to get at the photos of him and Margaret together. He must have developed the whole roll and found the lightning strikes. They were simply too good to throw out. A strange coincidence? Or Adam's legacy?

'You wanted to shut Adam up,' I say.

'I didn't mean to kill him, just startle him enough to grab his camera for a minute.'

'Without evidence he had no story,' I say. 'Oh my God.'

Paul nods.

'Were you even drinking?' I ask.

'Yeah. I knocked back half a bottle of that fancy champagne he was carrying on the spot. I was only trying to calm my nerves. When the cops breathalysed me, I was marginally over the limit and they assumed reckless driving. I was hardly going to correct them now, was I?'

Barely composed, I have to ask. 'Why did you keep the lightning strikes? You could have thrown them out years ago.'

Paul smiles. 'Ah, that was just a little fun. To fuck with your head. I couldn't help myself. You know, we could have been happy, Susan. If you'd just grieved like a normal person. This isn't how I wanted this to go.'

I wrap my arms around myself and all I can think about is the last time I saw Adam, and now the last time I saw Amelia. I've lost everything.

Chapter Forty-five

Now

Paul's lips press against mine. I try to pull away but his fingers slide through my hair and keep my face pressed against him. I feel sick. He lets go as suddenly as he pounced, and I stumble but I don't fall. He flings open the knife drawer and pulls out a carving knife as I'm gaining my balance.

'Now, sweetheart. It's time for everything to go back to normal. It's time to bring Amelia home.'

I eye up the door in the tiny flat, but it suddenly seems so far away.

'Where is she, Susan?'

'I don't know.'

'You're lying,' Paul says, raising the knife.

I scream. 'Deacon took her.'

'Deacon,' he sneers. I know I could make it down the concrete steps ahead of Paul, but I'm trying to calculate if I could get out the door at the bottom fast enough, or if he'd chase me out on to the street with the knife. Surely he wouldn't, not with witnesses around, but there's madness in his eyes and I can't be sure.

'Deacon,' Paul repeats.

'He wants to protect her,' I say, my heart aching as I realise it's true.

'From me?' Paul takes a step forward and his grip on the knife tightens.

'No.' I shake my head, not taking my eyes off the blade. 'From me.'

'I don't believe you.' He takes another step forward. 'Deacon isn't capable of something like that.'

'She's gone, Paul.' I swallow, broken, and don't bother to back away. I close my eyes. I don't even care any more if he brings the blade crashing down. I just hope he makes it quick.

'Drop the knife,' a female voice shouts.

I open my eyes. 'Langton.'

'Drop the knife, Paul,' she repeats.

The Gardaí charge in. Faces I don't recognise. Some I do. There's shouting and commotion and suddenly the tiny, always so depressingly quiet flat is heaving with people. I watch as three large Guards pounce on Paul. He bellows and swears as they twist his hands behind his back to cuff him. He bucks and fights as they bundle him out the door of the flat.

'Are you okay?' Langton says, hurrying over to me, shielding me from the sudden frenzy all around. She notices my cut knuckles and the dried blood matted into my hair. 'Oh Susan. It's okay. He can't hurt you any more.'

'I . . . I . . . I don't understand,' I say. 'He called you. He told you not to come. Why are you here?'

'We had an anonymous call. Someone tipped us off.'

Deacon, I think, but I don't dare mention his name aloud.

'There's been a report of suspicious activity – the caller said they saw a woman fleeing this address and being chased by someone in running gear,' Langton explains. 'It's the same address Paul gave us. It all added up.'

'Jenny,' I say, genuine tears of regret trickling down my cheeks. 'The missing woman. She's my best friend – Jenny.'

'We have him, Susan,' Langton says. She gathers me into her arms and I cry hysterically for everything and everyone I've lost.

Epilogue

Five Years Later

A brightly coloured barge chugs along in the canal that runs parallel to the garden. There's a family on board. A little boy and girl sit on deck reading a story with a young woman I assume is their mother. Their father is at the front, steering the barge. He waves when he notices me looking up from my gardening.

'Lovely day, isn't it?' he hollers, his distinctive English accent wafting towards me.

'Yes, indeed,' I shout back. 'It's supposed to rain later. I hope you stay dry.'

'Ah, a little rain never hurt anyone,' he shouts, smiling. 'Bye-bye now,' he waves as the barge chugs on.

The children and their mother all wave too as they float away. I wave back until my arm grows tired and they're long out of view.

I smile, knowing another boat will be along soon and more friendly people enjoying a lazy afternoon will wave or smile or chat. It's my absolute favourite thing about the little villa in sunny Provence. I'm never lonely with an abundance of tourists floating by all summer.

'Tea is ready,' my mother calls, coming to the back door of the villa that overlooks the long, winding canal.

She doesn't come outside much any more. The garden is set on a steep incline that leads to the water, and she took a fall over some garden stones six months ago and broke her hip. It's still bothering her and she prefers to stay inside now. She'll come as far as the deck, of course. We eat most of our meals out there and spend our evenings playing cards by candlelight. And every night before we go to bed she says the same thing.

'I'm so glad you finally came to visit me, Sue. I always knew you would.'

She first said that five years ago. I haven't left since.

I stand up from kneeling on my soft gardening cushion. My hip creaks and groans, reminding me of an old injury. I pick up my cushion, shake off the bits of moss and muck and tuck it under my arm as I straighten up.

'Beautiful,' I say, staring at my tall sunflowers, my pride of the garden. 'Just beautiful.'

'You really do love those,' my mother says as she places a teapot in the centre of the table, and the smell of fresh tart and home-made strawberry jam makes my mouth water.

'You know how much I love yellow,' I say. 'And they're taller and brighter than ever this year.'

My mother and I chat and enjoy our food as several more boats pass by on the canal. I'm gathering up our plates and cups when I notice people at the end of the garden. I crane my neck to investigate. A barge is moored nearby.

'Bloody nosy tourists,' I say. 'Don't they realise this is private property.'

'They probably didn't know,' my mother says. 'No harm done. I'll finish cleaning up here, you pop down and ask them to be on their way.'

I make my way down the incline, squinting to get a better view of the uninvited visitors. It's a man and a child. He's tall and thin with shaggy grey hair. Without seeing his face, I guess he's about my age. I can't tell what age the child is, not from this distance, but I know she's a girl with shiny blonde hair that cascades halfway down her back like a beautiful waterfall. I look around for her mother, assuming an entire family has invaded my private space.

The child leans in to smell the sunflowers and to my surprise she picks one.

'Don't do that,' I shout, furious and waving my gardening apron about as I try to catch their attention.

I pick up speed but it's hard to run in flip-flops.

'They're my special yellow flowers,' I warn, getting closer. 'You can't pick them.'

'I'm sorry, I didn't know,' the girl says, turning to face me. A clunky disposable camera dangles around her neck. 'They're just so pretty. I love yellow.'

'Oh my God,' I say, jumping back as I look into her huge blue eyes. I go over on the edge of my flip-flop, my bad hip jars and I fall over.

'Are you okay?' the girl asks. She is speaking to me but she's looking at the man for reassurance. I've startled her, no doubt.

'Yes,' I nod, barely even feeling the pain in my hip as I stand up. 'I'm sorry, I thought you were someone I knew.'

'I'm Amelia,' the child says, extending her hand.

'Hello, Amelia,' I say, shaking it, delighted by her wonderful manners. 'Nice to meet you.'

'Amelia,' my mother shouts from the deck. 'Is that you? Oh, I can't believe it's really you.'

'Grandma,' the young girl says. She hurries up the hilly garden to where my mother stands with her arms stretched wide and the two embrace.

I've dreamed of this moment for so long, and now that it's actually happening I can't quite believe it's real.

'Deacon,' I nod, forcing myself to say that name after all these years.

The grey-haired man turns round and his smile is as familiar as ever. 'Hello, Sue,' he says. 'How have you been?'

I swallow. I have no words.

A barge floats towards us on the canal, drifting close to the edge. The captain beeps his horn and enthusiastic passengers wave.

'*Salut*,' he shouts happily.

'Oh fuck off,' I grunt.

Deacon laughs. 'I see you haven't changed one bit.'

I turn and face my mother and Amelia sitting on the swing chair on the deck. They rock back and forth, chatting and wonderfully comfortable with one another.

'Look at them,' I say, smiling. 'Meeting at last.'

'Are you ever going to write back to her, Sue?' Deacon asks. 'You reply to mine but not hers. Why?'

I shake my head. 'My mother writes to her. I think they've reached the stage of sending a letter a week now, maybe even more.'

'Amelia draws her pictures too,' Deacon says.

'I know. Mam puts them on the fridge,' I say, remembering how she would proudly display Adam's and my school art on the fridge when we were kids.

'They share photos too, sometimes,' Deacon adds. 'Your mother's are usually out of focus, but Amelia treasures them nonetheless. But there's never any of you.'

'I know that too.'

Deacon slides his hands into his pockets and stares around the picturesque garden. 'Beautiful flowers,' he says. 'No surprise they're yellow.'

'I like yellow,' I shrug.

'She asks about you,' he says. 'More and more all the time. I'm not sure what to tell her.'

'Tell her I love her,' I say.

'I do,' he nods. 'But she's nearly eight. She wants to know more than that. She wants to know you.'

'Is that why you're here? So my daughter can get to know me?'

Deacon takes a deep breath. 'I've met someone,' he says, switching his gaze from the flowers to my mother and daughter swinging on the deck.

'Oh,' I say, bending to pick up the broken flower Amelia dropped.

'She's amazing, Sue. You'd like her. She's bubbly and quirky and talks a lot.'

'That's great, Deacon,' I say, and he tilts his head as he watches me. 'I'm happy for you. Really.'

'And she's wonderful with Amelia,' he adds, his face lighting up as he talks about her. 'They paint each other's nails and go shopping together. All the girly stuff I was never very good at.'

Amelia giggles on the deck and the sound carries down to me, wrapping its arms around me like a warm hug. My sense of missing out is overwhelming, even worse than usual.

'She's happy,' I say, pointing towards my daughter.

'Yeah,' Deacon nods. 'She is.'

I bend and pick several of the shorter-stemmed sunflowers, adding them to the one already in my hand. I bundle them together and take the brightly coloured belt off my apron and tie it around them, securing them into a haphazard bouquet.

'Tea, Deacon? Or are you hungry, would you like some tart?'

He makes a face, confused, as he looks me up and down. 'Susan, I'm trying to tell you that your daughter needs you and you're asking if I'm hungry?'

'My mother made it herself, it's delicious.'

'Susan, I can only imagine how hard this must be to have Amelia suddenly so desperate to be a part of your life. But she needs her mother.'

I shake my head. 'She needs *a* mother, Deacon. And by the sounds of it you've found someone wonderful to fill those shoes.'

'Susan—'

'Deacon, please. This is already so hard. Don't make it worse by trying to reason with me.'

He shakes his head and a sadness washes over him.

'Do you remember the text you sent me the day they arrested Paul for murder?' I ask.

'Vaguely,' Deacon says.

'You told me to get help.'

'Ah yes,' Deacon smiles, 'my pearls of wisdom.'

'But I already had help,' I say. 'I had someone who put Amelia first when no one else did. I had you.'

'I love her as if she is my own,' he says.

'I know.' I pass him the makeshift bouquet of sunflowers. 'And that's why I know you'll put her first again now. She can't be here, Deacon. It's too dangerous. Someday Paul will come looking . . .'

'He's in prison for triple murder, Susan.'

'I know. But someday will eventually come. It always does. Amelia deserves a family, Deacon. With real parents, not the selfish biological ones she was cursed with. She doesn't remember me, does she?'

He shakes his head, and although it's the answer I needed I wasn't prepared for how much it would hurt.

'Good,' I say, flicking away a tear that trickles down the side of my nose. 'That's good. Now, let's have this tart.'

Acceptance creeps across Deacon's face as he places his hand on my shoulder.

'And then you can tell Amelia that I'm the nice lady who looks after her grandmother's garden, and you can be on your way.'

'Sue . . .' He looks as if he is about to object, then he sighs. 'These are beautiful,' he says, shoving his nose into the centre of the bouquet and taking a deep breath. 'Amelia will love them.'

'You won't be back, will you?' I ask, choking back tears.

Deacon shakes his head. 'No.'

'Can I take your photo?' Amelia says, skipping towards me.

'She loves nothing more than taking pictures,' Deacon explains.

I smile but my heart is aching.

'She's really very good,' he adds proudly.

I know, I think. I've seen the ones she sends Mam. And Mam says she's even more talented than Adam was at that age.

'Okay,' I nod nervously. 'Just give me one moment?'

'Okay,' Amelia says.

I rush back to the house. In the kitchen I open the corner cupboard and glance up at the top shelf, beaming with satisfaction when Adam's old camera stares back at me. I pull over a chair, climb up and take a deep breath as I reach for his pride and joy.

Amelia is happily snapping shots of my sunflowers and the canal when I return to the garden.

'There's something I'd like you to have,' I say, offering her Adam's camera.

'For me?' she says, wide-eyed and giddy with excitement as she takes it. 'Look, look, Deacon. How cool is this?'

'Very cool,' he says.

'Thank you. Thank you,' Amelia chirps. 'I'll take such good care of it.'

'You didn't have to do that,' Deacon whispers.

I nod happily. 'Yes. Yes, I did.'

I position myself next to the beautiful yellow sunflowers as Amelia raises the camera, her small fingers managing it masterfully.

'Say cheese,' she says.

I smile brightly. 'Cheese.'

ABOUT THE AUTHOR

Janelle Harris penned her first story on scented, unicorn-shaped paper. She was nine. A couple of decades, one husband, five children, two cats and a dog later Janelle wrote another story. Unfortunately the paper lacked any fragrance but that didn't hinder *No Kiss Goodbye* from becoming an international bestseller. Janelle now writes psychological suspense for Lake Union and women's fiction for Bookouture. She is always on the lookout for aromatic notepads.